Who was attacking me, and how could she control the water?

I scrambled to my feet, heart pounding, and took off in a sprint. On my third step, I was back on the ground. This time, when I turned my body, the figure stood over me. I reached out slowly, trying to find a rock or a branch, anything that would help me to get away but there was nothing. Under my left hand was decent size puddle. It didn't make sense, but I didn't get to think about it long before my attacker motioned at my left hand. The water around my palm slowly retreated.

"Why are you different?" The voice was high and shrill sounding, which meant it was a she.

"What?" Unable to do anything but focus on getting the hell away, I didn't worry about what was coming out of my mouth.

"What does he see in you? You're human."

This time her hand snaked out and curled around my neck, hauling me up until my feet left the ground. My hands flew up to her cruel grip, scrabbling for purchase. My breathing became shallow as I fought for air. Her strength was unbelievable. Squirming, I dug my nails into her skin, desperate to escape.

"Answer me!" she screamed and then threw me to the ground.

Something in my wrist popped as I hit. Rolling over, I got to my hands and knees. I tried to push up, but couldn't move. Water covered my wrists, the pressure holding me in place. It made no sense. Even stranger, the water turned to ice, and something slammed into my upper back. My face kissed the dirt. I tried to get up, but couldn't muster the strength. Hell, I could barely lift my head. As I fell back down, panic closed in. I couldn't move.

Maisy Karolson walked into to class and fell—literally, an arm-flailing kind of fall—right into arms of the prince of an extraordinary breed of humans, and her future boyfriend. She just didn't know it yet. Maisy is your typical college senior. She works hard in school and loves her job as a waitress at the local college bar, Woodys. But her social life isn't all that great, and her love life is non-existent. That is, until she meets Linc Floodpoika. He's everything she should stay away from—arrogant, tattooed, and gorgeous. Exactly what Maisy needs.

Linc comes from a very powerful family in the Veden world, a special race of humans that can manipulate water. He's next in line to be king, and his family isn't all that enthused about the blonde human he's brought home. Not to mention that she bares the mark of a Fiskare, another special race of humans designed to take out Vedens. His family isn't the only ones who aren't thrilled about their relationship. Someone has made it their mission to tear Maisy away from Linc, and they won't stop until they get what they want...

KUDOS for *Across the Creek*

In *Across the Creek* by Brittany Tollison, Maisy Karolson is a college student in rural Alabama. When she meets Linc Floodpoika, she thinks he's a jerk and wants nothing to do with him. But Linc is persistent, and Maisy doesn't stand a change. Then things get interesting. Maisy soon discovers that her new love isn't even human...well, at least not a *normal* human but is a special breed of humans called Vedens who can manipulate water. In addition, one of Maisy's best friends is a Fiskare, another special breed of humans who hunt the Vedens. As if it isn't bad enough that she has to deal with learning there really are monsters out there who can kill normal humans with a wave of their hand, someone is out to get her, and Maisy has no defense. With a solid plot, fun and fascinating characters, fast-paced action, and plenty of surprises, I had a very hard time putting this one down. A really great read. ~ *Taylor Jones, The Review Team of Taylor Jones & Regan Murphy*

Across the Creek by Brittany Tollison is the story of an average college senior in Alabama who has a not-so-average boyfriend. Maisy Karolson is unaware that the guy she is dating is special. Yes, he's gorgeous, a hunk, and sexy as hell, but as far as she knows, he's human, just like she is. But Linc Floodpoika is not just like she is. He is a Veden, a race of humans who can manipulate water. He doesn't want her to know, but after she is attacked by another Veden, marked by a Fiskare—another special race of humans with magical powers—and sees Linc do things no human can do, she is forced to admit the truth: he has powers she can't even comprehend. Naturally, her first reaction is fear, and then she wonders what the heck he is even doing with her in the first place. But what really concerns her is that someone seems determined to kill her, someone with power like Linc's. *Across the Creek* is well written, the characters both well developed and realistic, the action fast and tense, and the story full of twists and turns that will keep you on your toes. I really hope there is another book coming soon, because I couldn't get enough. ~ *Regan Murphy, The Review Team of Taylor Jones & Regan Murphy*

ACKNOWLEDGMENTS

Thank you to the awesome team at Black Opal Books for all their hard work and making one of my dreams of having my work published come to life.

I wanted to say thank you to my husband, family, and friends who let me bounce ideas off them and for reading draft after draft. I would have never had the courage to submit this book without them.

Across

the

Creek

Brittany Tollison

A Black Opal Books Publication

GENRE: NEW ADULT/PARANORMAL ROMANTIC THRILLER

This is a work of fiction. Names, places, characters and incidents are either the product of the author's imagination or are used fictitiously, and any resemblance to any actual persons, living or dead, businesses, organizations, events or locales is entirely coincidental. All trademarks, service marks, registered trademarks, and registered service marks are the property of their respective owners and are used herein for identification purposes only. The publisher does not have any control over or assume any responsibility for author or third-party websites or their contents.

DEDICATION

For my husband, Wade.
Thank you for being my biggest supporter.
I love you!

Chapter 1

Having class at seven in the morning sucked balls. Luckily for me, that was when most of the Humanities courses were scheduled. It was exactly six-thirty in the morning, and I was in the car, ready to go. Unfortunately, my best friend and roommate, Sarah, was not. Ugh. Sarah, love her to death, was the most unorganized, scatter brained, carefree person I knew. Which was probably a good thing, because I, on the other hand, cringed at the thought of not being structured and organized. She kept me fun.

Seriously, what the hell was she doing in our rented three-bedroom home? I sat there, staring into the woods behind our house, tapping my fingers on the steering wheel, and thought about what too cook for dinner. Pasta maybe? Oh! Or Mexican!

She finally came out and locked the door behind her. She ran toward my car, pulling her thick brown hair up into a messy ponytail. When she opened the door, I gave a noisy huff so she could tell I was annoyed. Her green eyes were bright with humor. "We're fine, Maisy, it's only like six-forty-five or something."

"It takes at least twenty-five minutes to get to school, and you know parking is going to be a bitch," I whined.

"Not if you drive fast." She checked out her bright

red nails and then looked in my direction and waited.

We both stared at each other, her smiling, me not so much. I shook my head and started up my old Toyota Camry.

It was the beginning of the school year, so it was mid-August, which meant, even this early in the morning, it was already warm and humid for our little northern Alabama town. My hand dropped to my coffee mug full of scorching coffee. Taking a sip, I instantly regretted not making it iced. For once Sarah was quiet. When we hit a red light, I glanced at her. Her straight white teeth were nibbling on her bottom lip, and those red nails were restlessly tapping her knee. As a glass-half-full kind of girl, the collection of nervous movements was out of character.

She came from a good home with a loving family and had no shortage of friends, male or female. Being gorgeous didn't hurt, and she lived for the male attention, loving every bit of it. At five foot six with tan skin and minimal make up, she was rocking the cut up jean shorts and flowery tank. She always looked perfect.

I, on the other hand, was a hot mess. I stood two inches shorter with blonde, frizzy shoulder-length hair, blue-gray eyes, the one thing I did have going for me was my boobs—all natural, even if they did a great impression of implants.

Sarah raised a perfectly groomed eyebrow. "What?" The defensive note in her voice indicated she was anticipating a snarky comeback.

Whoops, I was staring again. "Are you feeling all right?"

My unexpected question caused her to frown. She let out a long breath and gently tucked a piece of hair she missed behind her ear. "Yeah, fine, just not ready to start school. I feel like summer just started, and we're already going back. And I'm a little disappointed that I don't really get to see Todd as much."

"Yeah." It was the best thing I could possibly say to that statement. Todd was an ass who basically used Sarah as a trophy. He would parade her around to his friends and family and then treat her like shit later. Then there were his anger issues. He constantly got mad at Sarah for wearing the wrong clothes, laughing at things he considered inappropriate, and made these digs about her body until she was highly self-conscious.

"I hope there's eye candy in this class," she said, snapping me out of my thoughts. "Because something needs to keep me awake, or I'm definitely going to fall asleep and end up failing the class

"You and me both." I pulled the car into a parking spot that was at least a mile away from the school. Great. We were already late, and it would take at least fifteen more minutes to get to class. I hated being late, but being late on the first day of class was torture because you became an instant center of attention. I hated that. Sarah, on the other, didn't mind.

We grabbed our bags out of the back seat and headed for class. I beeped the car lock. Twice. Sarah turned and gave me a funny look as I sped up and passed her. "Just making sure criminals know I mean business."

A few steps behind me, Sarah said loudly, "Seriously, Mais, chill, we're already late. We don't have to sprint to class."

I slowed my pace. "Well, I hate being late, and next time if you're not ready, I'm leaving you."

She blew out an exasperated breath. "No, you aren't."

She was probably right. Since it took us less than ten minutes to get to our class, maybe I exaggerated a bit on the mile-away-parking job. Still, I made Sarah walk in first. That way everyone would look at her and not watch me sneak by in the back of the classroom.

I held the door open as she gracefully walked into the room. Our professor was a larger, older lady with shiny silver hair. It was all I caught because I made a bee-line for the back. Honestly, if the professor couldn't put my work with my face, it would be a win. I preferred to be invisible.

Sarah, of course, chirped right up, "Hi, Professor McNolan. Sorry we're late. I'm Sarah Rodriguez, and the girl running to the back of the classroom is Maisy Karlson."

Welp, there went my invisible plan.

"Welcome to Humanities Two-Thirteen," Professor McNolan said. "Please take a copy of the syllabus."

Hopefully, Sarah grabbed one for me. If not, I could make a copy of hers.

"Thanks!" Sarah smiled at the professor and joined me at the back of the class.

Looking around the back of the classroom, I couldn't find two seats next to each other. Fine. I let Sarah take the closer seat and headed for the one three seats back. Making my way back to the empty seat, I heard something fall behind me. Shoot, it was probably my phone. I touched my back pocket—yup, definitely my phone. I turned around, and my foot caught on somebody's bag, throwing me off balance. My arms flailed, and I sucked in a deep breath waiting to hit the floor. Great, this would cause a huge scene—exactly what I was trying to avoid in the first place.

I braced for an impact that never came, or it did—it just wasn't the floor. Something wrapped around my waist and tugged me against something hard. My eyes flew open to discover that a male chest dominated my vision. I didn't know what was worse—falling and face planting, or falling and having some random guy catch me. He pulled me up slowly, and I stared at his chest to avoid making eye contact, but it didn't stop me from noticing how his muscles bulged through his shirt because of my weight. I wasn't fat, by any means, but I wasn't a stick either.

Mumbling, "Thank you," I tried to turn away and escape, but he didn't let go.

"Are you okay?" His voice was low and a bit husky.

It ran through me, leaving goose bumps in its wake. "Yup. Totally fine. I...uh...just tripped." I winced. *No shit, Sherlock.* As much as I didn't want to meet his eyes, it was weird not to look when someone talked to you. I lifted my gaze. *Shit. Really shouldn't have looked. Dammit.*

His eyes were the color of honey, and his messy light-brown hair fell over them. I never liked brown eyes. They were boring and normal, but this guy was definitely rocking 'em. There was scruff on his face, as if he hadn't shaved in a couple days. His plain black T-shirt totally showed off his muscular chest, and I'd bet my life that there were abs under it. Gosh, I wanted to be that shirt. His jeans hung low on his hips.

"I got that." His comment snapped my attention back to his face.

I caught his smirk. Damn, was there drool on my chin?

"Next time, let's try to function like a normal human being," he said.

Wonderful, he was hot and an asshole. I shimmied out of his hands, picked up my phone, and walked to the seat behind him. No way in hell would I say thank you now.

I sat down, still irked at what happened. Staring at his stupid head in front of me, I considered chucking my pen at him. Not worth my time. I turned my attention to the classroom. It was basically a big brown box made of tan walls with a little white board at the front. The rest of the room was lined with individual desks. You could easily fit sixty students in the class. Professor McNolan went over the syllabus, and I was stoked we didn't have any papers to write, just three tests and a power-point presentation. Sweet.

I looked up at Sarah. She wore a full-fledged grin and was trying to stifle her laughter. She raised her eyebrows, and mouthed, "Whoa."

I pretended to ignore her but stole a glance at the jerk in front of me to make sure he didn't notice her. Yeah, whoa was right. He was good looking, if you were into the rugged-cave-man thing.

The professor passed out papers, but since I wasn't paying attention, I missed what it was. Douche Bag turned and handed me a sheet. When I refused to look at him, I heard a deep chuckle. I scanned the paper. It was for a project, with a list of names grouped in pairs. Great, a group assignment. Locating my name, I discovered I was paired up with some kid named Lincoln Floodpoika.

"For the rest of the class time, please meet up with your partner and get to know one another," Professor McNolan announced. "You guys will be working with each other the rest of the semester."

Everyone started getting up and asking people who they were, trying to find their partners. I, being the socially awkward type, sat there and waited until the majority coupled up. In front of me, Douche Bag wasn't moving either. *Please don't let me be partnered with him.*

At that very moment, he turned to look at me. "I think we're partners." He sounded bored.

Great, I totally jinxed it. "How do you know? I don't remember telling you my name."

I tried to sound nonchalant but failed miserably.

"When you walked in, your friend said her name and yours out loud. Something you must have missed when you were running to the back of the classroom and tripping over your own two feet."

Unsure how to reply, since I tried not be confrontational, I gave him a blank look. "So your name's Lincoln?" *Why am I Captain Obvious today?*

"I go by Linc," he mumbled as he continued to look over the assignment.

Okay, after class I would talk to the professor and beg her to switch my partner. Maybe if I explained I could get more work done if I was working with, say, Sarah, who lived with me. Sounded good to me. Until then, I'd go through the motions.

"How do you want to do this? Do you want to exchange numbers, or emails, or we could just meet—"

"Numbers." He pulled his cell phone out of his pocket. "What's your number?"

The way his biceps flexed with the movement mesmerized me, but I managed to give him my number. Right after, he got up and started walking away. What was he doing?

"I'll text you," he grunted over his shoulder and walked out of class.

I stared after him, completely confused.

Seriously, what the heck was his problem? He didn't seem to like me, which made no sense. We'd barely spoken, and tripping over his bag wasn't a play for his attention. The only opinion he could've formed about me was that I was clumsy.

As soon as the door closed behind him, I bolted to Professor McNolan.

"Professor, is there any way to change our partners? I live with Sarah Rodriguez, so it would be a lot easier

just to do the project with her, since we know each other's schedules."

"What was your name?" The old woman squinted in
my direction. "I'm sorry, I just have so many students."

"Maisy." I gave her a little wave, don't ask me why.

"Okay, Maisy, I understand it would be more con-
venient for you to work with Sarah, but this is college,
and it's about meeting new people and trying to form relationships. Once you get an actual job, you're not going
to like everyone you work with, so you'll just have to
stick it out."

Stunned by her assumption, I blinked. Since I had a
job at a local bar where I worked and waited on people I
didn't like all the time, I was offended. Still, she was my
professor, and no use shooting myself in the foot before
the semester even started. "Okay."

I gave her a fake, polite smile and went back to my
seat, fuming. Throwing myself on the floor and having a
temper tantrum wouldn't do a damn thing. When the professor finally let class out, I found Sarah waiting for me
right outside the door.

"How are you feeling, boo?"

Since I basically ate shit in class and got the worst
partner possible, I grimaced and shoved my hair out of
my face. "Fine, it was a good way to start the week. Being late, falling—"

"Having that hot guy catch you!" she said, filling in
the list of what went wrong.

"What's his name?"

"Douche Bag?" I replied dryly.

"Mais, be nice." Wide eyed, she hit my shoulder and
then smiled, showing off her straight white teeth. She
loved those teeth-whitening strips.

"Linc, but Douche Bag is more fitting." I rubbed my
shoulder. "And that hurt."

She gave me a puzzled look but shrugged her shoulders and began walking to her next class, which was right next to mine. She started talking about what a good semester this was going to be, and how we had to make the best of it. Blah, Blah, Blah. I wanted to be done with school. Going to college for five years was long enough for me. At twenty-three, I should have had my life together, but that wasn't the case.

We walked up to the building our classrooms shared, and Sarah finally wound down enough to say, "I'll see you in a couple hours, unless you wanted to get lunch in between?"

Since she was going to meet Todd after this class, no thank you. "Nah, I'll just meet you at the car."

"Well, have a good first day!" She bounced around and through the doors of her class.

"Yeah, you too." I turned and walked into my next Humanities class. Being a Humanities major was pointless, but I loved the classes. There was a huge range of topics to choose from. For example, my first class with Professor McNolan was on romantic love. The one I was headed into was called The Power of Jazz. Every topic was unique.

I walked into the room, head down, and didn't notice anything or anyone. It was not that I didn't like people, but making new friends wasn't high on my list of goals. I was content with the good friends I already had. Since class didn't start for another five minutes or so, I took out my notebook and started doodling with a black pen. My horrible morning would make a good story later. That almost made me giggle, but that urge quickly died when I looked up and locked gazes with a set of gorgeous brown eyes. Douche Bag was back.

Once again, I imitated a deer in headlights, staring at Linc. The moment he saw me, his face darkened. *Won-*

derful. He walked to the back of the classroom, and I tried not to watch, but it was hard not to focus on someone that delicious. Muscles, scruff, tattoos—tattoos? For the first time, I noticed the tattoo on his left bicep. It was hard to tell what it was because half of it disappeared under his shirt, but it resembled a tentacle. He sat a couple of seats down in the row behind me.

I didn't remember a thing the professor said because I was too busy trying to ignore the hot man behind me. I glanced back a couple times and caught him looking at me once. This resulted in me turning around instantly while heat washed over my face. Once the professor dismissed of class, I bolted for the door and didn't look back.

With an hour and a half before my next class and Sarah's decision to hang with Todd, I went to my car, hoping to take a nap or read. Once in the car, I reclined the seat and stared at the sky, eventually dozing off. When my phone buzzed, I jumped so high my knee hit the damn steering wheel.

"Crap!" Ugh. That frickin' hurt.

I checked my phone, but it was an unknown number.

It's Linc, Library tomorrow. 8pm.

Yeah, not happening.

I work till 11. Any other time?

Where do you work? I'll meet you on your break.

Seriously? We had all semester to figure out our presentation. Why did it have to be tomorrow?

Can't we just do a different day?

No. Busy.

Fine. I work at Woody's bar. My break's at 9.

When he didn't text me back to confirm, I assumed he'd be there or not. With fifteen minutes until my next class, I grabbed my bag and started walking. This semester was going to suck. Between a super-hot partner who seemed to hate my guts for no apparent reason, and Sarah spending most of her time with Todd instead of me, the next few months stretched endlessly before me. I could get a boyfriend, but if my choices were guys like Todd or Douche Bag, I didn't need one. I just needed a hobby.

Chapter 2

After my last class, a required science course, I headed back to my car. Since I wasn't a fan of science anything, I decided it would be best if I took that class in my last semester.

The college sat up on a hill and the path down to the parking lot was lined with massive trees wrapped in kudzu, a vine that took over everything, dotted with tiny purple flowers. I enjoyed my walk because this time of year everything was still in full bloom and green.

My stomach rumbled. Pasta was definitely for dinner tonight. When I got to my car, Sarah was still not there, not surprising, and she got out a half an hour earlier than I did. I checked my phone. No missed calls or texts. I started texting her.

"Looking for me!" Sarah said in a high-pitched voice. My head snapped up, and I saw her walking with Todd, hand-in-hand. *Great.*

"Yeah, you ready?" I glanced at Todd, *please don't invite him over.*

"Yup, Todd's going to stay at our house tonight, that okay with you?"

Damn. "Sounds good." Not.

We all got in the car. Sarah started talking about her classes and how she felt it was going to be an easy semester. Todd was sitting in the back, texting on his phone, being quiet. Maybe he was keeping his mouth shut because he knew I wasn't fond of him. If so, it was a good choice.

"So how was the rest of your day, Mais? Did you see King Douche Bag again?" Sarah was wearing the biggest grin on her face.

Todd looked up from his phone and glanced at me in the rearview mirror.

I sighed. "Yup, he's in my jazz class too."

"Did he talk to you?" Her question was way too enthusiastic.

"No, he sat on the other side of the room."

Sarah frowned at my answer. It had been a while since I had a date, and she was determined to set me up with whatever guy I decided to talk with, didn't matter if we just met or not.

To head her off, I added, "He texted me though, he's coming to the bar tomorrow night. We're going to figure out what we're doing for the assignment on my lunch break."

Her eyes lit up. "I work tomorrow, too! Does that mean I get to meet him?"

"Um, if you want to go up and introduce yourself to him, fine, but I'm not doing it. I don't think he likes me much. It feels like he thinks I'm annoying or something."

"He has good taste then," Todd bit out.

My "Fuck you," came at the same time Sarah said, "Todd, that's mean."

He snickered and looked away.

Glaring at him through the rearview mirror, I snapped, "Don't you have a car? Next time, use it." God, I hated him. The rest of the ride home was quiet.

℃℈℃℈

The pasta Sarah made for dinner hit the spot perfectly. So fat and full, I decided to at least look at the assignment Linc and I would be working on. Thanks to my over-full stomach, I waddled to my bedroom and shut the door behind me. Leaning against my door, I closed my eyes.

My room was my safe place. It was small, but I loved it. There was a white dresser on the right wall and a bed with a pink and green comforter against the other wall. A small closet nestled by the door, and I was surprised it fit all my clothes and shoes. By the bed was a white desk. Decorations were pictures of my family and friends from back home in California.

Sitting on my bed, I pulled out my notebook and flipped through the tabs to the Romantic Love Class. Finding the paper outlining the assignment, I reviewed it. It seemed simple enough, form a hypothesis on something to do with love then, through observations, surveys, and other types of data collection, prove or disprove the hypothesis.

We could do this without even talking with one another. Nice. We could figure out a problem or hypothesis tomorrow, gather our own data, and then I could write the paper based on both of our findings. "Sounds perfect," I muttered. Tension began to bleed out of my shoulders, and I slumped against my pillows.

There was a knock at my door, and then Sarah poked her head through. "Wanna watch a movie with us? I'm thinking the new *Star Trek*." Her hair was down and framing her face as she flashed a bright smile.

That was the absolute last thing I wanted to do. "No thanks. I think I'm going to go running in a minute." Since I just ate, it wasn't the best idea, but I didn't want to be cooped up in my room all night either.

"Well, go soon, it's getting dark. Do you want us to

go with you?" Her offer was out of character. She hated running.

"Nope." It came out a little mean, and I winced.

Ever since we moved here, she'd been weird about me running by myself. Maybe it was our new environment. Back in California, we lived in a city, but our current house was basically in the middle of nowhere. Our nearest neighbors were about a half mile in both directions, so, technically, we weren't alone. It just felt that way. Honestly, nothing bad ever happened in this little dinky town, so there wasn't a threat.

Sarah smiled, but it didn't reach her eyes like normal. "Okay, well, let me know before you leave and when you get back home."

"Of course." I grabbed my hair and pulled it into a high ponytail.

Changing into my favorite purple running shorts, a T-shirt, and my gray and purple Nikes, I ran out into the living room. Todd and Sarah were curled up on the couch. His arms were around her, and her head was on his chest. They looked cute, happy, and, for a second, I felt a pang of jealousy but immediately shook it off. What was I thinking? I knew their relationship, and there was no way I wanted what they had going on, but it would be nice to have *someone*. Time to go before I decided to stay in my room and pout.

"I'll be back," I announced and then opened the wooden door.

"Be safe," Sarah whispered.

I stopped in the driveway, which was just a plot of dirt we parked on, and stretched. The sky was blue, deep red, and streaked with purple, but you could see the faded, full moon. Unlike midday, the air was still warm, but it didn't feel like an oven. If I'd tried to run earlier, I was pretty sure I would've died of heat stroke.

Standing up, I stretched my back one more time and then took off down the driveway. My feet pounded over something that passed as a paved street in rural Alabama but would be considered a dirt road by California standards. I ran my usual path that took me roughly three miles toward town.

My mind kept wandering, even as I tried to take in the scenery or count trees, so I wasn't thinking about the mechanics of running or the day's stresses, this was my time. Despite my best efforts, my mind kept returning to intense brown eyes, full lips, and brown wavy hair. Blah, what the hell was my problem? I didn't even know the guy, and I was running and...and fantasizing? *Is that what I'm doing? Ugh. I have issues.*

Maybe it was his attitude problem that bothered me the most. I never had someone be so angry at me and not know why. Maybe he'd had a bad day, and he decided to take it out on me because I was unlucky enough to tripping into him.

Right before I hit the town, I veered off into the wooded area, following an old trail. I never told Sarah about it, nor did I plan to. She would freak. The temperature dropped considerably since there wasn't much light in the woods. The giant trees covered the sky only allowing glimpses of dark blue and purple between the thick leaves. It was nice, calming.

Running up to the small stream, which was my turn around point, I heard someone walking down the stream. The sound pulled me up short. The footsteps sloshed in the shallow water, as if pacing in the stream. It didn't make sense. The stream was tiny. It would only take two, maybe three, steps to get to the other side. I'd run this trail for four years and hadn't seen a single soul. Now I could hear them, but couldn't see who or what it was.

I could feel the pins and needles flood my body, urging me to turn around and sprint back toward the road, but my curiosity won, and I took a couple steps down stream to look around a tree. A giant figure stood in the middle of the stream.

What is he doing? I took a step back and water soaked into my Nikes. I glanced down at the water now covering my shoe. I swallowed and stared, shock holding me still. "Shit."

Instead of its normal path of flowing downstream, the water was running upstream. *What the fuck?* I blinked once to make sure I wasn't seeing things, but nope, the water was still going the wrong way.

Taking a timid step back, I prepared to run and squished a branch or leaf underfoot. The small noise made the giant turn around. I barely caught a glimpse of his bare, muscular shoulder before I took off. I'd never run faster. The entire forest became a blur of greenish-brown darkness. When I finally hit the road, a half-mile away from the creek, I didn't stop but ran all the way back to the house.

Once safely inside, I slammed the door and put my back to it, breathing heavily, as my heart slammed against my chest. My legs trembled and collapsed, sending me to the floor.

"Mais? Maisy!"

I heard Sarah yell, but she sounded far away, and I couldn't exactly see her, just an outline of a body before everything went black.

"*Maisy!*" someone shrieked.

My eyelids weighed a ton, but I finally got them open to mere slits. Why was I on the floor, looking at the ceiling? Better question, why was Todd yelling at me? Why the hell was I in his lap?

"What?" I tried for annoyed, but it came out breathy and soft.

Everything came back to me—the man in the water, the stream acting weird, and my five-mile sprint home. Shit, I must have passed out. I tried wiggling out of Todd's hold, but he tightened his grip.

"Maisy are you okay? Here's some water. Drink."

That was Sarah's voice, but I was still a little woozy and didn't know what direction it was coming from. Cold, hard plastic pressed against my left hand.

"Thanks." I put the plastic cup to my lips, letting the water dribble into my mouth and slide down my throat.

The coolness felt amazing. Until that moment, I hadn't realized how thirsty I was, or how great water actually tasted. Finishing the whole cup, I sighed and looked over at Sarah.

Her eyebrows were drawn together as she ran a jerky hand through her hair, her green eyes wide and full of panic. "Are you okay?" she asked.

"I'm fine, I think I was just pushing myself too hard and overdid it." No way would I tell her why I overdid it, she'd think I was crazy. Besides, it would give Todd more reasons to think I was a nutty bitch. *Speak of the devil.* "I can sit up on my own now." I sounded annoyed as I started to sit up.

He let go immediately and gave me a little push, as if he touched something vile. I sat on the floor for another minute or so before I stood. Sarah watched warily, as if she didn't believe I was actually fine. I walked out of the kitchen and back to my bedroom, leaving them and their unasked questions behind.

After taking the longest shower in history, I settled into bed. My brain kept replaying what happened. It didn't make sense—the water moving in the wrong direction, the giant man standing there. Maybe he was a crazy bum. Yet a little voice in my head whispered, *Since when did bums have muscles like that?*

❦

The next day went by in a blur. After my two morning classes, I went running again and took time out for lunch. Now I was on my way to Woody's for my three-to-eleven shift. It was the perfect time-slot for me, I'd be there early enough not to get stuck closing at two in the morning, but late enough to enjoy the tips from late-night partiers

The uniform—cut off jean shorts, open flannel shirt over a tank top, and cowboy boots—wasn't bad either, and it blended well with the locals. Plus, it was totally comfortable.

I parked my car behind the bar and noticed Cindy's car was already there. Sweet! I loved working with Cindy, because she had her shit together at work and did her part. Some of our waitresses used their jobs just to meet guys and did as little work as possible.

I walked in through the back and put my purse in bar owner's office in a drawer where we all kept our belongings. When I got to the back of the bar, I noticed Seth, the bar owner, was already behind it with a notepad, checking our stock, and Cindy was cleaning tables.

Exposed wood made up the entire room, with a huge bar you couldn't miss when you walked in the front door. Bottles of alcohol lined the shelves. Very old school. Instead of booths, there were eight long tables, which could seat about twenty people apiece. The last four tables were usually mine and while the other waitress took the remaining four. With only three people in the bar, it was slow for the moment, so I went over to Cindy.

I came up behind her. "Hey, girly."

"Hey. How are your first days of school goin?" Cindy tucked her fire red hair behind her ear. Her hair color was awesome next to her bright green eyes.

"Umm, they're okay, nothing special. How's life without school?" Sometimes I envied the fact she'd decided against the whole college thing.

"Good. I got a puppy yesterday! A little brown one with floppy ears. Poor guy was walking on the side of my driveway." She made a little pouty face.

"At least, he's in a good home now. Oh, by the way, during my break at nine, do you think it would be all right if I took like a half hour, rather than fifteen mintues? I'm meeting somebody."

She didn't answer right away. Instead, she studied me for a moment and then did a little happy dance, complete with a smile like a kid caught with their hand in the cookie jar. "Oh my god, you finally have a boyfriend!" She did a hop that made her curly hair bounce, adding to her enthusiasm.

Stunned, I wondered if she spoke a foreign language. Why would she think I had a boyfriend? "Not really, more like a partner in one of my classes."

She arched an eyebrow. "Guy?"

Catching on with where she was going, I shook my head "Unfortunately."

Undeterred, she kept on, "Hot?"

It was a losing battle, so I laughed. "You can judge for yourself when he comes in, but he's not really my type." *Liar!* Maybe not a total lie, since he oozed arrogance, which was not my type. But if I was to judge by looks alone, and if he kept his mouth shut, he'd be every girl's type.

"Can't wait." She smiled sweetly and wandered over to the other customers to make sure they were happy with their food and drinks.

Around five-thirty, more people started flowing into the bar, and by eight-thirty, the entire college baseball team sat in my section. I wasn't complaining, since I got to admire the scenery and flirt with athletes all night. College guys tended to be the best tippers, especially when they were a bit drunk. The only down side to my job was dealing with them when they got grabby.

One of the boys whistled, and I turned immediately. He held up the empty pitcher of beer and pointed. Instead of frowning, I nodded. That was their sixth pitcher. Per Seth's rule, I'd have to ask who was driving and then consider cutting them off.

"Here you go, guys. Which one of y'all is driving tonight?" I pitched my voice over the noise, set down the full pitcher, then started cleaning up their dirty plates and empty beer pitcher. One of the guys held up his glass of coke he'd been nursing, answering my designated driver question. One guy's plate still had fries, so I asked, "You finished, hon?"

He wore a red flannel, jeans, and sneakers, and when you added in his sandy-blond hair and blue eyes, he was attractive.

Those baby blues were glassy as they roamed up and down, stopping at my chest before being joined by a goofy smile. "Not nearly," he slurred.

Perv. Suddenly, his attraction factor plummeted, and his ick factor skyrocketed. "You just let me know then."

Turning quickly, I went back to the bar. As soon as I got there, Sarah was waiting. She was scheduled to bartend and then cover my tables when I left. She was hot in her brown-heeled cowboy boots, daisy dukes, and black tank top. A black and white open flannel shirt completed her uniform. Her stomach was exposed, so the end of her dangling belly button ring showed. Her long brown hair fell in large ringlets down her back. She pulled off sexy without looking like a complete skank. I envied her confidence.

When she saw me, a grin broke out. "Hey, girl, hey."

I leaned my elbow against the bar with a wide smile.

"So, it's almost nine. Where's Mr. Tall, Dark, and Gorgeous?" she exclaimed.

"I thought you said he wasn't your type?" Cindy chimed in as she helped Seth pour drink orders.

"That boy is everyone's type." Sarah giggled. "Don't listen to Mais." She walked off to check out the tables and make sure there was room for Todd and his friends, who always came in when she worked.

Cindy stared at me, but, thank god, she didn't open her mouth. I left and went to check on my baseball table to see if anyone needed another round. They did. As I was taking the orders, I noticed their…girlfriends?…play things? What did you call girls who managed to hook up with boys in a matter of minutes?

Despite doing it twice, it was something I didn't understand. In my limited experience, it made me want a man more, which was depressing. Sarah's advice was to consider it satisfying a need and then move on. Easier said than done.

Plastering a smile on my face, I got to work. "You ladies want to order anything? Drinks? Or food?"

Unsurprisingly, they ordered different flavored margaritas, but no food.

"I'll be right back with those." I put some effort into sounding more cheerful, so I'd get better tips.

Once the girls arrived, it became harder to get good tips.

Back at the bar, I gave Seth their drink order and started helping him make strawberry and raspberry margaritas.

"Hey, uh Seth, I'm meeting one of my classmates tonight, for school. We have a project together, and I was hoping to take a thirty rather than a fifteen, if that's okay. I already cleared it with Sarah and Cindy."

With hazel eyes, short light-brown hair cropped close to his head, and his bulging muscles, he screamed scary and possibly ex-military. Not that he talked about his personal life, but he was pretty intimidating. Even the football players looked like five-year-olds next to him, but he was a big pushover.

"Yeah, no problem. It's not that busy yet."

"Thanks, if you need me, I think I'm going to take him to the tables outside in the front." I checked the clock it was almost nine-fifteen. If I was lucky, he wouldn't show. Of course, with that thought, he waltzed through the door

And he wasn't alone.

Chapter 3

Linc was with two other guys, who were almost as alluring as him. Linc looked good in a brick-red shirt, dark blue jeans, and black biker boots. The trio sat at the end of one of my tables. Turning away, I focused on something else before I started drooling.

"You're so full of shit, Maisy," Cindy whispered in my ear. "If one of those guys is your partner, don't care which one, I would just start taking my clothes off now to see where it got me."

"Slut," I muttered with a smile.

She winked and walked away, adding a little extra sway to her hips. I headed back to their table, only to stop when I realized Linc was staring at me. It wasn't in the sexy I-want-you way, but as if he was more annoyed at my presence. *Break eye contact now.* Before I could do that, someone jumped in front of me, making me jump.

"Hey, sweet cheeks, I was wondering if you'd like to hang out after your shift? Maybe get a drink?"

It was the guy who basically eye-fucked me earlier. Did he just call me sweet cheeks? Ew.

"Can't, I, uh, I have plans already," I lied, hoping he'd leave me alone. Twirling the end of my hair with one of my fingers, I studied it.

"Maybe next time," he said.

Sweet, I got off easy. Sliding past him, I jumped when a hand clutched my ass and gave it a squeeze. I turned to look at the idiot, but he was already back at his table, fist bumping his friend. For someone who was piss drunk, he moved freaky fast.

Rolling my eyes, I sighed and turned back to Linc, who was now staring daggers at the handsy baseball player. I walk up to Linc's table and smiled.

"Did you guys want a drink first, and then I can take my break?" My question brought Linc's whiskey-colored gaze to mine.

One of Linc's friends broke our staring contest. "Sure. I'll have whatever you have on tap."

I turned to him, practiced smile firmly in place. "Bud, okay?"

With his buzzed brown hair and brown eyes, his dark green jacket over a white T-shirt and dark jeans gave him an outdoor ruggedness. He nodded, and I turned to the next, equally gorgeous man.

This one was your typical surfer with shoulder-length blond hair, blue eyes, and a super tan exposed by a white T-shirt and worn-out light blue jeans with sandals.

"Same." Surfer Boy offered me a glimpse of gorgeous pearly whites.

The breath-taking testosterone factor increased and made me bite my lip and look away, as heat crept under my cheeks. I smiled tightly at Linc, my stomach full of confused butterflies. I couldn't decide if he made me nervous, or if I was still embarrassed by my near face plant at school. "And you?"

"Water's fine." His gaze flicked from me to Surfer Boy, his expression hardening.

Okay, who drinks water at a bar? As I went to turn away, I remembered something. "Sorry, can I see your IDs?"

Linc's friends grinned and pulled out their wallets. Checking the IDs, I noticed both were from the state of Alabama. Brown Eyes was twenty-four and Surfer Boy was twenty-two.

"Thanks, I'll be right back." I only made it a few steps away from their table, before one of them called out.

"Oh hey!" It was Surfer Boy. "Can we get some cheese fries too? Please?"

He flashed another smile, one that was the most perfect smile I'd ever seen. The way his face lit up made me want to take Cindy's advice and strip off my clothes. Between his face and body, it was a safe bet that he left a trail of broken hearts behind.

"Yeah, of course, and the name's Maisy if you need anything else." Was that considered flirting? I doubted it, but giving him my name counted, even though it was part of my job.

"Thank you, Maisy." He said my name like it tasted good on his tongue.

I stole a glance at Linc. He was staring again, but this time, it wasn't as if he wanted to kill me. It was more curious than anything.

Scanning the bar as I grabbed the two beers and poured Linc his water, my gaze crashed into Cindy's as she made her way over to me. She was grinning from ear to ear.

Before she could comment, I said, "I think I'm going to take my break now

"Uh huh," she hummed.

Shaking my head, I made my way back to Linc's table.

Passing out their drinks as they all said, "Thank you," I held on to Surfer Boy's beer a little longer than normal. When he held my gaze, I dipped my head down but felt my lips pull up slightly at the corners.

"You ready?" Linc cut in and got to his feet.

Blinking away from Surfer Boy, I offered, "Yeah, wanna go to the tables out in front?"

He held his left arm out to let me pass. "Lead the way."

Even this late, it was pretty warm. I sat at the small metal table, and he sat across from me. We didn't say anything for what felt like forever but was probably just a few uncomfortable minutes. Why was I so nervous? My hands wanted to tremble. and I reminded myself to hold it together.

"So, how do you want to do this?" I tried to break the awkward silence. He didn't say anything, just continued to sit there, his face expressionless. Unwilling to play his silent game, I continued, "I sort of came up with a thesis we could use."

He raised one of his dark eyebrows, and…was that a smirk? Why was he smirking?

Stunned, all I could so was stare as I tried to decide if he excelled at being a complete asshole to people he barely knew. Watching his lips curl into a definite smirk, I decided to plow ahead. "Okay, what if we focus on girl/guy platonic relationships? Can people of the opposite sex be friends without being attracted to each other, or will they always get romantically involved?" My words tumbled out so fast they were garbled.

"Thanks for the vocabulary lesson." There was a hint of humor in his voice. "So how would we test our theories?"

"We pick two people…or use ourselves, as examples…I don't know." I winced at how hard my voice sounded. Avoiding his gaze, I started playing with my hair.

He ran his hand through his curls. "Fine, let's use

ourselves. Say two people of the opposite sex can have a completely platonic relationship. It wouldn't be hard to prove."

It was my turn not to say anything, because I didn't know how to react to that. Did he not find me attractive at all? Maybe he had a girlfriend. Did he mean to be insulting? Because it sure sounded like it. Even more worrisome, why did the fact he didn't find me attractive matter? It didn't, dammit, not at all.

"How about no? We can keep that theory and people watch around campus. If we don't have enough to write about by the middle of November, we can use ourselves." That way we didn't have to spend a lot of time together.

Getting up, he muttered, "Sure."

Since he decided we were done talking, I followed behind him. He opened the door for me, and, as I stepped through my damn boot caught the edge of the tiny lip. I stumbled but managed to catch myself at the last moment. I glanced up to find him almost laughing. Giving him my best dirty look, I tried to ignore the funny things his laugh did to my head. It was official, Surfer Boy had nothing on Linc.

He held up both hands, his brown eyes still dancing with laughter. "I didn't say anything."

If he didn't wipe that look off his face, I was going to smack him. Over at the bar, Sarah started busting up as she watched us, while Seth gave me a sympathetic smile. Shaking my head, I continued on toward Cindy, who was enjoying the attention of my baseball table. I tapped her shoulder to let her know I was back on the floor. Hurrying to the bar, I grabbed my rag and order book. From the corner of my eye, I noticed someone trying to flag me down. It was Surfer Boy. Not wanting to go back over to that table, I closed my eyes and inhaled, trying to calm myself. It was no use. I gave up and stalked in their direction.

Standing at their table, I was miffed when Linc wouldn't look at me. He seemed to find his water more interesting. Surfer Boy, on the other hand, wore a big smile aimed at me. It was ridiculously hard not to smile back.

"What can I get ya…um…sir?"

His smile went colossal. "I'm Thomas, but my friends call me Tommy. Could you get us three more beers, please?" He nudged the empty plate of cheese fries. "And another order of cheese fries."

"Of course." Unsure of what he wanted me to call him, I didn't add his name to the end of that. We weren't friends, so Tommy wasn't appropriate, but Thomas sounded too formal. Clearing their table of the empty glasses and plates, I tried my hardest not to look at Linc but failed.

At the bar, I checked the time, ten-fifteen. Thank goodness, I was almost off.

Sarah came up behind me. "Hey, Mais, can you watch Todd's table for a sec? I got a voicemail from my mom."

"Yeah." I gave my order to Seth and then made my way to Todd and his friends.

"Hey, guys." Hopefully, I sounded cheerful.

Todd didn't pay me any attention but his friend, Jake did.

"Hey, Maisy, how you been?" Jake stood up and gave me a hug, lifting me off my feet. We'd dated briefly freshman year, but he wanted to have fun and not be exclusive. It didn't hurt my feelings, because I'd left a relationship the summer before and was in the same boat. Jake was cute, more lean than muscled, with vibrant blue eyes and brown hair. He was pretty awesome.

I heard Todd huff but ignored him. "Good, you?"

"Great!" Jake ran his fingers up and down my arm. "What time are you off? There's a party tonight. You should come."

"I'm off at eleven, but I'm going to have to pass. I'm tired." I stepped back just a bit, offering a tiny smile to take the sting from my rejection.

"Come on, Mais. If you don't go tonight, you have to come with me to the party this Saturday. Todd and Sarah will be there." He laid it on thick, giving me puppy-dog eyes which made him look absolutely ridiculous.

I laughed. "Fine, sounds good. Did you guys need anything?'

Jake was the only one who answered. "Nope, I'm good, but I'll text you later."

I nodded and went back to the bar to pick up the order for Linc's table.

"Here you guys go." I handed Linc and Brown Eyes their beers first and then turned to Thomas. The glass slipped from my hand and hit the table hard. I grabbed my towel to take care of the spill, leaning forward to wipe the table. "Crap, sorry, Thomas."

"It's cool. You didn't spill it on me. And it's Tommy."

Lifting my head, I saw the beer in his hand, still filled to the brim. *How did that not spill?* I'd basically dropped it. I grinned at Tommy. "Let me know if you guys need anything else."

As I walked away, I heard Linc's low, "What the fuck, dude?"

I kept walking and checked on my other tables.

When I checked my watch again, I was excited to find there was only five minutes left in my shift. "Cindy, I'm off in five," I yelled over the bar.

"Okay, give me a minute, and then I'll walk around with you."

She finished up what she was doing. Seth thought it was common courtesy to introduce people to their new waitress if we left and still had customers.

I introduced her to my tables, and then we headed over to Linc's table.

"I'm off," I announced to the three men. "This is Cindy. She's going to take over your table."

Cindy was all smiles. If I didn't know Linc was some sort of an asshole, I probably would have been the same way.

"I hope you all have a good rest of your night." I smiled and bowed out, not looking at Linc.

Saying bye to Seth, I went to his office to get my purse.

"Maisy?"

I jumped and almost dropped my phone. Whipping around, I found Tommy standing in Seth's office doorway. I reached out to grab my purse. "You frickin' scared the crap outta me."

"Sorry about that. I was wondering if you had work this Friday night?"

I stared at him. "Yeah, I work till eleven again."

"Wanna go out after your shift?"

Did he just…

"I don't really think anything's going to be open at around eleven, unless you plan to take me to another bar."

He laughed and moved his hair out of his eyes. "Who said I wanted to take you anywhere?"

Once again, I was left staring.

"I'm kidding, Maisy. We could get a drink here or drive around until we see something interesting."

He was asking me out? I stared at him, confused. *Say*

something! "Uhmm." *Not what I was hoping for.*

"It'll be fun, I promise. I'm pretty awesome."

Try arrogant. My lips tipped up at the corners. "Yeah, okay."

"Cool, I'll see you Friday." He turned on his heel and walked back out to the bar.

I left Seth's office with a small smile on my lips. I just said yes to my first date in months. Instead of dreading a date, I felt giddy.

On the drive home, I mentally ran through my week, trying to figure out if anything was due in the next couple days. It was only the first week of school, but some teachers still believed in the introduce-yourself-paragraph due the second week of classes, and it counted for roll. I drove past my running trail, and chills broke over my skin. Memories of that bum still haunted me, and I didn't know why. Maybe it was the thought of what could have happened if he followed me. Or maybe it was the water part. Crazy as it was, I didn't want to admit it happened.

I was relieved to finally park in our driveway. Once inside, I headed straight for the tub. I loved bubble baths and really needed one to erase the smell of smoke and beer. Inching into the scorching water, I slowly sank to the bottom. I slipped under the water and stayed there for about a minute before coming back up for air. Lying there, I relaxed and, eventually, my eyes slid closed.

I woke up to someone turning on the faucet and rummaging around in a drawer nearby. Opening my eyes, I found Sarah had made it home from work, so it had to be close to three in the morning. Stretching my arms, I noticed the water was lukewarm.

"How long have you been in there?" She managed the question around her toothbrush stuck in her mouth.

I squinted up at her. "Couple hours, maybe."

Glancing at me, she chuckled, "Cold much?"

A quick peek down revealed the bubbles from earlier were gone. Although the water temperature wasn't cold, my nipples decided it was below zero. I stood up and grabbed the towel Sarah held out to me. "Shut up."

"Night, Mais." She left me to dry off.

"Night."

Chapter 4

The next day flew by. Sarah was actually ready to go at six-thirty—kudos for her—and I went to class and didn't talk to Linc at all. During the two classes we shared, he barely even acknowledged me, which was fine. Back home after school, I decided to run before dinner, since Sarah and Todd were going out, leaving me dining solo.

I sat on the porch to put my shoes on and then stretched. Stretching felt good. I took off in a sprint and kept my pace at a fast run. The trees and dirt resembled green and brown watercolors that had run together. I kept running.

Once I got to the trail, I slowed, resting my hands on the back of my head and walked in circles to cool down.

Peering into the shaded forest at the trail I had avoided the last couple of days, I whispered, "I can do this." Catching my breath, I jogged into the trees, being extra attentive to my surroundings.

Paranoia left me imagining someone standing behind a tree or a bush, watching, but I shook it off. I'd run this trail a million times in the last four years. No one was out here.

A heavy hand landed on my shoulder. "Maisy?"

I screamed and tried to run faster.

"Maisy, it's me, it's Linc." He pulled my shoulder until I spun around to face him.

"What the fucking hell is your problem?" I yelled, trying to catch my breath. "Are you following me?" My voice shook, sounding breathy as hell.

He shook his head. "You wish. I was on a run, and I saw you ahead of me, so I thought I'd say hi."

"You thought you would say hi? You had two classes to say hi! Yet you decide the best time to share was to creep up behind me while I was running?"

"I was not creeping up behind you. Besides, I'm feeling friendly now." He ran a hand through his sweat-soaked hair as he smiled.

"Okay...um...hi." I pulled away, gave him my back, and started jogging again.

He kept the pace next to me. "So, do you run here a lot?"

"Yeah, almost every day, you?" Running and talking wasn't something I was good at so it was hard to keep my voice normal.

"Nope. I usually stay on the street, but I saw you turn in here."

"So, you were following me." Those damn butterflies in my stomach were back. I tried not to analyze it too much.

He shrugged. After a couple of minutes, he said, "I heard Tommy's taking you out tomorrow night."

How was I to respond to that? "Yeah."

"He's a pretty cool guy, fun."

Was he trying to talk his friend up? If so, he sucked at it because his voice sounded pissed off.

"He seems fun." I snuck a glance at him, and our eyes met.

His lips were pushed together in a hard line. Our conversation ground to a halt until we arrived at the small creek. I slowed down and studied him. "Um, I usually turn around here, did you want to keep running with me?"

"Sure."

Something told me he had slowed his pace to match mine, but he did follow me all the way home.

"Well, this is me," I announced, walking up the driveway.

"Do you live here all by yourself?" His question sounded like a parent scolding a teenager for doing something stupid.

"No, I live here with Sarah, the girl I sit by in our Romantic Love class." I tried to catch my breath as I forced an even tone.

He nodded. "Good."

We stood in the driveway, facing each other. I could feel the weight of his stare, even though I was examining the dirt at my feet. "Do you want to come in for some water? Or dinner? I was going to make dinner." *Shut up, shut up, shut up, Maisy.*

"Lead the way, gorgeous."

My heart stopped, and the butterflies took flight, until a small smile pulled at my lips. Heading toward the house, I heard him chuckle behind me, and that sound made my fingers fumble with the house key.

As we went through the living room and kitchen area, I watched him take in the house with our worn furniture and Sarah's questionable decorating skills, which consisted of enormous amounts of framed pictures filling the walls and any available surface.

While he was distracted checking out the house, it gave me a chance to check him out. He wore black running shorts, a gray college T-shirt, and blue running shoes. Gray was one of the colors on my what-not-to-wear-while-working-out list, as it showed sweat lines.

However, he could definitely pull it off. His shirt clung to his well-muscled chest and biceps. His mysterious tattoo was only partially visible, but there was definitely a tentacle wrapped around his bicep. My gaze lifted to his wavy hair that was still wet and plastered to his face. Then I noticed his eyes were on me. Shit—

"Did you want water or dinner? I'm not really sure what you agreed to," I looked away as heat crept into my cheeks.

"Both." His eyes drifted from my face to my chest and then back. They were darker, deeper, if that was possible, and the butterflies in my stomach moved lower.

It'd been a while since I had felt that particular feeling.

"Sounds good, do you want chicken or pasta? Oh! I think I also have pork chops somewhere."

"Chicken's good."

"'Kay." Was that breathy, high-pitched, and girly tone mine?

"Did you have somewhere I could rinse off at?" He leaned against the kitchen counter.

"Bathroom's second door on the left," I instructed.

He nodded and disappeared down the hall, leaving me standing there like an idiot in the middle of my open, country kitchen.

When I finally heard the water turn on, I inched closer toward the hallway. The bathroom door was cracked. Proving my feet had a mind of their own, I somehow ended up right outside the bathroom door, like a creeper. Peering in, I could only see the outline of huge male body inside my shower. The bathroom was filled with steam, but the mist or fog or whatever, looked funny as it hung in perfect circle above the shower. It didn't cling to the mirror or the walls, simply hovering over the shower…weird. When the shower suddenly shut off, I was jerked from my condensation puzzle and literally sprinted the entire way to the kitchen.

I leaned against the island's, both hands pressed to the white tile patterned counter top as I listen to the door open and then heavy footsteps head down the hallway.

Linc appeared in the entryway. "That felt good. Did you want to go shower and I could start dinner?" He raised an eyebrow. "Are you okay?"

Guess my panting clashed with my casual pose, but it wasn't entirely caused by the mad dash back to the kitchen. Oh, where the hell did his shirt go? Normal guys weren't supposed to look like this. Guys who put Beckham to shame were definitely not supposed to be in my home. My frickin' hormones were going crazy, urging me to tackle him. Finally, I got a glimpse of his tattoo, a giant octopus wrapped around his bicep and up his shoulder. Its head lay on his chest.

"Yeah, why?" I tried to remember how to breathe normally and hide the gulps of air I needed.

"You look tense, and you're out of breath."

Because I didn't think *I was watching you shower and I got all hot and bothered* was an acceptable answer, I chose to ignore his remark. Instead, I grabbed the chicken out of my freezer and put it in a pan.

"A shower sounds good. Just put the chicken in the oven at three seventy-five." I walked past him, feeling his eyes on me the entire time. "Help yourself to anything you want."

Those deep brown eyes did another once over, and an involuntary shiver ran over my body. His gaze stopped at my mouth. Feeling awkward and insecure, I nibbled my lower lip. His gaze met mine searching for something, and a knowing grin curled his lips.

"Don't offer me something I can't have again."

Um...what? I held his intense gaze for a second

longer before tucking my hair behind my ear and making my way down the hall.

When I got to the bathroom, I realized I was wearing a giddy smile, but it quickly faded. What if he was messing with me? Instead of staring at him like a girl fan seeing Luke Bryan for the first time, why couldn't I come up with something witty? I took my hair out of the ponytail and got undressed. I turned the water on scorching hot and stood there under the stream. After a few minutes, I realized I had company and couldn't afford to be rude. I shampooed and conditioned my hair in record time. Turning off the shower, I reached out for my towel only to find it was soaked. He used my towel? Well, I guessed that was okay, because I hadn't given him one. But now I was out one super soft, cotton green towel. My attempt to dry off didn't work since the towel was drenched.

Spying Sarah's towel on the rack, I went to grab it and then stopped. What if Todd used this towel? Ew. New plan, I'll run to my room directly across from the bathroom. If Linc is in the kitchen or living room, he won't be able to see me. I peeked out of bathroom slowly and quietly. No Linc. I made a run for my bedroom.

"Hey, Maisy, do you have Cajun seasoning for the chicken?"

I stopped like a deer in headlights. Shit, fuckin' shit. We made eye contact.

"Shit, Maisy!" he yelled. After another moment of staring at my naked body, he threw his hands over his eyes and turned away, giving me time to get away.

Slamming my bedroom door, I ran for my drawer and pulled out a clean towel to dry off with then found a dark T-shirt and another pair of clean running shorts. *Shit on a stick. What the heck?* I dragged my hands down my face. *He saw me naked. Naked. Fuck. Now, what am I supposed to do?*

I racked my brain for the best possible solution. Nothing came back that wouldn't be awkward. *Great.*

Fully clothed, I stood in front of my bedroom door and breathed. *Just walk out there like nothing happened. You can do it.* I stepped into the hall and headed down at a snail's pace. When I got to the kitchen, he was leaning back against the counter, water bottle in hand, staring at the oven like he was watching his favorite team playing.

"How's the chicken coming?" I asked hesitantly.

"Fine. Hey, listen, my brother Craig—you know, the guy with the short hair that was with me and Tommy at the bar last night? He just called, needs a ride, so I'm going to head out." He turned toward the door to leave, despite still being shirtless.

"Did you need a ride? Or do you want your shirt—" He was basically out the door before I could finish my questions.

"No, and keep it. I'll text you over the weekend about our project." He shut the door before I could even get the word "bye" out.

I paced the kitchen the entire half hour it took the chicken to cook. I didn't know what to do. The guy I found completely attractive just saw me buck-ass naked and basically ran out of my house.

I seriously contemplated taking my clothes off and looking in the mirror to see what he found so repulsive.

Maybe when Sarah got home from work, I could ask her what was so bad about my body to send a guy running. I wasn't stick skinny or overly attractive, but, when I took my clothes off, guys usually didn't flee.

The oven dinged, but my appetite was gone. *Great, maybe flashing a guy can be a new diet trend.* Unfortunately, I loved food way too much, so even my self-consciousness couldn't stop me from eating a chicken breast with that stupid Cajun seasoning he couldn't find and some green beans.

Pushing my hair out of my face and trying not to be overly emotional about the whole weird situation, I decided to believe he was telling the truth and his brother…whatever his name was…really did call him to get a ride. It had nothing to do with him seeing me naked. But by the time I'd finished most of my chicken, I was convinced it had everything to do with seeing me naked, and he was just an asshole who didn't find me attractive.

My phone vibrated while I sat at the table pushing green beans around my yellow plate. One sentence lit up my phone.

Thanks for letting me run with you, I had fun.

I stared at my phone, trying to decide how to respond. He saw me naked and ran away so fast he didn't even put his shirt on. Which reminded me…

I went into the bathroom, grabbed Linc's shirt, and then went to my room for my dirty clothes to throw in the washing machine. He could wait for a response.

After I started the small load of laundry, I texted him back. One word.

Sure.

There, that should do it. It didn't sound mean, or overly nice. Seconds passed before another text lit up my screen.

See you tomorrow.

I raised an eyebrow at my phone. No, he wouldn't, because we hadn't made any plans to do so. Or did we? Worried, I racked my brain, going over our conversation during our run. I couldn't remember him saying anything about seeing me tomorrow. Maybe he was just confused. Since I had no clue what he was talking about, I didn't text back.

Back in my room, I decided that nine-thirty wasn't

too early to go to bed. I was tired from our run. No need to go into why I felt the need to pick up my pace and go faster than normal. Nope, I wasn't going to think too much on the whys behind that. Changing into an oversize T-shirt, I lay down and was out before my head hit the pillow.

ↄ✺ↄ

I yawned, stretching my legs to the end of the bed and extending my hands to the top, holding it for thirty seconds. Today was Friday, and I didn't have anything to do till three, which made for a happy morning. Today's run would be somewhere different, and longer. I threw my blonde messy waves into a high ponytail and grabbed some workout clothes. On my way out the door, I remembered Linc's shirt was in the washing machine. Running into the laundry room, I threw most of the clothes into the dryer, hanging his shirt because I didn't know if it would shrink or not. No sense getting blamed for ruining it, even though he told me to keep it.

It would be dry by my shift, and I'd bring it to work and give it to Tommy before our date. That wasn't weird, right? Giving your date his friends' shirt? I laughed a little but knew it was going to happen because I didn't want it. Plus, it would be creepy to keep it.

I stretched in my driveway and took off, feeling an immense amount of energy, so I was really moving. I hit the spot where I usually veered off and decided to run past the small creek. Even though the trail went farther than the creek, I never did. The woods felt cool on my skin, the contrast of the temperature drop gave me the chills.

Checking my watch, I was thrilled to see I hit the creek in under thirty minutes, perfect. Stopping at the water's edge, I bent down to dip my hand in the cool liquid. I missed the beach back in California. I loved water. My friends back home teased that I was part fish. Anything to do with swimming, surfing, diving, I did it. The creeks, rivers, and random ponds out in Alabama didn't cut it, but there was this really gorgeous lake that the entire school went to every weekend. I tried swimming laps there, but there were too many people who I knew and I ended up talking to them and getting distracted. So, I settled with running.

I cupped the cool water in my hands and splashed it on my face, the contrast of the cool water felt amazing against my overheated skin. I crossed the small creek, surprised to find it was a little deeper than I thought when it came up to mid-shin.

My depth perception was super off, since I thought it was ankle deep. Closer to the other side, it was almost over my knee. Hopping up onto the bank, I found the well-worn trail. Weird to think that many people ran it because, except for the bum, I'd never come across anyone else here.

Shrugging it off, I picked up my pace and ran another mile or mile and a half before noticing a big sunny patch just ahead. Maybe it was the road on the side of town. Once there, I stopped and almost gasped, like in those cheesy movies. It wasn't the side of town. It was a huge meadow. There was long green grass surrounding a small lake in the middle. Trees lined the outer edges. It was beautiful. Sporadically placed tiny white flowers dotted the meadow, and everything was so green.

How did I not know about this? If I hadn't stopped at the damn creek every time, I would've found it sooner. I walked over to the pond and took in the pretty steady descent of the shoreline into the water. It must be a pretty decent-sized depth, considering the darker color toward the middle of the lake. It probably had a ton of snakes in it though.

After checking my watch again, I turned back around, prepared to head home. Two hours was long enough for a run. Rough estimates put my initial run at almost seven miles before I found the new pond. Kind of a personal record. I hauled butt home.

Being the damn klutz that I was, when I got back to the creek, I slipped on a rock and fell forward, drenched in seconds. Getting up super-fast, I couldn't help but look around, which was dumb because no one was out here to witness my embarrassing fall.

Testing my elbows and wrists, I discovered small aches. My right elbow sported a gorgeous big scratch, which would leave a scar. Yay. At least the drenched clothes felt good in the sun as I came out of the trees. I closed my eyes and kept running, picking my knees up a little high, so I wouldn't eat shit. Opening my eyes, I tried to run faster, but my legs were almost to the point of shaking, and they hurt.

Once inside my home, I grabbed two bottles of water and drank them both. I lay on the couch, not wanting to move ever again. My run had to be close to fifteen miles, and I could feel new blisters on my feet. Turning my head, I stared at the DVR box. Ten-twenty-six. Great, I still had a couple more hours till work this afternoon. Time enough take a long shower, eat something, and maybe do some homework, or sleep. In the hot shower, I discovered a new cut on my elbow as it burned at the contact with the scorching water. My long shower turned into a five-minute one.

Putting on a big shirt, I walked to the kitchen and heated up the other chicken breast from last night. It tasted fantastic, probably because I was really hungry. Grabbing my binder, I went to my room. I swear I started in a sitting position, but ended up in a horizontal position, under the covers. The bed felt so good, I just wanted to stay in it, sleep, and forget about work.

Thoughts swirled in my head. I still needed to make sure Linc's shirt was dry and figure out what I was wearing on tonight's date. It would have to be cute, but working at a bar meant I couldn't dress up that much. Maybe cut off shorts and my black tube top with my brown boots? I could bring extra shoes to change into. That was my last thought for the next three hours.

Chapter 5

Jolting awake to find it was two o'clock, I scrambled up, trying to find my phone. Crap on a stick. I needed to leave in thirty minutes. Running around my room, I grabbed my cut offs and my strapless black bra and then ran into the bathroom to do my makeup. Throwing on some cat eyeliner and mascara, I added Sarah's red lipstick. Darting into the laundry room, I grabbed Linc's now dry shirt and hightailed it back to my bedroom to find my black tube top. Finding it in my closet, I pulled it on. With a sweetheart neckline, it was sexy. Walking to my floor length mirror, I spun for a full check. Not bad, my legs looked a little thick, but other than that, I was acceptable. Grabbing a turquoise statement necklace, I hobbled into my brown boots. One last hair check in the bathroom confirmed my side bangs were sticking out everywhere. I pinned them back because there was no fixing them.

When I got to work, I put my wristlet into Seth's office and almost walked right into him. He grabbed me around the waist, so we didn't topple over. I gave a silent groan. *Way to go, Mais, take out two hot guys in one week with your grace.*

He let go fast and cleared his throat. "Hey, Mais." He checked out my outfit. "You look nice. Occasion?"

"Yeah, I have a date after work," I answered with a grin.

"Have fun. Oh, can you do the bar tonight? I have to go over the bar's accounts and shit."

"No problem." Sweet! I loved working the bar. Besides my over-worked legs would thank me.

Walking out to the floor, I found Sarah coming in.

"Hey," I called to her.

She smiled and did a little spin wave thing then went to the back to put her purse away. I went over to where Cindy was punching in someone's order into the computer at the bar. Walking up behind her, I pinched her butt.

"Hey, love," she said unfazed. Her fiery hair was in spiral curls today.

I leaned against the counter next to the computer. "Hey, you off?"

"Yeah, it's been slow. You going to that frat party tomorrow?"

"Yes, ma'am. I'm going with Sarah. Are you actually going to a party?"

Cindy never went to parties, which, when we first met, surprised me. Her personality screamed wild.

"I was thinking about it." She smiled in my direction, showing her tooth gap. It was small and gave her face more character.

"Come to my house before, and we can all go together."

"Sounds good, I'm off at eleven, so I'll be there around eleven-thirty?" She bit her pink bottom lip.

"Perfect, I get off the same time."

"Yay. Can't wait." She giggled and headed out the back to get her purse before leaving.

Grabbing a rag, I started wiping down the bar, which was pretty much clean. I'd only bartended once, so I was good if customers wanted beer, wine, or margaritas. Anything outside of that, and I was clueless. I'd be asking customers "what's in that" to all of their drink orders tonight, but it was good practice and fun.

The next four hours went by super slow. Ten, maybe twelve, people came into the bar the entire time. Since all they wanted was beer, I was safe.

Sarah and I talked the entire time about tomorrow's party.

She was getting off earlier than Cindy or me and would wait for us to get back to the house.

"Are you excited about Tommy tonight?" She wiggled her perfectly shaped eyebrows.

"Sort of. I hung out with Linc yesterday, and feel a little weird." I didn't meet her eyes as my face turned red.

"You didn't tell me that," she yelled. "What did you guys do?"

I rolled my eyes at her excitement. "We just ran and then went to the house."

"And what sort of activities went down at the house?"

I blushed. "Umm, I was making him dinner, and he saw me naked."

She smiled like the Cheshire cat from A*lice in Wonderland.* "And how did that go?"

"He ran away," I admitted, my voice barely a whisper.

She started cracking up, to the point of snorting. Between snorts, she got out, "What?"

"He said his brother called him for a ride, but he didn't have a car, so he ran back to where ever he lives and grabbed his car. He even left his shirt." I put my face into my hands groaning with embarrassment.

"Well, I've seen you naked, and I highly doubt he was running from you."

That made my lips turn up in relief. "Yeah, I'm going to give Tommy Linc's shirt to give back to him to-night."

She started to say something, but Todd and Jake came in and took her attention.

"Hey, guys."

"Hey," they both said in unison.

I met Jake's bright-blue gaze. "Drink?"

"Just a coke."

I crinkled my nose.

He laughed and grasped the back of his neck. "I'm driving."

"Okay, hon." I turned, filled a cup of ice with coke from the dispenser, and then handed it to him.

He looked me over. "What are you doing tonight?"

"I'm hanging out with a guy I met earlier this week," I answered, looking up at him. He was easily six foot.

"Do I know him?" His eyes searched my face, and his tone didn't sound happy.

"His name's Tommy. He was in here the other day with Linc, my partner for class."

Jake's eyes darkened a bit, but then an easy smile formed on his lips. "I don't think it's a good idea to go out with someone you just met." His tone was just a bit too big-brotherly for my taste.

"It's fine. He seems harmless."

"Doesn't matter, still not a good idea." He took another sip of coke.

"Back off, Jake. She's finally going out. Leave her alone," Sarah chimed in even as Todd's arms encircled her small frame.

Jake grumbled but shut up and drank his coke. I helped a couple other customers at the far end of the bar. They each ordered a beer, easy. A few beers and hours later, the door opened, and in walked Tommy, Linc, and some chick with brownish red hair. Her arm was looped through Linc's. Girlfriend? It would make sense if that was why he ran away.

"Hey, Mais." Tommy took a seat at the bar, and Linc and his girlfriend sat down next to him.

Tommy's shoulder length hair was pulled back in a small bun. "You ready for tonight?"

"Yeah." I nodded and blushed a little but snuck a peek at Linc before snapping my head back to Tommy. "You guys want anything? I'm not really good at making drinks, but I can pour a really good beer. Oh, and I'm Maisy, by the way." I stuck out my hand out to the girl sitting between Linc and Tommy.

"I'm Eva," she said, taking my hand.

"Yeah, that's my little sis," Tommy chimed in.

"I wouldn't have guessed that. It's nice to meet you. So, beer?" They all agreed, and I checked Eva's ID. She just turned twenty-one two days ago.

"Oh, happy birthday!"

Eva smiled shyly, and I went to the bar's other end to pour their beers. Linc still hadn't said a word to me. Fine. Whatever. He would have to talk to me sometime. I filled their beers to the brim and headed back.

"Thanks!" Tommy took a drink from his beer. "You're going to get off right at eleven, right? I was thinking we could go night swimming maybe."

Well, I got pretty for nothing then, but I love swimming, so score. "That sounds fun." I beamed at him and then turned to the other two. "So, what are you guys doing tonight?"

"Swimming is starting to sound good," Linc said, as his lip twitched.

"You guys should come with us." It spilled out before I even thought about it. Crap. I looked at Tommy and offered an apologetic smile. "If that's okay with you."

"Yeah, that's fine." He didn't sound totally thrilled.

Well, shoot. "I have to go get my swimsuit, though, I didn't know we were swimming."

"No problem, I can ride with you. Linc and Eva can meet us there." Tommy's cheeks dimpled slightly.

I heard Sarah call my name. "Well, I'll see you in a bit."

I headed over to Sarah who was dropping off a drink order. Her deep, brown hair was in a messy bun, and she wore a green, plaid shirt with dark jeans tucked into black boots.

She leaned in. "You can take off if you want. Seth's done with whatever he was doing, so we've got it."

"You sure?"

"Yeah, go have fun!" She pushed me toward the door.

"Okay, I'll see you at home."

I turned and got maybe three steps before I heard Sarah whisper, "Mais, remember, you're on a date with Tommy, not Linc."

Shooting her a dirty look over my shoulder, I went to Seth's office to get my wallet.

When I got back to the bar, I walked over to Linc, Tommy, and Eva. "You guys ready?"

"Yeah," Tommy said, as Linc grabbed his wallet to pay for the beers.

I put my hand over his huge one and pushed downward. "Don't worry about it." My hand lingered a little longer than what was socially appropriate.

His gaze held mine captive. "Thanks."

"Okay, well, we'll meet you there," Tommy cut in.

We said our good-byes and Tommy followed me through the back to where I parked. I didn't realize how big Tommy was until we got into my car. He filled my entire car and looked cramped.

He stared out the window toward the bar. "How long have you've been working here?"

"Little over a year. What do you do?" I snuck a peek at him.

"I work for mine and Linc's family. It's a landscaping company."

"Sounds cool, does Linc work there too?"

"Yeah, and so does Craig, Linc's bother. Do you remember him? He was the other guy with us last time."

"I thought Linc and Craig were the same age, so are they twins?" Well, that was a bit creepy, I shouldn't have remembered their ages.

"Naw, they're not related biologically. Linc's family took Craig in when we were younger."

"Oh. That's nice of them."

"Yeah, they're cool."

An awkward silence settled between us. Trying to break it, I asked, "So, where are we going swimming?"

"The lake that everyone goes too, that okay?"

"Yep." We pulled up to my house and got out of the car. As we walked inside, I realized I hadn't done the dishes this morning. They weren't high on my to-do list since I wasn't planning company.

"Sorry 'bout the mess, want anything?" I threw over my shoulder as I made my way back to my room.

"I'm good."

I grabbed my floral bikini, wiggled into it, covered it with my shorts, and put on flip-flops. I went to my dresser and grabbed a green V-neck T-shirt. I picked up a towel from the bathroom and was ready to go.

"Ready?" I walked toward Tommy.

He held out his hand, and I took it. "Definitely." He spun me and never let go of my hand.

Considering I hung out with his best friend yesterday, I almost felt bad.

We headed out, locked the door, and got into the car. Opening my trunk, I moved Linc's shirt over and put my towel down.

Behind me, Tommy reached over, picked up the shirt, and held it up. "Is this Linc's shirt?" He sounded appalled and slightly confused.

"Yeah, we went running, and he left it at my house. Um, how did you know that?" Tommy knowing the shirt was Linc's was super weird.

"It has our work's logo on it. Since I know it's not mine, I'm guessing it's his." An awkward silence surrounded us.

"Not to sound demanding or anything, because you can do what you want, but why exactly was his shirt off?" His voice was low.

"Umm, he showered—" *Crap.* "—after our run and came out with his shirt off, shorts on, though." *Unfortunately. Shit, stop thinking.*

"All right." And, with that, Tommy became quiet.

Minutes passed before I blurted, "Nothing happened. I know he's dating your sister, and it was nothing like that, honestly."

"He's not dating my sister." He sounded disgusted. "I'd chop off his—"

"Okay, sorry," I cut it in. "It just sort of looked like it from where I was standing."

"We're all like family. It wouldn't happen."

I drove the rest of the way with my mouth shut. I felt him watching me, though, the entire way. When we got to the river, he grabbed my towel and my hand and started walking towards the riverbank where Linc and Eva were. Eva was slung over Linc's shoulder, and when he looked up, our gazes locked long enough to be noticeable. Tommy squeezed my hand, and I broke eye contact first. I gave Tommy a smile. In the distance, a loud splash

sounded. Without checking, my money was on Linc toss-
ing Eva into the water.

When we came to where Linc and Eva's clothes
were, Tommy took off his white T-shirt. Man, he was
ripped. Goodness, I really didn't want to take my clothes
off now. He stepped closer and tugged my hips toward
him.

"You can swim right?" He didn't move his hands.
His touch felt weird as if I should like it, but I didn't.
There was no rhyme or reason to it, Tommy was sweet
and drop-dead gorgeous.

"Yeah, I love the water." I put my hands on his and
tried to move them off. He took it the wrong way and
stepped in closer.

"Tommy, get in here! You too, Maisy," Eva yelled.

Tommy made a half chuckle and took my hand
again.

I pulled back just a little.

"Go ahead, I'll be there in a minute."

He ran into the water and about took Eva and Linc
out. I stared at the three of them as they laughed. Eva was
gorgeous in a wine colored two-piece bikini, proving the
two siblings definitely hit the genetic jackpot. They even
had matching triton tattoos on the right side of their tor-
sos. I slightly envied their closeness. I didn't have siblings, but totally wished I did. I mean I had best friends.
There was just a different type deep connection that siblings had that I had never experienced.

I started to peel my shorts down my legs and looked
up. Tommy and Eva stood in the water close to the bank
talking. Linc was farther out, the water up to his chest,
and he was staring at me. It was dark, but I couldn't
shake the weight of his attention. I pulled off my green
V-neck and waded into the water. It was warm and felt
good. Passing Tommy and Eva, I heard Tommy stop talk-

ing, and he grabbed my hand again, stopping my descent into the dark water. I gritted my teeth. The water hadn't covered my tummy yet, and I didn't want to stand where the three of them could see my far-from-perfect body.

"Do you come out here often? I've only seen you a handful of times down here at the parties?" Eva asked me.

"Sort of, Sarah is dating one of the guys from the frat that usually throws those parties."

"Cool, which guy?"

"Todd, he's friends with Jake." Jake was more well-known than Todd, so it made sense she'd know Jake.

"Oh." Her voice sounded surprised.

"Maisy, come over here," Linc called.

It was the longest string of words he said to me tonight. Tommy let go of me, and I swam out to Linc. The water was over my head at this depth, and I had to tread water when I got to him. His dark hair clung to his forehead and face. He looked good wet.

Once in front of him, I tried for casual. "Yeah?"

"Do you want to hang out tomorrow?"

I didn't know what to say that wouldn't be awkward, considering I was here on a date with his friend.

"And start our research?" he finally added.

"Sounds good to me. Text me when you wanna hang out."

I was starting to get tired, so I sank to the bottom and came back up. When I started treading water again, it felt different, as if the water had gained weight, and I could sit there and float forever. Tommy and Eva's heads snapped in Linc's direction, and then Tommy went under the water. I went to ask Linc what was wrong, but I felt arms grab onto the back of my thighs and launched me into the air, whipping my wet hair back. I crashed into the water and came back up to see Linc punch Tommy's arm.

"You good, babe?" Tommy yelled, smiling from ear to ear.

I gave him a thumb's up and began to swim toward them.

Tommy grabbed Eva and tossed her into the air. "Incoming," he yelled as soon as he let go of her.

She crashed into the water right next to me. She pulled her definitely dyed auburn hair out of her face and beamed. "Good perk of having an idiot jock brother. You never have to feel fat because they can toss you like you weigh nothing more than a thimble."

I laughed and followed her back to the boys. I stopped in-between Linc and Eva, across from Tommy, which was where I wanted to be but would never admit out loud. We swam and played, the boys throwing us around while we talked about nothing. It was wonderful. So different from what I was used to. I'd never had friends who all got along.

We stayed out in the water for close to two hours. We were talking in the deeper part where I couldn't reach the sandy bottom, and I was treading water between Tommy and Linc. A hand grabbed mine and held it straight down so I could put all my weight on that arm and rest. The hand was from Linc's side.

We stayed there for another ten minutes before Linc asked, "You guys ready? It has to be close to two in the morning."

The other two nodded. I yawned.

"I think we wore her out," Eva chuckled

I liked her. She was sweet and seemed to accept me, which was nice. In my experience, girls were usually total bitches, at first, before accepting a new addition to a social circle.

"Maybe a little," I replied softly.

Suddenly I was airborne again, and my stomach

came down on something hard. It turned out to be Tommy's shoulder, and now my ass was in the air. *Awesome.*

"You can put me down, I can make it to the car." I tried to be nice. This was terrible.

"Trust me, carrying you is more than fine."

I could hear the smile in his voice.

"Put her down, Tommy," Linc ordered.

Surprisingly Tommy did. He took my hand and pulled me out of the water with him.

My legs felt like Jell-O, and my body was about to collapse. I was surprised I was able to swim the entire time, especially after my crazy run this morning. We walked to our clothes.

I peeked over my shoulder and saw Linc and Eva walking up behind us. It was the first time I'd actually seen Linc from his chest down. His black swim trunks sat indecently low on his narrow hips. His tattoo, that wrapped around his well-defined bicep and went over his shoulder to his chest, seemed to move with the contraction of his muscles. He shook his head, and water droplets went flying.

"You good?" Tommy asked.

His arm tugged my elbow, and I felt warmth crawling up my neck into my face at being caught appreciating his best friend's smoking-hot body.

"Yeah, do you want me to drive you home?" Avoiding his gaze, I wrung out my hair and pulled on my clothes.

"It's fine, I can just get a ride home with Eva and Linc."

"I'll go with her," Linc offered. "It's like two in the morning, and she doesn't need to drive that far alone."

"Don't worry about it. I only live twenty minutes away, and it's an easy drive."

"You sure?" Tommy shot a glare in Linc's direction. "They could follow us over there."

"Don't worry about it." I smiled as I moved toward Eva to give her a hug. Afterward, I turned to Linc, unsure whether a hug or just a bye would work, but he came forward and scooped me up into a bear hug. The grooves of his hard abs pressed against my stomach.

"Text me when you get home," he whispered in my ear.

"Gotcha," I whispered back.

He put me down, and I followed Tommy to my car.

"Thanks for inviting me. I had a lot of fun." I sent a silent plea he wouldn't try to kiss me because, honestly, I wasn't really into it.

"No problem. I'll see you later?"

"Yeah."

He bent down, kissed my cheek, and took off toward the other car. That I could deal with. As much as I liked Tommy, we'd be better off as just friends, since I couldn't stop staring at Linc. Giving them a little wave, I turned my car around and left the river behind. The drive home was uneventful, and Sarah's car was in the garage when I pulled in, so I wouldn't be alone tonight.

After taking a long shower and settling into bed, I fell asleep pretty quick, my body exhausted from all the activity.

My phone vibrated, waking me with a text from Linc.

You home?
Yes, sir, already in bed.
Good, I'll see you tomorrow.

I left it at that, and, a minute later, my phone lit up again.

I liked your swimsuit.

I was pretty sure I turned every shade of red, and I lay there in my bed, smiling like an idiot, before drifting back to sleep.

Chapter 6

Since I didn't wake up till almost ten the next morning, I decided to give my body a break and not work out. I was sore all over, my abs, arms, and thighs, even my ass. It was a good sore though. I staggered out of my room and into the kitchen. Sarah and Todd were already there.

"Morning," Sarah chirped, her brown hair a mess. It probably mirrored mine.

"Hey, coffee?" I asked.

"Yeah, there should still be more. How was your date with Tommy?" She was way too enthusiastic this morning.

"Good, we went swimming with Linc and Tommy's sister, Eva."

She flashed her cheesiest smile. "Oh, that sounds super fun, did you get any?"

I stayed expressionless, too sore to roll me eyes. "No, but it was fun. Linc's coming over today to work on our project."

"Haven't you hung out with him enough?" This came from Todd.

"Todd, leave her alone," Sarah scolded. "She's finally hanging out with guys."

"Well, she doesn't even know him," he said.

"Do you know him?" I faced him, folding my arms over my chest. *Note to self, next time put a bra on.*

He made a sound of disgust. "No, but I hear he's sort of a dead beat and does anything with legs and a vagina."

"Well, there isn't going to be any doing, except our project, so calm down." Was Todd actually concerned for my wellbeing? That was completely out of character.

He shook his head and turned to Sarah. "What time do you have work?"

"Eleven-thirty. Ugh, I should start getting ready." She bounced away from the table and disappeared into the hallway.

Todd mimicked my current stance and folded his arms over his chest. "What time is Leon getting over here?"

"Linc," I corrected through gritted teeth. "I don't know, probably not for a couple hours."

Todd shook his head and followed Sarah into her room. I was making eggs with spinach and tomatoes when yelling erupted from Sarah's room. Then the door opened and slammed.

Sara came storming out of her room with Todd on her heels. "Todd, my clothes are fucking fine. I'm not changing."

"Yes, you are. Get your ass back in there. I don't need everyone staring at my girlfriend's tits the entire day."

He grabbed her arm and pulled her back. They stood there staring at each other. I stepped closer, staring at Todd, daring him to drag Sarah back into her room. His gaze darted between the two of us before settling back on Sarah. I think he felt outnumbered because he threw her arm away and left, slamming the door. It wasn't long before tires peeled out of our driveway.

"Sarah, has he done that before?" I asked her

carefully because I could already see her eyes getting glassy.

"Butt out," she choked and then stormed out, slamming the front door.

I started doing the dishes with a sick feeling in my stomach, not knowing if I should try to help my friend or stay out of it. All bets were off the moment she came home with a bruise of any kind. Only then, could I legitimately go after him. I went to my room to check my phone, nothing. Since it hurt to move, I took another super long, hot shower trying to get my muscles to relax, and the water felt good. I did my morning routine and then some more chores around the house until I was sweaty again, and considered another shower.

Instead, I grabbed my binder, determined to go through what was due for the next week. There was just the three-page paper for the Humanities class Linc and I shared, explaining what issue we were going to explore. Easy. My phone vibrated, and I felt around my unmade bed for it, butterflies taking flight in my stomach, until I saw the screen and they dropped away. It was Jake asking if I needed him to pick me up for tonight. I sent him a quick text letting him know I was going with Sarah and Cindy and didn't need a ride. It was almost noon, and, with no word from Linc, I wondered if maybe we weren't going to hang out today. Since I was gross and sticky from all the cleaning, I headed to the bathroom to rinse, taking my phone with me. As soon as I stepped into the shower, I got a text.

Incoming.

It was immediately followed by a knock on my front door. Shit, I jumped out of the shower and jerked my clothes on. No need for a repeat of earlier this week. Running to the door, I pulled it open.

Linc stood there, with his lips tipped up and those

deep brown eyes lighting for me. "Hey."

"Hey." I was out of breath and moved aside so he could come in. Out in the driveway, there was a blue, jacked-up Ford truck. *Figures, redneck.* The butterflies were back. I waved him to the couch and went to grab my binder from my bedroom. Sneaking a quick check in the mirror, I decided it would be weird if I changed now so my yoga pants and razor-back gray tank would have to work. As I entered the living room, I felt his gaze the whole time and actually enjoyed the fact that he was watching me. I sat down next to him, with my right leg propped up under my other one, so I could face him.

"Oh, did you want anything to drink or food or anything?" I said, grabbing my hair and gathering it to one side.

He studied me with that half grin that was growing on me. "Naw, I'm good. You work today?"

"Yeah, at three."

"Cool, maybe I'll drop by." He moved his hair out of his face. "What time do you get off?"

I grinned. "Stalking me?"

He laughed. "You wish."

I loved that laugh. It was deep and throaty and all kinds of hot.

I blushed and focused on my binder. "Eleven, I get off at eleven."

He got up and went to the kitchen sink to put his hands underneath the steady stream of water. I stared while he washed his hands as if it was the most interesting thing I'd seen all morning, which honestly it was. Him doing anything interested me.

"Sorry, I'm on my lunch, well sort of." He lifted his wet hands. I guess he thought they were dirty.

"Oh, yeah, Tommy told me you guys worked for your parents' landscaping company. How's that going?"

"I love it. You get to be outside and work with your hands, plus it pays well. You don't get a lot of opportunities like that, unless it's farming, and I'm never doing that shit."

I nodded. "So what time do you go back?"

"Whenever Craig calls me. He's going to a client's office to talk about the landscaping they want around a couple new buildings their company is opening."

He walked back to the couch and sat down, closer than before, which I had no problem with. His proximity gave me goose bumps—the good kind, though.

"Your morning good?" I said, trying to procrastinate.

"Yeah, I ran and then headed over to our first job. Afternoon's turning out to be better." He glanced over, and his eyes flickered to my shirt and then back to my face. No matter how inconspicuous guys tried to be, when checking out a girl's chest, the girls always knew.

"Good." I bit my lower lip, forcing my gaze back to my binder. "So, um, did you still want to do what we talked about?"

"No," he replied.

I looked up from my papers questioningly.

"Got a better idea?"

He gave me a half smile. "Oh, yeah, it's brilliant."

I waited, but he didn't say anything, just sat there like a really badass-looking dork.

"Care to share your brilliant idea?" I prompted.

He leaned closer so that our lips lined up, and I instantly licked mine, my gaze riveted on his mouth before drifting back up to meet his eyes. His smile disappeared, and a different look slipped over his normally hard face, softening it. I really liked that look. It meant I affected him the same way he affected me—as hard as that was to believe since I was me, and he resembled one of those guys who should be airbrushed in a sports magazine.

His eyes closed and, when his lips made contact with mine, the little prickles of his scruff against my face thrilled me so much that a shiver ran through me. The kiss started out slow and timid, with tiny kisses, until he flicked his tongue over my lips, asking permission. *Yes, please.* I opened my mouth, our tongues twisted and swirled together, and the butterflies from earlier move down to my lower stomach. Our lips were the only part touching, and my body ached, needing more from him, so I took a fistful of his shirt and tugged him forward. Slowly, I reclined until he hovered over me, supporting his weight on one arm resting by my head. His other hand was against my hip, caressing my skin where my gray tank rucked up. His hand glided up, taking the shirt with it. I arched my back, pressing closer until I could feel how ready he was against me. My hands explored his body, inching their way under his shirt until they were pressed flat to his perfectly muscled stomach. I went to grab his shirt and pull it over his head when something vibrated against the inside of my thigh.

He pulled back, looking annoyed. "Sorry, could be work." He was out of breath as he sat up, pulling me up with him. "What?" he bit out, answering the phone. "Uhh, yeah, I'll be there in five." He ran his hand through his hair, shut off the phone, and looked at me. "Work, I gotta go," he said, waiting for my answer.

"Yeah, okay." I was panting and wasn't surprised, but it was almost embarrassing.

We walked to the door. He pressed another kiss to my lips, light and fast, but my body still reacted. It had been too long, because trying to keep my hormones in check was exponentially hard, and I wanted to pull him back into the house.

"I'll see you later," he promised and then turned and walked to his truck.

"Are you going to be at the river tonight? There's a party?" I yelled after him.

"You going?"

"Yeah, I'll be there around midnight."

"Then, yeah, I'll bring Craig and Tommy."

My stomach started doing flips.

"See you tonight," I called and then shut the door.

Leaning against the door, I smiled like an idiot and did a little happy dance. Checking the time to find it was almost two, I ran to the bathroom to get ready for my shift at Woody's.

ℰↃℰↃ

After putting my wallet in Seth's office, I went to the bar where Sarah was, to tell her to go take her lunch.

"Hey, hon." I reached out and touched her shoulder.

She gave me a hug and held me for a little bit. "Sorry about earlier. I was mad at him," she explained, pulling back.

"It's fine, just let me know if you ever need help, or anything."

"No, we're good. It never escalates, so no worries."

I shrugged. "Well, it's your lunch, so go get some food."

She nodded and walked to the back. Standing there, I checked out the bar. It wasn't too crowded for a Saturday afternoon. Cindy was supposed to be here by now to man the bar, but she was always late. I studied the sitting area checking in with each table, but they were all good. Not many people drank at three in the afternoon, except our regulars, so there wasn't a big need for a bartender.

Cindy strolled in a half hour late, apologizing pro-fusely. She leaned over the bar. "So, how's that partner of yours?"

"Good," I said, trying to act nonchalant but failing miserably. I felt the heat instantly rise to my cheeks.

Her green eyes doubled in size. "What happened?"

"Um, we kissed," I squeaked.

"What?" she all but shouted. "I need details please!"

"It's nothing, we just kissed on my couch, and then he got a call and had to go into work."

"What's he do?"

"He's a landscaper."

"Sweet, is he going to be there tonight?"

"Yeah, I invited him," I replied, playing with the ends of my hair.

"Wait, you little slut, didn't you have a date with his friend? The blond one who was here with him?"

"Yeah, but I'm not really into him, and it was only one date, which doesn't really count. He kissed my cheek at the end, which means he can't take it that hard or anything, right? And Linc didn't seem too concerned, so—"

"Cheek kiss? Trust me, you don't want one of those. I think I got more action in the second grade. If they try to feel you up, they should be good, right?" She winked, and I smacked her arm.

The rest of our shift went fast, the crowd running a bit on the older side, probably because of the party. Sarah took off around seven thirty and said she'd meet us at home. Todd and Jake would meet us at the party. On my break, I walked to the back to check my phone and smiled because Linc had texted me.

Did you need a ride at all? I can come get you.

It was cute he offered at all.

It's okay, Sarah and Cindy will be with me.

Less than two seconds later, he sent, *You sure? We can pick y'all up?*

I thought it over and decided to ask Cindy if she rather catch a ride with Linc and his friends. I ambled over to where she was filling a drink order. "So, Linc wants to know if we all want a ride from them."

She was focused on her beer task. "Them?"

"I think him, Tommy, and Craig."

"Yes! If Craig was the one here last time with them, then, yes."

"Okay, I'll let him know. What time? Midnight?"

"Sounds good to me."

Returning to the back. I sent a text, asking him to be there around midnight. He confirmed. Those butterflies took up a permanent residence in my stomach, their presence constant now.

It was slow for a Saturday night and, by the time the other waitresses came in, we were able to leave an hour early. Cindy and I grabbed our wallets and bags from the back. She brought a huge bag full of her clothes, make up, and hair products.

Her bright red hair bounced with her movements as we settled into my car. "So, you excited?"

"About?" I asked, acting like I didn't know what she was talking about.

She gave me a knowing smirk. "Linc. You should hook up with him tonight. How long has it been for you? Almost a year? Your vibrator probably wants a break."

"Cindy!"

Her smirk turned apologetic, and she shrugged.

"I've only known him a week," I said. "I'm not that hard up for it. And it's been closer to six months." The last part came out in a hush.

She laughed.

"So what are you wearing tonight?" I asked, so I could start mentally planning my outfit.

"I think I'm going to wear some white jean shorts and my silky purple shirt with my brown strappy sandals. You?"

Purple would look awesome with her hair.

"How about jeans and maybe a tank? I don't know yet. Since we're going to the river, I don't want to get that fancy, but Linc's going to be there."

"Don't worry, we'll find you something. If anything, you can wear what you said and just do your make up a little bit heavier. That'd look cute."

"Yeah, maybe."

Chapter 7

The drive home was short as Cindy and I laughed the whole time. Cindy was all kinds of inappropriate. I loved it. When we got there, Sarah was watching a reality show and eating popcorn in one of Todd's T-shirts. She grilled salmon for dinner, which turned out delicious. Afterward, we all ran into my room, since it had the biggest mirror, and decided on our outfits, Sarah opted for a blue razorback sundress patterned with lacy flowers and added brown sandals. I paired my tightest jeans with a see-through black tank with a black lacy bandeau under it.

There was nothing I could do with my hair, so I pulled it back into a ponytail, letting it flip out. Applying minimal make up, mascara and gloss, I added, like the other two, brown sandals. We all looked good, both my friends were gorgeous. Cindy's shorts made her legs look like they went on forever. Sarah's deep chestnut hair hung in ringlets down her back, perfect as always.

About a quarter to midnight there was a knock on our door, and we giggled like we were ten. Skipping to the door, I stopped and took a long deep breath before opening it.

My breath stalled, something I thought only happened in movies. I stared at all three males like I'd never seen a man before and I needed to use them. Now. "Hey guys."

I held the door open for them to come in. Linc came in first, followed by the other two. Tommy gave me a kiss on the cheek. All three wore dark blue jeans, with T-shirts. Linc's was black, Tommy's was green, and Craig's was black with some kind of tribal design. It looked like a wave symbol, but one you'd find on the inside of some exotic cave. The other two girls came into the kitchen as the guys entered.

"Oh, um, this is Sarah and Cindy, that's Linc, Tommy, and Craig." I introduced everyone, they all exchanged hi's.

"Do you guys want to take shots before we leave? Or have a beer?" Sarah offered, holding a bottle of Jack.

"Shot sounds good to me," Craig answered. It was the first time I actually heard him talk.

"We have tequila or whiskey," Cindy chimed in biting her lip and making eye contact with him.

All three boys said whiskey at the same time. I stared at Linc and, when his eyes found mine, a smile rose to his lips as he held out his hand. I hesitated then finally took it.

He pulled me toward him and bent his head down toward my ear. "I talked to Tommy already. He wasn't necessarily happy about it, but he's fine," he whispered in my ear.

I swear I tried to pay attention to his words, but his lips kept brushing my ear, and all I could think about was getting his lips on the rest of my body. *Whoa, nope, back up. On my lips. Sheesh, whore.*

Sarah poured our shots and handed them out.

"To fun," Cindy offered, holding up her glass.

We clinked and threw back. Yuck. The warm liquid slid down my throat slowly, causing it and my nose to burn. I remembered why I hated whiskey. Someone chuckled. I looked at Linc who was trying hard to not laugh but failing.

I gave him a dirty look. "Something funny, mister?"

"Not a damn thing," he said. He turned to the rest of the group. "You guys ready?"

As we left, I locked the door. Linc waited as the other four headed to his way-too-big of a truck.

"Call shotgun," Linc whispered in my ear, putting his hand on my opposite hip.

"Shotgun!" I called.

"Shotgun right side!" Sarah yelled almost immediately.

"Dammit," Tommy yelled.

"I'm totally fine sitting with these two in the back." Cindy threw a mischievous look in Craig's direction.

He returned her smile.

Linc followed me to the passenger side and opened the door. Staring at his passenger seat, I pondered how the hell to get into the car. No way would my leg reach up to the step. As I stood there figuring out my point of attack, hands gripped my hips, and then I was airborne. Linc swooped me up and set me down on the seat, solving my dilemma.

I scooted over, laughing. "Read my mind."

He chuckled while he grabbed Sarah and tossed her in next to me. Craig and Cindy entered from the other side.

Sarah looked at me after being tossed in and mouthed, "Oh my god!"

Giving her my biggest smile ever, I gave myself a mental pat on the back, because I kissed that man.

The drive over there was fun. Music played, and Tommy, who stole our whiskey, was giving everyone shots, except Linc, who was driving. Linc kept his hand on my thigh the entire drive, and every so often I would grab his hand or wrist, just to encourage it not to move. By the time we got there, I was pretty sure we three girls were feeling the alcohol. My initial plan was to only have one drink at the actual party, because when I got drunk, I got horny, and I didn't want to maul Linc. Well, I did, but I would rather do it sober.

When we got there, Sarah jumped out, and I followed. She texted Todd immediately. I turned around, and Craig had Cindy in his arms.

"I call this one!" Craig walked off with Cindy to get drinks.

Everyone stared after them for a minute

"Is Eva going to be here?" I asked Tommy.

"Yeah, she should be here soon." He didn't look at me and walked away.

All right.

"Todd should be here in a minute," Sarah announced as we stood in a tiny triangle, Linc leaning on his truck and both of us in front of him.

"How long you guys planning on staying?" he questioned as he pulled out his phone to look at something.

"Umm, probably just a couple hours." I looked at Sarah. "Is Todd coming back to the house?"

Her brown eyes lit up. "Yeah, I think so."

Trying to stifle my sigh, I turned to Linc. "So, I can just catch a ride with them, at the end, since we're all going to the same place."

"I'll drive you," he said.

Sarah bumped my shoulder but didn't look at me.

"Hey, ladies." Jake's voice came from behind us, and we turned to see him and Todd walking up. Sarah threw herself into Todd's arms. Todd was in a red shirt, and Jake was in a gray one. Both guys wore dark jeans.

Jake came up and wrapped his arm around my

shoulders. Linc straightened, a frown darkening his face.

"Guys this is Linc, Linc, this is Jake and Todd."

None of the guys offered hands, but rather stared at each other.

Linc tried a smile, but it was obviously forced. "Hey."

The other two nodded.

"Mais, you want to go get a drink? I saved you a cider." Jake tugged me in the opposite direction.

"It's okay, um, I think I'm gonna hang out with Linc for a bit. I'll find you," I lied.

"Come on, Mais." Jake moved his hand down to my forearm and gave a little tug.

I opened my mouth to tell him "No" more sternly, but Linc's hand snaked out and jerked Jake's arm away, throwing it back, before I could respond.

"She'll find you later." His voice was deep as he stared at Jake. They stood there engaged in a pissing contest. Todd left Sarah and went to stand by Jake, probably in an attempt to scare Linc off, but Jake backed off first.

"I'll see you soon, Mais." Jake, Todd, and Sarah walked away.

Sarah gave me a weird look before they left. I just shook my head.

I turned to Linc. "I didn't realize you knew them."

He didn't look at me. "I don't."

Uh huh. I let it go.

"Want to go find something to drink?" he offered and put his hand out.

"A drink sounds wonderful."

I put my hand in his, and he pulled me into his side. We walked together, his arm wrapped around my shoulders. We saw Craig and Cindy sitting at a wooden picnic table, talking and laughing. I was happy to see her having fun. We passed them and came to a huge rock perched half in and half out of the water. Linc scooped me up, as if I weighed nothing, set me on top, and then lifted himself up. I appreciated a chance to ogle him without him noticing. The tentacle on his left arm moved as his biceps strained against his shirt.

Once he was situated, he turned toward me. "Thanks for inviting me, I'm glad I came."

He clinked our beers together, took a sip, and lay back on the rock. He placed his free arm behind his head and just stared at me. I took a swig of my beer and wondered what he was thinking. I thought the staring thing would be awkward, but it wasn't. Still, I broke eye contact first, and my gaze went straight to the piece of flesh showing between his jeans and his black shirt.

"So, how do you know Jake?" he asked as he looked out towards the river.

"He's Todd's best friend, and Sarah and Todd have been dating since freshman year."

"Cool. Did you guys ever do anything?"

Well, that was forward. I lifted my gaze to give him a look that said it's none of your business, but his eyes were closed.

He opened his eyes into slits. "Does that silence mean yes?"

"Not that it's any of your business, but we went out a couple of times. We're friends." That sounded acceptable. He didn't need to know we slept together. Wanting to change the subject, I asked the first thing that popped into my mind. "Why the sea monster, octopus tattoo? I've never seen a guy with that before. Usually its crosses or birds or something."

"It's sort of like my family's crest. All the guys in our family have one."

"Craig has one too?"

"No, he doesn't. He was welcome to get one like

mine, but he wanted a different one that reminded him of his family. It sort of looks like that wave on his shirt, and it's on his back, between his shoulder blades. Do you have any tattoos?"

"No, I might be a little terrified of needles." I laughed, but those things *were* terrifying.

"Really? I didn't expect that since your belly button is pierced."

"I was forced! I wanted one, but Sarah had to basically hold me down so the piercer could stick the needle in."

"So, what do you like to do for fun? Besides stare at my stomach," he teased.

My gaze snapped back to his face and heat rose over my skin. I didn't even notice I was looking. *Shit.* I racked my brain for something clever, but nothing came to mind.

He grinned. "It's okay, I have a nice stomach. I would take my shirt off for you, but you'd probably not pay attention to the conversation anymore, and I want to get to know you more."

"I could so pay attention to the conversation." I hit his leg and muttered, "Cocky bastard."

He laughed and stretched his legs. His brown eyes looked up at the star-soaked night sky. "So what's your favorite color?"

"You serious?" Was he crazy?

"Completely, I kissed you earlier and plan on doing it again, but like I said, I want to know more about you first. Your favorite color is definitely a need to know thing."

I laughed in disbelief. "Okay, it's green. What's yours?"

"Blue."

I laughed again because this was stupid. A guy had never wanted to know my favorite color. The weirdest thing about this conversation was he actually seemed interested. Personally, I'd rather skip over the getting-to-know-you part and go straight to the kissing part. With him sitting so close, it was hard to sit still and not tackle him. Lying down next to him, I tried to turn onto my side, but it wasn't comfortable because we were on a damn rock. I stayed on my back, our shoulders touching, looking up at the stars. There were so many twinkling overhead—as if they were putting on a show just for us. In the city, you were lucky if you saw two stars. Out here in the middle of nowhere, there were hundreds of thousands. I'd lived here for four years and would never get used to it.

"Where are you from?"

His question snapped me out of my thoughts.

"How do you know I'm not from here?"

He gave me a knowing look. "Your accent for starters."

"I don't have an accent. I just don't say 'y'all' every other sentence."

"First off, it's 'y'all.' Say it, don't scream it. Second, we don't use it in every other sentence."

"I didn't scream it, and I'm from Los Angeles. Ever been?"

"Yeah. I have some cousins out there, but it's been a while."

"It's nice, if you like the concrete jungle sort of thing and lots of people."

"Which place do you like better? Here or California?"

"Definitely here, it's more me. Not a lot of people, tons of nature and outdoorsy stuff, and it's gorgeous and green. I feel like I was born in the wrong state."

He grabbed my hand and squeezed it lightly. We talked about meaningless things—classes, majors, and jobs—and time passed. I learned he was an environmental major, which could potentially help him with his job. His thumb made little circles on my hand, making it hard to pay attention to what he was saying. There was no sense to my acting like a hormonal teenager who couldn't control her body, but it didn't diminish the fact I hated our hands were the only things touching.

"Want another drink?" He sat up and patted my upper thigh, which sent zings to my lower stomach.

"Yeah a drink sounds good," I fumbled over the words, focusing on where his hand was.

I sat up as he hopped off the rock to get us a drink. Instead of heading off, he turned and gently moved my legs apart. He was still taller, but not by much. He cupped my face with his left hand and then tilted it up. My heart rate picked up when his head came closer, and his breath feathered over my lips. My eyes fluttered closed when his lips met mine, and as fast as the kiss started, it ended. Instantly I missed his touch and gave him a pouty face.

He chuckled.

"I'll be right back, babe." Then he turned and walked away.

I sat there smiling like an idiot and finally lay back against the warm rock. I'd only known him a week, but every time he was around, my body hummed, butterflies taking flight in my stomach, and I actually looked forward to seeing him in my classes. It had been a long time since my last crush. Even when Jake and I hooked up, my heart never raced when I saw him. I liked this feeling with Linc. It was fun and thrilling. Despite knowing him for such a short time, and logic dictating I was nothing more than another notch in his bedpost, I couldn't bring myself to care.

Behind me, grass and rocks crunched underfoot. Anticipation hummed under my skin at how fast Linc got those beers. Images of me pulling him back between my legs and making that innocent kiss of before into something a little more risqué ramped my pulse and hormones. I turned and someone, who was definitely not Linc, loomed behind me.

A slender figure was walking up toward me. Despite the eighty-degree night, they wore black jeans and a gray hoodie, making them stand out since that definitely wasn't normal attire for the summer months. My body went into hyper drive, and my stomach dropped, leaving a sick feeling behind. The figure stood there, staring at me, no drink or anything else in their hands.

"Hi." My greeting came out overly loud. I tried to sound friendly, but I was mentally freaking out.

Linc needed to hurry the heck up. The person remained silent and unmoving, then they cocked their head to the right side, as if studying me. Shit, their strange behavior reminded me of all those damn murder mystery shows Sarah was addicted to on TV.

Wanting to get back to where people were, I hopped off the rock and started scooting past the figure, toward the party. I could see the people and the light from various car headlights, so if I screamed, they would hear me. Probably. The dark figure turned as I walked past them and their gaze weighed on me the entire time.

Just as I was about to break out into a run, something wet grabbed my ankle and tripped me. I hit the ground hard but managed to turn to my back immediately. The figure was still a hundred yards away, but their hand was out in front of them, in a fist. Something about their stance sent fear through every cell of my being, choking off my scream.

I scrambled to my feet, heart pounding, and took off in a sprint. On my third step, I was back on the ground. This time, when I turned my body, the figure stood over me. I reached out slowly, trying to find a rock or a branch, anything that would help me to get away but there was nothing. Under my left hand was decent size puddle. It didn't make sense, but I didn't get to think about it long before my attacker motioned at my left hand. The water around my palm slowly retreated.

"Why are you different?" The voice was high and shrill sounding, which meant it was a she.

"What?" Unable to do anything but focus on getting the hell away, I didn't worry about what was coming out of my mouth.

"What does he see in you? You're human."

This time her hand snaked out and curled around my neck, hauling me up until my feet left the ground. My hands flew up to her cruel grip, scrabbling for purchase. My breathing became shallow as I fought for air. Her strength was unbelievable. Squirming, I dug my nails into her skin, desperate to escape.

"Answer me!" she screamed and then threw me to the ground.

Something in my wrist popped as I hit. Rolling over, I got to my hands and knees. I tried to push up, but couldn't move. Water covered my wrists, the pressure holding me in place. It made no sense. Even stranger, the water turned to ice, and something slammed into my upper back. My face kissed the dirt. I tried to get up, but couldn't muster the strength. Hell, I could barely lift my head. As I fell back down, panic closed in. I couldn't move.

As unreal as it sounded, the girl flipped me over without touching me. Even weirder, as I lay on my back I could see she was still a few feet away. Unfortunately, the surreal nightmare continued as water seeped over my face, like a floating bubble. Great, between fear and panic I was fucking hallucinating.

Closing my eyes, I tried to breathe, but all I sucked in was water.

When I reopened my eyes, the girl was standing over me, her hand out, palm down. She lowered her hand, and the water seeping over my face covered it completely. We locked gazes, and, on some remote level, I realized her eyes were bright blue. Her smile was cold and vicious as water forced its way down my throat and into my lungs. I tried to cough, but couldn't. *Great, this is how I'll die.*

As my consciousness began to dim, I accepted my impending death. Then some type of primal growl, sounding like tiger or a bear, cut in. Strange, there were no tigers or bears in Alabama that I knew of. Water rushed over my face and down my neck. My lungs started to burn, then I was coughing and breathing in precious air. I tried to lift my head, but couldn't. My muscles refused to cooperate, leaving me weak, and my head was spinning. My eyelids felt heavy and, when I finally got them to open, everything was blurry.

Looking over to the side, I watched the girl retreat. A tall figure stood in between me and my attacker. She drew her hand back, and a rush of water hurtled forward at the approaching bulky figure, as if a fire hose was turned to full force behind her. The force of the water's impact should have knocked whoever was heading over on their ass, but the broad body took it easily. They threw their fist into the stream and, suddenly, the water fell to the ground. None of this was making any sense. No one could take that kind of pressure and remain standing.

The latest arrival stretched out a hand, palm down, much like the girl had done before, and water appeared out of thin air. Little raindrops formed, frozen in mid-air, but their size increased rapidly. The collection of water froze instantly, turning into spear pointed icicles. The man, because it had to be a male, wound up his leanly muscled arm and threw his fist in the direction of my attacker. She turned to run, but the icicles flew after her.

Courting death had me was losing my damn mind. I tried to catch my breath, but my heart was pounding so hard, I couldn't. I needed to calm down, or I would pass out again. I did not want to pass out. *Stop, Maisy, you're fine, alive. Now focus on getting out of here.*

I kept repeating the words, but it didn't help. My body began to shake violently.

"Maisy!" I heard a voice yell. "Mais, you hear me? Look at me!" The panicked voice got louder, and then I was being lifted from the ground. A mass of golden hair took up my entire vision, but I couldn't focus. The guy gave me a little shake. "Come on, Maisy." He shook me a little bit harder.

"Is she responsive?" Linc's voice broke through my confusion. "Don't shake her, dumbass!"

There was more conversation, but I couldn't make out anything else. Finally deciding it was safe, my body gave in and let go. I passed out for the second time this week.

Chapter 8

I was spinning while someone blew air on my face. Either that, or it was super windy, but I was definitely spinning. When it stopped, I realized I was lying on something soft and warm. Peeling my eyes open took a hell of a lot more effort than it should have. Attempting to take in my surroundings, I realized I was in an unmoving vehicle, and my head was on someone's lap. I turned from my side to my back, and piercing brown eyes met mine. Linc's eyes, I sighed, and my body relaxed.

"Maisy?" He looked tired, with purple rings under his beautiful brown eyes and his face a little paler than normal, almost sickly.

"What happened?" I croaked, barely recognizing my voice. My throat burned as if on fire.

"You tell me," he said carefully. His gaze drifted over my body and came back.

"There was this woman, and she was drowning me, but I wasn't in the water." God, that sounded crazy. I clamped my mouth shut and thought about what to say. "I don't know what happened."

He probably thought I was losing it, but I wasn't. Whatever happened was real, my body felt bruised and battered, not something I could make up.

He furrowed his brow and studied me before he

spoke. "I found you in the water by the rock. I think you hit your head and passed out."

"No, that's not what happened."

"Then what did happen, Maisy?" His voice was hard.

Did he think I was fucking making this up? I was *attacked*, damn it. "I...I don't know," I stuttered while tears clouded my eyes.

I tried to sit up because I wanted to get away from him. I wanted to go home, maybe have some of that whiskey, and look myself over, but I didn't want to be alone. My heart thumped hard, and my breathing became erratic. I started shaking. His arms wrapped around my waist as he pulled me up onto his lap.

"Shh, you're safe," he said into my hair.

I wanted to get away from him. It pissed me off that he didn't believe me but being held started relaxing my body. It eventually stopped shaking, my breathing evened out, and my heart rate returned to normal.

"Take me home please," I practically begged.

"Yeah, just let me text Craig that we're leaving." He pulled out his phone.

I slid over to the passenger seat and buckled in.

Why would he say I was safe? Hell, why was he determined to claim I'd fallen off a rock? I didn't fall, and he knew it. He had to know what happened. I swore, now that I could somewhat think, it was Tommy's voice that was trying to get me to wake up back there. Linc had to have been there.

I wanted to demand answers from him, but I was in no shape to do so.

Linc started his truck and pulled out onto the main road, his hand rested on my thigh. "Do you want me to take you to a hospital to get checked out? Or do you want me to call anyone?"

"No, I think I'm fine. My body just hurts, and Sarah

should be home soon," I said more to reassure myself than him.

He nodded, and the rest of the car ride was silent. He pulled into my driveway, and I fidgeted with my seat buckle, but the thing wouldn't unhook. I pulled the seat belt hard and still nothing. Shaking it a couple of times, I tried the button again. Nothing. Frustrated tears gathered for the second time tonight.

"Easy," Linc soothed, reaching over to unbuckled me.

I jumped out of the car, swaying a little bit, but walked to the door as he hovered behind me. I unlocked the door then turned around and came face to chest. I wanted to lean into him and tell him not to leave, but I didn't know why he was insisting that I fell off the rock. I was too confused about what had just happened to have him come in. It wasn't because I didn't want to be alone. It was because I didn't want anyone else but him with me.

He frowned as he looked me over. "Are you going to be okay?"

"Yes." *No.*

"You sure you don't want me to stay with you? At least till Sarah gets here?"

"Yeah, I'm fine, I'll be okay." *Please stay.*

"Call me if you need anything." He reached for my face and placed his hand on my cheek. I fought not to turn into his touch. "Doesn't matter what the time."

He pulled me closer and kissed the top of my head. I didn't reply but watched as he turned and left. I leaned on the door until he pulled out of my driveway.

After he was gone, I slowly walked to the bathroom and turned on the shower. I didn't even bother looking at myself, I was too afraid of what I might see. Getting in the scalding hot water, I slid to the floor and started bawling until I was dry heaving. Sarah would be back soon, and I needed to get it together before she and Todd arrived. Or at least get to my room. I scrubbed my body until it was red, and I was a complete prune.

Getting out of the shower, I ran to my room, turned, and leaned on the door, locking it. *I will not cry again, I will not cry again.* I went to the closet and grabbed a T-shirt, tugging it over my head. Chancing a look in the mirror, I almost didn't recognize who stared back. It was barely human. My eyes were swollen and red in my white face, and there were dark bruises around my neck. Tilting my head back, I covered the marks with my hands, feeling the welts left from my attacker's nails. How would I hide this from people? September in Alabama meant the weather tried to fry people on the spot. It wasn't like I could wear a scarf or a turtleneck without drawing undue attention. I sighed, went into the bedroom, and got into my bed, pulling the blankets up over my head. Silent tears dripped over my cheeks until I eventually fell asleep.

છ৯છ৯

The next week passed in a blur. I took a week off from work and school because there was no way to hide the bruising. It took two days before the swelling around my neck disappeared. I was pretty sure I scared the crap out of Sarah, too. Every time she came home, I hid in my bedroom. She even kicked the door once, trying to get in. Eventually, she gave up and bought my story that I was sick and quarantining myself to my bedroom. She urged me to go to the hospital. That option was definitely out. On Wednesday, she went to stay at Todd's for the rest of the week.

I didn't want to analyze what happened the night I

was attacked until I was fully confident I wouldn't burst into tears. So the entire week I found comfort in doing tedious tasks that would keep my mind occupied. I washed my car, cleaned the entire house, organized my bookshelf so the books were in alphabetical order by author, and color-coded my closet.

Today was Saturday and exactly one week since the incident. I made green tea and decided to partake in one of the most well-known sports in the South, front porch sitting. Sitting there, in a lawn chair with my green tea, it was time to face what happened. I was attacked by something, although I wasn't sure what. No way could a human do...do what...manipulate water? It sounded flipping crazy, but it happened. I was sure of it. There was no way I fell off the rock and hit my head like Linc claimed. A fall didn't explain the bruises around my neck, which were just beginning to fade and starting to turn to yellow.

That night, Tommy was there, and I was pretty sure Linc was, too. I now remembered hearing Linc's voice before I passed out. Could he control water? I shook my head. No one could do that, no one. Instead of trying to figure out what happened, maybe it would be best to ignore it. I couldn't talk to anyone about it. They'd put me in the looney bin, for sure.

Throughout the week, Linc texted, checking to see how I was doing and where I was. He even offered to come over and make me dinner one night. I declined. I didn't want to see him. I wasn't sure what happened, but if I wasn't nuts and he could do those things, like pull water out of thin air, and turn it to ice without a freezer, I didn't want him near me.

Going back inside, I pulled out my notebook and started writing for one of my classes. At least now, I could do this. Before I couldn't even focus enough to write my name.

My phone buzzed. I grabbed it, certain it was Sarah asking if she could finally come home. I answered it without checking.

"Hey, hon," I sounded normal again, finally.

"Hey," answered a really deep, sexy voice.

Taking the phone away from my ear, I checked the name on the screen. Linc. *Shit, shit, shit.* I hadn't planned to talk to him for another couple days and wasn't actually sure I wanted to talk to him.

"Hello," he said.

I seriously contemplated hanging up and turning my phone off.

"Oh, um, I thought you were Sarah," I finally got out.

"How are you feeling?"

"Good, great." *Now, please leave me alone.*

"You working tonight?"

"No, I'm off until Wednesday."

He didn't say anything, and I was almost about to tell him I had to go, when he sighed. "Then why haven't you been at school the last week?"

Was he serious? I got fucking attacked and was left with meltdowns every five minutes. I didn't want to start crying in one of my classes or have someone question the bruising around my neck. Hell, I kicked out Sarah so she wouldn't suspect anything.

"I—I needed time to myself," I finally stuttered out.

"I told you to call me if you needed anything," he said, sounding frustrated.

"I didn't need anything."

"Like hell," he growled. "You haven't been to school or work for a week. I tried calling you, and no answer. I texted you but got nothing. I even went and hunted Sarah down to see what was up. You are not good, so stop bull-shitting me." He bit out the last sentence.

Yeah, it was time to end this conversation. I didn't need this and didn't need to be told how I was. "Okay, well, I've got shit to do around the house, so I'll see you Tuesday."

"Mais, I'm sor—" he started.

I hung up. My initial guilt at being so rude faded pretty quickly. I didn't want to talk to him. Who the hell did he think he was? We'd known each other for a couple weeks, and he expected me to run to him when I was having a mental breakdown. Plus, it wasn't like he believed me. I didn't need him. I'd tried opening up to him the night of the attack, telling him what I saw, and he wrote it off, as if I was crazy. I didn't need him thinking I needed help. I didn't. I went to the couch and turned on the TV as a distraction because the damn tears were back.

❧❧❧

It was finally Wednesday and the first day I was due back at work. I skipped school yesterday because I didn't want to see Linc. He sent me a text right after class, threatening to come over to the house if I didn't talk to him. I told him I was fine and not to come over because I wouldn't answer the door. He never came, which I was thankful for.

Checking the clock to find it was almost five in the evening, I sighed. My shift started at six and went to two in the morning. I hated this shift. If it wasn't a weekend, the bar was dead, but sometimes Seth would let us take off early since it was so slow. Since it was time to get ready, I went to the bathroom and checked my face. Nice, my eye swelling had gone down completely. I hadn't cried in the last two days, which was an accomplishment. I was fine. I settled for black skinny jeans, cowboy boots, and a black T-shirt that was a tad low cut.

When I got to work, I was happy to realize I was working with Cindy today. She never asked too many questions about anything. Perfect.

She greeted me with a hug. "Hey, girlfriend!"

Her crazy red hair got into my mouth as I tried to hug her back.

"Hey," I finally got out when she pulled away.

Her bright green eyes looked me over. "I heard you got some kind of flu of death. Feeling better?"

"Yeah much. How have you been? I feel like I haven't talked to anyone in forever!"

"I've been good. Nothing new, except I've gone out with Craig a couple times," she said sweetly.

"How's that going?" *Great.* As happy as I was for her, I really didn't want her dating Craig. But I couldn't say anything. At least, not yet. If Linc was some kind of water-controlling freak, I was sure Craig was, too. Maybe I should demand to know what happened again. Not yet, though. I was so not ready for that.

"Great, he's good." She winked, and I laughed.

A couple hours into my shift, Todd, Sarah, and Jake showed up.

"Maisy!" Sarah yelled, almost tackling me to the ground. She was lucky she was light, and I had a good lower center of gravity, or we would have hit the floor. Her brown eyes brightened. "You feeling better finally?"

I dipped my head at the other two boys.

"It's been nice, not seeing you for a week," Todd offered.

"Same to you, buddy, like a mini vacation," I cracked, proud of my comeback as he towed Sarah to the bar.

Jake came up and gave me a tight hug. When he pulled back, he left his hand around my waist. "Where have you been, pretty girl?" he asked, his blue eyes sparked with curiosity.

I forced my gaze away from his. "Sick, it sucked." I felt his eyes give me a once over.

He ran a hand through his short hair then across the back of his neck. "You sounded fine at the party. Did something happen with Linc? You never came over."

"Nope, nothing, I started feeling sick, and Linc took me home."

He raised his eyebrow.

"Shut up. I said I was sick." I hit him in his rock solid stomach, but it didn't faze him. I'd been up close and personal with that stomach. He had a great body.

He changed the subject. "Good, when you off?"

"Two." I pouted a bit.

"Sucks, want me to wait for you to get off?"

Booty call much? "Nope, I'll probably be tired."

"Maybe we can hang out tomorrow then?"

"That'd be nice. What did you want to do?"

The bar door opened, but I wasn't paying attention till I heard Cindy say, "Craig!"

My neck snapped around faster than a mongoose dodging a cobra strike. *Crap on a stick.* In walked Craig, followed by Tommy and Linc. My gaze met those dark brown liquid pools, and my body didn't know what to do. I stood there with Jake's arm around me while Linc's gaze moved from mine and went straight to Jake's hand resting close to my ass. Linc stared daggers at that hand, looking like he was contemplating removing it himself.

They took a table in Cindy's section, and Linc sat facing me. I couldn't stop watching him. Jake moved my body closer to his, and, instantly, I wanted out of his embrace. Instead, I froze in place.

"Want to go to lunch or grab a drink or something?" I heard Jake say in the distance.

"What?" I turned back to Jake, almost dazed.

"Lunch? Drink?"

"Drink, definitely drink." Speaking of alcohol, I needed some now.

"Awesome, I'll come get you at seven."

I nodded and finally got away from him.

I was behind the bar when Cindy came up to me with the guys' drink order.

"Two beers, and Linc wants a whiskey," she announced.

"Okay." I poured their drinks and set them on her tray, trying not to look over at their table for the rest of the night. It was the most difficult thing ever. My self-control was shot, and I failed in my decision within the first hour. After that, every time I peeked, my gaze would clash with Linc's.

It was almost eleven when I took my break. I grabbed a bottle of beer and headed to the back of the bar, where Seth had a table and a couple of chairs for us. I needed alcohol, my nerves were shot, and I just wanted to go home. I didn't like the idea of Linc being here. I didn't want to see him yet, and I hadn't planned to see him until tomorrow. Maybe I was taking this way overboard, but what was I supposed to say? What if he was right, and I did hit my head and imagined all those things? I shut that train of thought down. There were handprints on my neck, and there's no way I got those from falling into the water. No way.

"Maisy?" said a deep voice behind me.

I jumped and almost landed on my ass on the floor. Linc chuckled and sat down in the chair next to me.

How dare he laugh? I didn't even hear him walk back here.

"Employees are the only ones allowed back here."

I didn't look at him, as I played with the bottle cap

on the table. My hair fell around my face. He reached across the table and laid his hands on top of mine, to stop me from spinning the cap.

"You look better," he finally said.

"Am I supposed to say thank you to that?"

He gave me a hard look. "I just meant that—" He paused. "Forget it. Are you going to school tomorrow or did you drop?"

"Nope, I'll be there." I stared at our hands, mine were tingling from his touch. *Stop it.*

"Good, so this weekend, did you want to start the observations for the project?"

"Can we start later? I have a bunch of stuff I need to get done for my other classes this weekend," I said, trying to blow him off.

He nodded. "Mais, if you need to talk, I'm here, you know."

You have got to be kidding me. We are not doing this here, at my work.

"I don't need to talk," I said, pulling my hands out of his grip.

"What is your problem?" he demanded, the muscles in his jaw strained.

"My problem? The last time I attempted to talk to you, you wrote me off," I all but yelled.

"I didn't write you off. Did you hear what you were saying, Maisy? You implied that a girl who controlled water tried to drown you."

I stared him down. "I know what I saw."

"No, you don't," he bit out.

We sat there, staring at each other. Tears prickled behind my eyes, but I ignored them. I was not going to cry right now.

It would ruin my attitude.

"Maisy, I thought you might want company." Jake

walked through the door and then stopped and stared hard at Linc. "I guess you already have some."

"Nope, stay. Linc was just leaving."

Linc stared back at Jake but didn't say anything.

"You leaving, pal?" Jake said to Linc.

Linc turned to me, and his face softened just a bit. "We aren't done." He pushed back his seat and stood up.

When he walked through the door, he hit Jake's shoulder forcefully, but it didn't faze Jake at all.

"You okay?" Jake asked after Linc was finally gone.

I was so tired of getting asked that question. Yes, I was fine. I wasn't helpless, and I didn't need people to worry about me. Ignoring him, I stood up to head back in.

"How long are you going to stay for?"

"As long as you want."

"Good, wait till I get off." As I walked past him, I gave him a sly smile and patted his massive shoulder.

I finished by shift, wondering why I asked Jake to stay. It wasn't as if I planned on doing what I implied. He seemed to get under Linc's skin, though, and I liked that.

Linc, Craig, and Tommy left around twelve-thirty, and Linc didn't say another word to me. Neither did Tommy. Craig walked over to Cindy, gave her a kiss, and left. Cindy turned toward me and made a hand motion like she was fanning herself. We both giggled and got back to work.

I was kind of bummed by Linc's silent treatment, but what did I expect? I blew him off all week and then acted like I didn't want to be around him. Which I didn't, or so I tried to convince myself. Unfortunately, Linc was the only guy I'd felt any real interest in since my last boyfriend almost four years ago. Linc was hot beyond words, and when he wasn't acting like a jerk, he could be kind. Those two things usually didn't come together. If the guy was hot, and knew it, he was usually an arrogant dick.

When the guy was kind, they tended to be a regular guy, which wasn't a bad thing by any means.

Jake waited for me, like I asked. He tugged my hips forward. "Do you want me to follow you home?"

I crossed my arms over my chest, feeling uncomfortable. "Yeah, that'd be good." That way he wouldn't have to stay the night.

He gave me a quick kiss and headed out the front.

I went out the back to my car.

When I pulled out of the parking lot I saw his lights turn on as he started following me. What was I doing? I didn't want Jake at all. Ugh, I was the biggest slut on the planet. A couple of weeks ago, I was kissing on Linc. I still wanted him. I just couldn't trust him. Jake would work, though, as someone to help take out my frustration on and get laid. Especially since he didn't expect a relationship in return. Not that he could hold one down if his life depended on it. Altogether, it made him safe.

Turning onto my street, I spotted a truck in my driveway. Maybe it was Todd's? All the boys down here had those damn redneck trucks. When I pulled past it, I realized it wasn't black like Todd's, it was blue, like Linc's. Well shit, this was about to get a whole lot of awkward.

Getting out of my car, I mentally prepared to not yell and scream at Linc for coming over. I groused at the stupid butterflies in my stomach, trying to get them to go away. They had no business showing up right now. None.

Linc was already walking to my car door as I got out.

"What are you doing here, Linc? Stalking me again?"

"Don't flatter yourself. We weren't done talking."

"Well, I don't really have time for it right now. Jake's going to pull up soon."

"You invited him over?" He looked disgusted.

"None of your business," I said as sternly as I could. "Could we talk some other time?"

"No."

We both turned toward the headlights pulling up behind us.

Chapter 9

Jake jumped out of his car fast and stomped over to where Linc and I stood. He looked almost scary furious.

"What the fuck?" He looked at me, his vibrant blue eyes lethal.

I threw up my hands. "I didn't invite him."

Jake straightened. "Get lost, bro. She doesn't want you here."

"Maisy, please talk to me." Linc completely ignored a fuming Jake and basically begged me.

My voice softened. "Linc, not now, please."

Jake put his hand on Linc's shoulder and turned him around.

"You need to leave her alone. Don't come back here again."

Linc threw Jake's hand off and stood to his full height. Jake was a big guy, but Linc made him look as if he was a teenager. Jake was in shape. He was a gym rat much like Linc was. But Linc was more lean muscle, while Jake was more beefy muscle. My money was on Linc, though. He gave off a more badass vibe.

"What are you going to do, Linc? You can't defend yourself right now," Jake said, egging Linc on.

What was he talking about? Did Jake not see Linc's

arms? I was pretty sure Linc was more than capable of taking Jake.

Linc smirked in Jake's direction. "Maisy, go inside for two minutes."

"Um no," was all I could say.

Jake stepped up to Linc and got in his face.

It was my turn to intervene. If I was in the middle, they'd probably not start hitting each other.

I walked over and pushed Jake as hard as I could. He didn't even budge.

"Jake, come on, back off." I pushed harder, and he took a step back. "No one is doing anything right now. Just go home, both of you."

"I'm not leaving you here with him," Jake said.

"Shut up, Jake, he's leaving too. I'll see you tomorrow for drinks okay?" I pushed him again. "Go."

Luckily, Jake walked away and got into his truck. I turned to Linc. "Your turn to get into your truck," I told him.

"You're not getting rid of me that easily, darlin'," he said.

I just stared. "Oh, yes, I am. You're borderline creeping me out," I lied.

He took a step back as if I smacked him. "Mais, I'm not going to hurt you, or stalk you. I want to talk. I need to know you're okay."

I ran my hand through my hair as I met his gaze. "I'm fine. Look at me, I'm good."

He looked me over, and I mean *really* looked at me. His gaze worked its way from my face to my boots and then back up, pausing at my chest on the way down and the way back up. When his brown eyes met mine, they were darker, and my butterflies were back in full force and moving lower. I bit my lip self-consciously and heard him make a noise that sounded suspiciously close to a growl. I shuddered, and my nipples hardened. His gaze dipped again, and a knowing smile curled his lips.

I opened my mouth to say something, but a loud honk made me jump. Jake was just sitting in my driveway. Ugh. Once again, I felt like the biggest skank ever.

"Yeah, you're fine." Linc continued to blatantly stare at my boobs.

"Go home, idiot," I tried to sound mean, but my smile gave me away.

He laughed but did get into his truck. "I'll call you tomorrow."

I shook my head, my lips tipping up. I couldn't help my reaction. I was excited when I shouldn't be. Jake turned his truck around, and Linc followed suit. Walking back to the house, I went in and closed the door, locking it behind me. Amused, I shook my head and got ready for bed.

I woke to a different ring than my alarm. Who the hell was calling me at…I checked my clock…six in the freaking morning? I grabbed the phone. "This better be a damn emergency," I said, my voice still thick with sleep.

"Well, good morning," Linc's deep voice said, and I could hear the smile.

"Linc, it's six, I didn't get home until two something. What do you want?"

"Meet me down by the trail for a run?"

"I'm sleeping. No."

"Come on, Mais, it's cool out right now."

I groaned, mentally killing him. I hadn't run in the last two weeks, and my first class was canceled, so I didn't have to be anywhere until later.

"Fine, give me a half an hour."

"See you soon." He hung up.

I stumbled out of bed, grabbed my shorts and a T-shirt, and hit the bathroom. My reflection showed a hot mess. Throwing on the shorts and shirt, I brushed my teeth and put deodorant on. Back in my room, I grabbed my running shoes and caught my full body in the mirror. The shirt was frumpy. I needed something a little tighter. Taking off the T-shirt, I settled for a tight tank with a built-in sports bra. Satisfied, I left to go meet Linc.

On my way there, I silently scolded myself for changing my shirt. It meant I wanted something and was trying too hard. I didn't want to try too hard. Hell, I didn't want to try at all.

Okay, maybe a little bit. Damn, I was giving myself whiplash. Yesterday, I was mad at the man, and today I was excited to see him. It made no sense, but it was what I was feeling.

A half a mile from our meeting spot, I saw him and my stomach tightened. When I realized I was smiling, I stopped immediately. No smiling.

He wore black workout shorts, with a gray shirt with the sleeves cut off. It showed more of his tattoo, and my mouth started watering. Why did I find tattoos on men attractive? Who knew? But I bet most of the female population felt the same way. Throw in his lean, toned muscles, and scruffy look and he was a walking orgasm.

"Stop staring at me like that, or next time I'm wearing something less revealing," he said, snapping me out of my thoughts.

Only then did I notice I had stopped running. He looked me over, and I got goosebumps. My nipples went hard and pressed against the fabric of my shirt, which wasn't all that padded. Yay.

"Maybe you should too." His voice was thick.

After a moment, I finally managed, "You ready?"

He nodded. "I'll follow you."

I thought about the shorts I was wearing, they were a little tighter than the ones I usually ran in, and short. I completely regretted what I wore. "That's okay, you go ahead."

He stared at me for a minute, looking a little put out.

"Go on." I waved my hand toward the trail, and he took off.

Shit, he was fast. I was out of breath in the first mile. Though the view was nice and helped the run. Once I noticed his ass, being tired took a backseat. It was so not fair. He couldn't have a good everything. Most people had one, maybe two, awesome features, but he was like a damn Greek god. Everything about his body seemed perfect, and his personality wasn't too bad either. He was a little grumpy, but I sort of like it.

When we got to the creek, he slowed down and turned to me. I was so busy admiring the view I almost plowed into him. He moved out of the way easily and caught me before I went into the water. I really needed to pay more attention to what was going on.

Heat rose in my cheeks. "Thanks." I sounded out of breath.

He wiggled his dark brown eyebrows. "I look that good from the back, huh?"

"Shut up." The heat under my skin went hotter.

He laughed. "It's fine, you don't have to admit it, but I know the truth."

"Oh, my god, stop talking." I hit him in the arm, trying to hide my smile. "What did you tell me yesterday? Oh, yeah, don't flatter yourself."

He laughed, like a real laugh. It was the first time I heard it, and I stared at him in awe. His laugh was gorgeous, deep, and throaty. I shook my head. He bent down to the creek and splashed his face with water and the then shook his head. His dark brown hair splayed out everywhere, while tiny droplets hit everything within a two-foot radius, including me.

When he lifted his head, he wore a more serious face. Shit, I knew what was coming. Time to get it over with, though.

"I'm glad you're okay," he said. At least he didn't ask me if I was.

"Me too, thanks for caring," I answered.

"Nothing else has happened before, right?"

Wait, what? "What do you mean?" I sounded almost panicked. My stomach dropped, and I felt my heart start to race.

"Just...I..." He sighed as he reached out and grabbed me.

My face was pressed against his chest, and his arms swept up around me. I could feel his heart beating. My heart sped up for a whole different reason. He was holding me, and damn if I didn't like it. Wait a minute. Did he just admit that I didn't fall off a rock? I wanted to question it, but the words wouldn't come. I didn't want to ruin the moment.

He pulled back, put his hand under my chin, and lifted it up. "I'm really glad you're okay."

His voice was husky. His proximity stole my breath. He pressed his lips to mine, and, what started out as a sweet kiss, turned fierce. His tongue dove between my lips, and I opened my mouth until our tongues swirled together. He grabbed my hips and lifted me, as if I weighed nothing. My legs instinctively curled around his narrow waist, my arms wrapping around his shoulders as my hands fisted in his hair.

He moved until my back hit a tree. Letting go of my hips, he reached around grabbed my hands, lifting them over my head. All without breaking our kiss. He rolled his hips, and my whimper escaped. Pressed against me, he felt huge. He bit my bottom lip as he rolled his hips again, and I could feel myself already building. The sensations were mind-blowing, and we still had our pesky clothes on. I wanted them off, right now. I tightened my legs on his waist, and something between a curse and growl came out of his mouth. Fierce satisfaction rose in me as we devoured each other. I liked that he reacted to me as much as I did to him.

Yanking my hands from his grip, I clutched his shirt and pulled up, but it didn't really get far because my legs were still wrapped around his waist. His hands went to my ass and stayed there. I wiggled down, and he let me go, breaking out kiss for a fraction of a second so I could tug off his shirt, and throw it to the side. Lips reconnected and our hands started exploring each other. I placed my palms flat on his abs and then slipped them upward to his pecs and back down. This time, I didn't stop at his abs, or the V his hips made. I gripped him through his shorts feeling his tremor. Cold air touched my stomach as he pulled my shirt up inch by inch. I broke the kiss and went to tug my shirt off, when his hands grabbed mine.

"Don't. As hot as it would be to take you up against a tree, or down in the dirt, our first time is not going to be in the woods. And before you say a damn word, there is going to be a first time," he said out of breath.

"Cocky much," was all I could think to say, completely surprised my voice came out as even as it did.

"Confident," he countered.

He went to find his shirt, and I turned around, rubbing the back of my neck. When I turned around, he was holding up his shirt, and it was dripping with water. I started laughing immediately.

He ran his massive hand through his hair. "I'm glad you find this amusing."

"It's your own fault."

We stood there, staring at each other, for an eternity. I could get lost in those gorgeous brown eyes, something

I planned on accomplishing soon. He wrung the water out of his shirt and tugged it back over his head. Turning around, I touched my lips. They were tingling.

"Don't go out with Jake tonight," I heard him say behind me.

Oh, here we go. I rolled my eyes and looked back at him over my shoulder, almost giddy, because this meant he cared, right? He wanted me. Well, obviously, but I liked he didn't want anyone else to have me. Now facing him completely, I smiled. "Why? I've known him for a long time now. He's fine."

He grunted, and then his lips curved up on the right side as he walked toward me. Walked didn't even cover it. He swaggered over to me. I was in trouble. He grabbed my hips and pulled me close. Instinctively, my arms went around his waist. I watched his sexy scruffy face and waited for him to speak.

"I don't really like the guy, but that's not the reason I'm asking you not to go. I'm asking you to hang out with Tommy and me tonight. I think Eva will be there too."

"Be where exactly?" I stared at his mouth as I considered the idea of seeing him twice in the same day.

"Our house."

I blinked. Had he just invited me over to his house? In my head, I did a little happy dance.

"And what would we do there?"

"Anything you want." He pulled me tighter until I could feel him against my stomach.

I arched an eyebrow. Was this a booty call? Seriously?

He chuckled. "Kidding. I think we're ordering pizza and watching a movie, but if you don't want to do that, then we could go out."

I wanted to do what he was implying before, but I'd already made plans with Jake. It would be rude to cancel on him. Plus there were the other questions I needed to ask Linc about the night I was attacked. "How 'bout I meet you after I hang out with Jake?" Well, that made me sound like a whore. Whatever, Jake was a friend.

Linc's smile dimmed. "What time do you think you'll be done?"

"We're meeting at seven, so hopefully we can get a drink or two, and I'll be out of there by eight-thirty at the latest."

"I can pick you up."

"It's fine. I'd rather drive."

Linc picking me up probably wouldn't go over to well at all.

He nodded and our conversation basically ended. We decided to run back and once again he offered to let me go first. While his hands had been up close and personal with my ass minutes ago, I still rather him go first so I could enjoy the view.

ↄ✺ↄ

School went by pretty fast. During the classes we shared, Linc sat next to me and Sarah. Sarah talked up a storm and then decided at the end of the day that she liked him. I was thankful for her positive opinion. Other than the frisky business from this morning, which I spent all day replaying in my head, the day wasn't very eventful at all. Added bonus, I hadn't seen Todd today!

I shaved my legs before going to meet Jake, but it wasn't for him, it was for who came after him. Not that I was expecting anything to happen with Linc, but I was hoping.

When I got to the bar, I didn't see Jake anywhere, so I took a seat at the far end. No one ever sat at this end so we would have privacy.

"Isn't it your day off?" Cindy walked up to me. "What the hell are you doing at work girlie?"

"Meeting Jake."

"Fun, why?" She didn't sound thrilled with my plans.

I shrugged. "He asked."

She nodded, left to make a drink, and brought it back to me. "Here, it's a margarita, with very little alcohol." She winked.

"Why little?"

"To make sure you go home alone." She gave me a tight-lipped smile and walked away.

Guess Cindy wasn't a fan of Jake's, not that I'd ever noticed before. Still, as I thought back on it, they never really talked or said hi at parties or anything. Hmm.

Jake grabbed the stool next to me and sat down. "Hey, Mais! Sorry I'm late, had to get gas."

Startled by his sudden appearance, I jumped a little, but thankfully it went unnoticed. I gave him a half hug. "Hey."

He was wearing khaki shorts and one of our college red shirts, which did good things for his looks. After I realized I wasn't into one-night stands, he became the last person I was intimate with. Our one-and-only time we were both drunk, and it was sloppy, but satisfying enough. Nothing changed after that night, though. He continued to act like a really good friend, indicating he didn't do the relationship thing, and I just rolled with it. We didn't talk about it. Even when we woke up together, he hugged me, said 'That was fun, we need to do that more often,' and then I left. Nope, wasn't gonna happen again.

He ordered a beer and gave me one of his dazzling white smiles. "Your day good?"

"Yeah, just school. What about yours?" I wasn't going to share my early morning hot make-out session with Linc. Not only wasn't it Jake's business, they didn't need another reason to be at each other's throats.

"Same, school and the gym."

We just saw each other, so nothing really new was going on. There wasn't much to talk about, so we covered menial stuff while we shared drinks for the next hour or so.

"So, Linc still bothering you?" His face turned a little hard.

"Oh, um, nope."

"He hasn't texted you or showed up at your door again, right? Because if he has, I can talk to him for you." His last words were accompanied by a mean smile.

"Actually, we've been talking. Everything's fine now. I'm actually seeing him tonight." I looked away from him as I spoke.

"Are you fucking kidding me, Mais? The guy's dangerous You don't need to be around him."

Oh, here we go. Why I blessed him with that piece of information, I had no clue. I mentally kicked myself. "Don't cuss at me and, may I ask, how is he dangerous?"

"He—" Jake paused as if he was thinking about how to choose his next sentence. "—he showed up at your door after your shift, without being invited. How does that not scream dangerous to you?"

"Jake, that was my fault. He just wanted to make sure I was okay."

"Okay? Okay from what?"

"It's nothing." I wanted this conversation to be over and needed to get out of here. No way was I telling Jake what happened. I didn't need him thinking I was completely nuts.

He glared at me. "Why did he want to know if you were okay?"

Well, shit. I hadn't seen Jake this mad ever. Staring at him, I wasn't sure how to handle the situation or what to say. "I got attacked at the party," I finally said, not willing to go into the floating water or water freezing to ice in eighty-degree weather.

"What?" he yelled. "Why the fuck didn't you tell me? What the hell happened?"

"I don't really remember. Linc scared the attacker off. I didn't get a good look at their face, though."

"Did Linc fight him off?" His voice turned more curious than pissed.

"I think so, I'm not really sure, I hit my head pretty good."

"I don't think you should hang out with Linc anymore. The guy's weird."

Umm, why was he now more concerned with me hanging out with Linc? "Good thing your opinion really doesn't impact who or how I spend my time."

Jake's pinched the bridge of his nose, and his face got red.

"Well, I think I'm done." I pulled out some cash, set it on the counter, and hopped off the barstool. "I'll see you around."

His warm hand grabbed my forearm, hard. I spun around as fast as I could and glared. His usually vibrant blue eyes morphed into black. What the fuck?

"Let. Go." I coated each word with as much ice as possible.

His grip tightened until a whimper passed between my lips. Scared, I glanced at my arm in his hands. If he gripped any tighter, he would snap my bone clean in half. As it was, I was going to have a nasty-ass bruise.

"You're hurting me. Let go, now." I tried for the same stinging tone as before, but my voice faltered because of the pain. His nails dug into my skin. Looking back up at his eyes, which were almost completely black, the hairs on the back of my neck stood up, and my stomach dropped. What the hell was wrong with him?

I slapped him. My move caught Seth's attention.

Jake's eyes slowly turned back to their normal blue, even as an arm grabbed Jake's wrist and tore it from me.

Seth spun Jake around and threw him against a table. "You okay, Mais?" he asked through his teeth.

Shit. "Yeah fine, just a disagreement."

Seth didn't take his eyes off of Jake. "Touch her without her permission again, and you don't get to come back here."

Jake nodded.

I shoved past both men, suppressing the desire to grab Jake's balls and twist. He didn't say anything or try to stop me, as I stomped out of the bar.

Chapter 10

Crap my arm frickin' arm hurt like hell. What the fuck was Jake thinking? I contemplated not going to Linc's since my sore arm was already starting to bruise, and I didn't want to give him another reason to kick Jake's ass. Sitting in my car in the parking lot of Woody's, I searched for a jacket, sweater, anything with long sleeves.

What the heck was that all about with Jake's eyes? Since when did eyes change like that, where most of the white outside his irises turned black? It reminded me of crow's eyes, or one of those scary movies when the demon gets inside someone and possesses them. Just to review my encounters with the freaky, first there were people who controlled water and now my friend's eyes turned demonic black. Perfect. Maybe I was hallucinating? As I sat there and pondered the benefits of checking into a damn asylum, my phone went off.

You on your way?

Seeing Linc's message, my body began to relax. How did one person affect me so much? Didn't matter if I was grateful, it made no sense. I sent him my response, asked for his address, and then was on my way. I stopped at home first to change, since there wasn't anything long-sleeved in my car. Being a clean freak had some drawbacks. When I got home, it went from quick stop to quick change. I grabbed a pair of white shorts and a green and white tie-dyed long-sleeved shirt. Checking the mirror, I reapplied mascara and pulled my hair in a high, messy bun, which took five tries to get the right type of messy.

After plugging in Linc's address, I followed my phone's directions. When it announced I had arrived barely ten miles down the road, I was stunned at how close he lived to me.

During my drive, I tried to calm my ridiculous nerves. Stupid to be so nervous, I'd hung out with Linc numerous times over the last month. Maybe it was because I was going to his house, where he had a bed, something I wanted to make use of, like yesterday. Fighting the urge to go home and brush my teeth again, I found a piece of gum and popped it into my mouth.

I pulled into what I thought was his driveway, but as I drove farther back, there was no sign of his house. Instead, the woods got thicker until I couldn't see the main road. In my rearview mirror, the road seemed to stretch behind me. Was my GPS was broken? Maybe I should turn back? I went another mile then came across a house with two huge trucks and small red Mini Cooper, probably Eva's since I couldn't imagine either of the two boys being able to fit it.

Parking behind Eva's car, I studied the house. It was big and white standing two stories. Huge old windows went across the bottom and top stories until it looked like one of those old plantation homes, complete with a wrap-a-round porch. It was so beautiful. For a good five minutes, I argued with myself between walking up to the door and knocking, or texting Linc I was outside. *Stop being a chicken shit.* I shoved open my door and headed up to knock. Not doing so was borderline rude, unless they didn't know you were coming over.

I walked up their gravel path to the door, but froze before knocking. Why was this so hard? I checked my outfit again and noticed I was subconsciously rubbing my arm where Jake bruised me. Pulling my sleeve up, I frowned at the light purple coloring my skin. Great, this one was probably going to be a doozy. Tugging my sleeve down to cover it, I made a mental not to touch it while I was here. Linc was too observant when it came to me, and I didn't want him getting pissed. And he would. He wasn't a big fan of Jake's.

I lightly tapped the door with my fist and waited. I went to knock again, this time harder, when the door flew open. Eva stood there in cheetah feet pajamas.

"Um, hi?" I offered, staring at her awesome attire.

"Hey, Maisy! Come in here! Linc, your girlfriend's here!" Loud and excited, her voice bounced off into another room.

Girlfriend? Was that what I was? I blushed slightly. Their entryway opened into a large sitting room with a beautifully crafted wooden staircase attached to a loft. Linc walked out of the upstairs hallway, his lips tipped up at the corners. He wore jeans and snug fitting white T-shirt, which showed off his cut body nicely. He walked down stairs, our gazes locked, and I fidgeted under his stare.

Once he got to me, he pulled me close, and my arms instinctively wrapped around his waist.

"Hey," he whispered into my hair. "Sorry about Eva's introduction."

I smiled against his chest. "I didn't mind it." His body rumbled with his chuckle. I pulled back enough to see his face. "So, what movie are we watching?"

He let me go but kept a hold of my hands, our fingers laced. "I think one of the Bourne movies, that okay?"

Sweet! Those were my favorites! While I loved action movies, horror could scare me for days. The first and last scary movie I watched was *Paranormal Activity*. Afterward, I didn't sleep for days. I even crawled in bed with Sarah when Todd wasn't staying over.

"Yup, I love those movies."

The corners of his mouth slid upward as he pulled me through the house, our fingers still tangled. We passed a small dining room, a bathroom, and at the back of the house, there was a large, gorgeous kitchen. The kitchen was done in dark wood cabinets, granite countertops and had modern appliances. A good sized island perched in the middle separating the family room from the kitchen.

The family room was close to the size of my entire house. With vaulted ceilings, a brick fireplace, and one wall covered with beautiful dark wood built-ins acting as a bookshelf, I was totally in love. It was gorgeous.

Tommy sat in a comfy looking chair next to a couch. Eva was on the floor with a mountain of pillows, popping in the DVD.

"Hey, Mais." Tommy got up, walked over, and kissed me on the cheek. He was dressed in pajama bottoms and nothing else, his straight, dirty-blond hair was pulled back into a small ponytail.

This was slightly awkward, because I had chosen his friend over him. "Hey. No awesome footie pajamas?"

Tommy laughed. "Sadly, I couldn't find my matching cheetah one. Want anything to drink? We have water, beer, lemonade?"

"Lemonade!" Eva piped in.

"I'm okay, but thanks." My right hand pinched my left index finger. I was a bit nervous being here.

Linc pulled me around the island and plopped down on one side of the couch. I took the middle cushion next to him. Tommy passed out the drinks, including water for me. Linc flipped a switch just above the back of the couch, and the room went dark.

Linc leaned in and whispered, "What are you doing all the way over there?" His low, deep voice sent a zinging sensation straight to my lower stomach, which trembled as his breath hit the back of my neck.

"Hmm?" I pretended not to know what he was saying.

"Come here."

He pulled me up against his chest until we were spooning. I lay in front of him, my back pressed against his warm chest. Maybe he could take a page out of whatever book Tommy was reading and get rid of his shirt.

I wiggled and pressed my ass tighter against him, and his hand tightened on my hip in response. I heard his short intake of breath, and I felt front teeth pinch my bottom lip. I loved how I affected him. He grabbed a patterned blanket hanging from the back of the brown couch and threw it over us. Was he really cold? Despite the air conditioner, I was burning up.

He arranged the blanket almost to my neck. Honestly, the last thing I wanted to do was sweat while we were like this. Sweating with clothes off, yes, clothes on, ew.

Under the blanket's cover, his hand started moving over my body. He cupped my breast, giving a light squeeze. I shifted until I was almost facing him, and enjoyed the rising sensations. His eyes were still focused on the TV and not me, but his lips tipped up at the right side in my favorite half smile of his.

His hands drifted lower, gliding over my stomach and teasing the top of my shorts. My heart rate skyrocketed until I thought my heart might jump out of my chest. The butterflies in my stomach migrated lower. I sucked in my breath and held it. Was he really going to get frisky on the couch in front of his friends? Pulling the blanket over us was obvious enough, and I'd never been the quiet type, no matter how hard I tried.

His hands gripped the top of my shorts and pulled upward slightly until the seam of my shorts rubbed against that already sensitive area, making it pleasurable. I almost sighed, but quickly caught it. I debated turning back to him, because I wanted to explore as well. Unfortunately, that would be beyond obvious. His fingers slid my button free with an ease that made me wonder for a second, but my body didn't really care. Selfish skank. His rough hand brushed my scorching skin. With his touch, my body convulsed slightly, and he hadn't even done anything yet. Maybe I should've done a practice run before coming over, then I wouldn't be so wound up.

As he learned my body, I couldn't stop my short breaths from escaping, and the end result of a whimper escaped. *Shit.* Tommy's head snapped in our direction even as Eva tried to stifle a laugh. Well, this was awkward. To make matters worse, blood rush into my cheeks and my palms started to sweat. I pulled the blanket over my head as I turned toward Linc. He threw his arm around me and scooted me closer to him. His body rumbled, and I heard his chuckle. Asshole, this was his fault. I placed a kiss on his chest and stayed there, not wanting to come out.

"Poor girl," Eva said, and I could hear the laughter in her voice. "That wasn't very smooth, Linc."

"Not very incognito man, since I'm the expert that taught you that trick," Tommy added.

I stiffened. *Well, then.*

"You mean, you're the loser, not expert," Eva offered, sounding disgusted.

"Fuck off, both of you," Linc growled, but you could hear the smile.

Great, so I was just another girl, another notch in his

bedpost. *Fucking awesome*. Nice to know he'd done this before. I gave myself a mental smack because that wasn't fair since I'd done things like this before too. It still hurt. I wasn't sure what to do or say, so I slowly turned around, uncovered my head, and then re-buttoned my shorts. Everyone was diligently watching the movie. What part were we even on? Linc's arms snaked around me again, but I brushed them off and pushed the blanket down. If I couldn't keep my noises to myself, I wasn't doing that again. He grumbled, but stopped and held me. It was nice.

The movie ended, and Eva bounced up. "I'll see you guys in the morning." She gave Tommy and Linc a kiss on the cheek and disappeared.

"Yeah, me too," Tommy added. "Have a good night, guys." His eyebrows shot upward, and a big ole cheesy smile broke out.

We said our goodnights, and I blushed the entire time. I sat up and stretched, arching my back. It felt so good.

Turning to Linc, I found him staring at me, his face and his lips turned upward.

"Do that again," he commanded.

Smiling, I crawled over to him until I was half laying on him. "Do what again?" I asked in the most mischievous voice I could.

"Stretch."

"I already did that."

"Then stretch something else." His voice was deep and thick with desire.

Getting an idea, I bit my lip, as I sat my hips back, and stretched my arms out on his chest, while my ass rose in the air and my back arched. After a moment, he made a grunting noise, and my head snapped up. His eyes were darker, and his smile was gone. His breathing stopped completely, before picking back up.

I chuckled and, in less than half a second, he flipped me onto my back. His hips pressed into mine until I could feel him. Honestly, a human should not be able to move that fast.

"I think that was my favorite stretch, by far." His breath mixed with mine.

"It was?" Oh gosh, my voice was all breathy and girly. My arms went to his chest, and my hands tugged on his shirt.

"Mmmhmmm, it made me start thinking." He grabbed both of my hands in one of his and placed them above my head, his hold tight.

"About?" I needed to know, there was nothing more important than what was going to happen next.

"I need to get me some of that." His lips came crashing down on mine.

He let go of my hands, and they instinctively went up to his back. I got a good hold on his shirt and pulled. He rose to his knees now conveniently settled between my legs and ripped off his shirt. He tossed it on the floor and stared at me.

He devoured me with his eyes, which was fine, but I wanted him to actually devour me, so his eyes weren't good enough. I reached out and unbuttoned his jeans, but he took my shaking hands in his.

"Not really fair, babe, you get to see all of this—" His head dipped as he scanned his own body. "—and you still have your clothes on."

He wanted to see me? Hell, he didn't have to ask twice. He could see me. Sitting up, I tore my shirt off, wincing a little as it tugged around my sore arm. I tucked it against the couch so he couldn't see.

"What are you doing all the way over there?" I copied his words from earlier and his face smoldered with intensity.

His body came down on mine, but our lips never touched. Instead, his lips went to my neck, where his tongue traced the line of my collarbone. I shivered with a full-blown shudder. His teeth nipped the inside of my breast. His arm curled under my back, and he lifted me slightly. Next thing I knew, my bra was off and had joined our shirts on the floor somewhere in the direction of the fireplace.

He trailed kisses between my breasts and down toward my navel, where he pressed a single, hot kiss right above my shorts. He looked up, smiling like a kid who had a master plan to eat the entire pie sitting on the windowsill.

"This okay?"

Weirdo, you've come this far, why would I stop you now? "Yes, god, please don't stop," I finally squeaked out.

He chuckled as he undid the button on my shorts, and I squirmed. My body was humming with anticipation, and I almost whimpered. His warm mouth glided over me, and I instantly melted, my fist wrapped around his light brown hair. This time I did whimper. The tension started building and gained momentum and, when his fingers rhythmically pulsed into me, all my insides tighten with satisfaction.

When I went over the edge, my body collapsed, like so much mush. I pulled him to my lips and started on the button on his jeans, without breaking contact. When the button finally opened, I reached in and gripped him. He made a low animalistic noise, and I smiled against his lips. I could love that sound. He was huge and my excitement rose once more, butterflies hitting my lower stomach as if they were on a mission for freedom.

He lowered one of his hands between us and grabbed my arms. He touched the sore spot, and I winced. Thank goodness, he didn't notice and stop. He stood, pulling his jeans and black boxer briefs off, then settled between my thighs. Goodness, he was gorgeous and hard. I needed him now, needed to feel him, and so I sat up, grabbed his arm, and lowered back down, bringing him with me.

He kissed my neck and left more trails of kisses down to my breasts. He captured my left arm, held it over my head, and sank into me. I could feel him against my core, teasing me, making my breath catch. Against my neck, his lips curled up, and his other hand drifted along my arm, hitting that damn spot. I let out a whimper that wasn't sexual, and he stopped instantly.

His gaze went to where his hand touched.

"What the hell is that?" Rage washed over his body. "What the fuck is this?" he repeated, holding my arm up to my face.

On my forearm, there was now a black welt. *Well, shit.*

Chapter 11

He scooted away, lightning fast, as if I had some contagious disease, and started putting his clothes back on. He threw my clothes at me, his jaw was clenched, and with every movement, the muscles in his arms and chest looked strained. He looked enraged. He gave me his back as I dressed. Crap on a stick, everything was going so well, and now he couldn't even fucking look at me. What the hell?

"You're fucking marked." He whipped around to face me. "Did Jake do that?" he demanded.

If looks could kill, I was the walking dead.

"Maisy, did Jake fucking touch you?"

"Yes." I shrank back. "But he didn't mean to."

"Why didn't you tell me?" His voice rose.

"I don't need to tell you every aspect of my damn life, Linc. You barely know me."

"Bullshit. When someone touches you, I need to know. You need to tell me those things." He knelt down in front of me, taking my arm, and studied it. "If someone physically hurts you, I need to know. Besides, I do know you, so don't play that shit."

Behind us, footsteps came through the kitchen. Tommy came into the family room. "Seriously, guys, people sleep here, and as much as I want to fist bump,

Linc, at the moment, you guys need to shut the fuck up and act like quiet bunnies, not horny hyenas."

Linc stood, glaring at Tommy. "She was marked." His body was physically shaking with rage.

"Trust me, bro, I heard you. No need to piss around her, too."

"No, she was marked by a fucking Fiskare," Linc yelled.

Tommy's face went white.

Wait, Jake wasn't a…what did they call it, a Fiskare?

Tommy held out his hand. "Let me see, Maisy."

I gave him my arm. He turned it, flipping it over to trace the inky line of the welt. I'd never seen a bruise do that, not even an Indian burn.

"Does your family know of a way to get it off? I didn't know they could mark humans," Tommy said.

Linc turned on him. "Shut up, Tommy." He turned to the hall and bellowed, "Eva!" He avoided my gaze the entire time.

Eva joined us, and, when she saw my arm, her reaction was the same—her face went totally white.

Eva scooted closer getting a better look as her auburn hair fell over her face. "What happened to her?"

"Marked," Tommy answered.

She stared at her brother with a stunned look. "I've never seen one up close before."

"Eva, take Maisy home, please." Linc finally faced me. "I'll come to get you in a little bit."

I stared at him.

What? I didn't want to go home, I wanted to know what they were talking about and what was happening to my arm. Besides, I could drive myself home.

"Linc, I'm not going with her. What is going on?"

He ignored me and turned his back, his cell phone at his ear, his voice so low I couldn't hear what he said.

Even Tommy looked put out.

"Come on, Mais." Eva wrapped her hand around my elbow and gave it a little tug in the direction of the door. "Everything's fine."

Linc still wouldn't look at me. I was scared, mad, and sexually frustrated. Why wouldn't he meet my gaze? It made no sense, none.

Eva drove, and the car ride home was quiet. Memories of the attack at the lake a couple of weeks ago came back, I could swear it was Linc who saved me. And I was beginning to believe it wasn't a hallucination, but that he could control water. And he and Jake seemed to absolutely loathe each other for people who claimed not to know each other, but I honestly thought it was just because they were interested in me. Oh god, could Jake do something similar? Was that what this was all about? What was I thinking? Jake and I had been friends for years. There was no way he was whatever Linc was, right? Until today, Jake was perfectly normal Still, I needed Linc to admit I was attacked and then tell me what was going on.

My gaze wandered over to Eva. I wondered if I could ask her about the attack, but it was probably best not to. Linc should probably be the one I talked to. "Eva?"

Her gaze flickered towards me, then back to the road. "Yeah, hon?"

"What's happening? Why did Linc act like I was repulsive after seeing my bruise? Because up until that point, I definitely wasn't repulsive to him."

She let out a shaky laugh. "Don't worry about it. I can't really tell you much because that's the hole he decided to dig, but Linc will fix it. He always does."

Fix it? What was 'it'? I didn't need fixing, and the bruise or whatever would go away with time. It wasn't a big deal. Why everyone was determined to get their panties in a bunch over it was beyond me. Things were getting too weird. As much as I really liked Linc, it was just my luck that he had a bunch of fucked-up secrets I couldn't puzzle together. His reaction to the bruise and calling me marked didn't excuse him from going all alpha male. The strangeness of it all was frightening.

I stared out the window of the car and decided to ask Linc what the fuck was going on, and if he wouldn't tell me, I'd cut him out of my life completely. I wanted the first option because he made me feel good, and not just physically. Every time I saw him, my stomach and chest tightened, and my head spun. I wasn't sure if those were simply signs of the lust coursing through me, or something more. Either way, I wanted to ride it out, if there was even anything to ride out, at this point.

"You've got to be kidding me," Eva muttered.

I blinked, and through the windshield, I noticed a truck and a Jeep parked in my driveway. Jake and Todd.

"Maisy, I need you to stay in the car. Call Linc and tell him that they're here," she hissed as she pulled her Mini Cooper to a stop. She reached into her back seat and grabbed two water bottles. She opened the first one. Water flowed out and floated into her open palm. The water in the next bottle did the same to her opposite hand.

My eyes widened in shock, and my mind screamed to get the hell out of here and run. Unless I'd reached a new level of crazy, this shouldn't be possible. There was no way in hell I was crazy. Obviously, what happened during my attack was real. My body started to shake.

I reached for the door handle, but the water in Eva's palm curled over my hand and pulled me back to face her.

"Maisy, I need you to calm down. Jake and Todd are not good guys, so running to them would be useless. I need you to call Linc and tell him to get over here fast. You have to calm down."

I just stared at her. *Say something, dammit!*

"What are you?" It was the first thing to come out of my mouth.

"Not a good conversation to have at the moment, hon. Linc will explain it to you, after. Call him. Now." She enunciated her words, leaving no room for misunderstanding.

What I didn't understand was how the hell she was controlling water with her hands.

Slowly she slipped from the car and stood in front of it, hands at her sides, her palms, with the freaky water, out toward the boys.

I reached for my phone and dialed Linc's number. No answer. Well, shit on a stick. I called Tommy next.

He answered on the first ring. "Mais?"

"Jake and Todd are at my house. Eva's in front of the car doing a weird water thingy, and I—I don't know what to do. Linc didn't answer." I was rambling and noticed I was shaking again.

I heard him cuss, then the line went dead. I watched Eva over the hood of her tiny car. She hadn't moved and was still standing in front with her hands extended to her sides, as if she expected a confrontation. Jake's gaze snapped up, and his eyes immediately went to me. Something close to regret lined his face. Suddenly, as if donning a mask, his expression changed. He looked lethal, standing straight and eyeing Eva with a deadly grin.

"Give me Maisy, and I'll think about letting you leave," he snarled.

When he spoke, the hair on the back of my neck stood up. What the hell was going on? Jake was my friend, lovable and caring. Not this. God, why didn't I see this coming?

"I don't think so." I couldn't see Eva's face, but I could hear the smile in her voice.

"You know, there's two of us. We could just take her, and leave you for your brother and Linc."

Oh, hell no. I got out of the car before I could think about what I was doing.

"Jake, what's going on?" My voice faltered a bit.

"Maisy, get back in the car, now," Eva ordered, but of course, I didn't plan on listening.

Jake walked toward me. "Everything's fine, Maisy. Just come over here, and I'll explain."

"Maisy, get your ass back in the car," Eva said again.

"If I come over, you'll let Eva go, right? I mean, she can go home?" I urged.

"Of course," Jake said immediately.

He held out his hand, urging me to take it.

I breathed in slowly, deciding he wouldn't hurt me. I took his hand. I wasn't aware my eyes were closed, but they were because I felt the air swoosh past me, and I hit something hard. Blinking my eyes open I discovered it was Jake. He had thrown me into his body. I looked up into his face, and his pretty blue eyes started to darken. I wanted to move away from him but didn't. I didn't want to end up with another welt.

He dragged me back toward the house, and when we passed Todd, whose eyes were already black, Jake mumbled, "Get rid of the other one."

I put on the brakes instantly and tried to fight him. "Eva, go!" I yelled as a hand went around my stomach and lifted me up.

Eva threw her hands out toward Todd, and the water became an extension of her. It flew toward Todd, turning to ice a second before it crashed into him. He stumbled back and then stood up—and up. God, what was with everyone being so damn tall? A serial-killer smile hit his lips, and he ran toward her, holding a glistening knife dripping with some type of oily substance.

Eva brought the water up off the ground and threw it at him with a raise of her perfectly pink polished pointer finger. She moved her entire arm toward her, and the water came barreling back. It wrapped around her body and then stopped in front of her. Her hands went up in the air, fingers splayed.

The water turned to ice and made a razor sharp spear point. Eva sent them, one by one, at Todd's head, but he was fast. She barely nicked the side of his cheek. Red blood flowed.

Still struggling in Jake's arms, I tried to wrap my head around everything that was happening. I couldn't tear my gaze away from Eva and Todd, even to fight Jake.

"Do you see what they're capable of Maisy? They could kill you."

"They never held me down against my will or marked me," I said, trying to act like I knew what I was talking about.

Jake smirked and looked at me. "The marking thing was an accident, but I don't think being my mate will be all that terrible."

Hold on a second, mate? Who the heck talks like that? I was so not his mate. Especially after this shit. No way in hell. I shuddered at the thought. "Mate?"

"Yeah, you're mine now." He picked me up and began dragging me into the house.

I elbowed him in the gut as hard as I could and earned a grunt from him. Good. I tried it again, but his hand snaked out, wrapping around my elbow and twisting. I dropped to my knees and heard screaming. My scream.

"Do that again, and I'll knock you out," he hissed in my ear.

I wanted to spit in his face but didn't have the energy

anymore. My strength was gone, thanks to my previous struggles.

A body flew behind Jake and smacked into the wall of the house. Jake turned, his hand still holding my elbow. Todd lay on the ground, out cold. My head snapped to where Todd had stood moments ago, and my gaze clashed with furious whiskey-colored eyes.

The look on Linc's face more than expressed his rage—if looks could kill.

"You try to run, I will find you. Your mark comes with a nice tracking system," Jake whispered into my neck.

Recoiling at those words, I winced. He laughed in my face, right before slamming me against the wall. A rush of warm liquid dripped down my forehead, and I reached up instinctively. When I brought my hand back, warm gooey blood filled my palm. I gulped. Shit. I placed my hand back on the gash to try and stop the bleeding.

An animalistic growl that belonged to Linc sounded, but it was deeper, rougher, nowhere near the smaller, pleasure-fueled one. This was the I'm-going-to-kick-the-living-shit-out-of-you-till-you-beg-for-death type.

"You touch her again, and I will kill you." Linc's voice was low, lethal.

Jake let out a laugh. "Like this?"

My body was ripped away from the wall, and my back hit Jake's chest. He put a bloody knife to my neck. I prayed it wasn't someone else's blood.

"You don't know who you're fucking with, Linc. I'm one of the most powerful Fiskares in the Southern states. I will kill her, which would be a waste. She's a pretty decent fuck. That's why I'm not too terribly torn up about marking her. Could be worse, right?"

My body started shaking again, my fight or flight

mode getting a serious workout. Tears swelled, and I tried to keep them back, but one fell and then another. Didn't matter how hard I tried, I couldn't stop them. There was pain in Linc's eyes for a split second before he turned his attention back to Jake.

Linc's hands were at his sides, and they curled into fists so tight his knuckles showed white. He threw his hands out toward us, and the knife began to move away from my neck. Jake's grip around me loosened enough I was able to scramble away.

Jake was on his knees, gasping in pain. His eyes were totally black. "What the fuck?" he spit out, breaking my frozen haze.

I took off toward Linc and stood behind him. He brought his hands down to the ground. Jake's body followed the motion of Linc's hands.

"You clearly don't know who you're *fucking* with. Did you forget my last name?" Linc growled out before turning to me. He looked me over from head to toe, then grabbed my shoulders, and pulled me close. He half turned back to Jake. "You look—actually, you even fucking think about her again—and I will put an end to every single person you love and let you watch. Then I will torture you until you beg me for death. I don't give a shit if you marked her, she is not yours." He slammed his free hand in a downward motion.

Jake's head bounced off the concrete, and he didn't make another move.

"Did you just kill them?" I asked between sobs.

"Nah, they'll wake up in an hour or so, but we need to leave now."

He tucked me into his arms. His body shook, and I wondered if he would pass out. We got to Eva's Mini Cooper.

I panicked, scanning the lawn and driveway. "Oh my god, Eva!"

Linc ran his hand through his light brown hair. "She's fine. Tommy grabbed her."

We drove to his house where Tommy and Eva waited. They both ran to the car. Eva pulled me inside the house while Tommy put one of Linc's arms around his shoulders and shuffled in behind us.

Eva basically dragged me upstairs, since my legs wouldn't work. My body didn't want to do anything else tonight, and my head felt like it would implode. We got to a blue bedroom with a massive king-sized bed.

"This way, Mais," Eva said softly and pulled me along.

We went into a large bright bathroom, and I recoiled. The lights were too bright.

Eva's gaze skimmed my face. "Sorry, they need to stay on while I check your head out." She sat me on the toilet lid and started picking through my hair, blood started to drip onto my knees and the white-tiled floor. "Well, it looked worse. I think you're okay." She walked over to the roomy bathtub and started the water. "Go ahead and get in. I'll set some clean PJs on the bed."

I nodded as she left the room. I peeled back my shirt that was dripping with sweat, dirt, and blood. Ugh, it felt like a truck had hit me. Stepping out of my shorts, I limped toward the tub, stepped up over the edge, and sank into the warm water. It burned, and I almost jumped out—almost. Scrapes and bruises covered my entire body. How was I going to cover this up? I couldn't miss any more work or Seth would fire me. Besides, I was already two hundred dollars short for this month's rent. No way could I ask Sarah to spot me more than that. Not to mention Sarah's boyfriend just went psycho and wasn't human.

I sank all the way down into the tub, so the water covered my head. The blazing water on my face was welcomed. I could stay under here. I didn't want to deal with what just happened.

I came up for air, letting the water settle around my neck. *Time for a reality check.*

Linc and his friends could control water. How did I begin to start processing that statement? I wanted to get away fast, but, honestly, where would I go? I couldn't go home since Jake and Todd were another fucking crazy species.

I wasn't surprised by Todd, but Jake? He'd threatened me. How could he do that? I slept with the damn bastard. Not to mention knowing him for four years. I would've dated him if he could've handled it.

Ugh. Just ugh. What was with all that talk about me being his mate? I was definitely no one's mate. I wasn't even anyone's girlfriend. I thought I was close to being Linc's, but that ship had definitely sailed. My heart ached. Maybe I'd get lucky and go into shock by morning, and then it wouldn't hurt so much.

Since my fingers and toes were shriveled like raisins, it was time to climb out. I walked to the mirror by the sink. I looked like death, like actual death. I was white as a ghost, with big dark circles under my eyes, and nice deep purple bruises forming on the right side of my forehead, along with little nicks and scrapes from where Jake shoved me against the house. My money was on the rest of my body looking the same.

Opening the door, I peeked into the room. No one was there, but there was a large shirt on the bed. I ran over and yanked it on. I should leave, but when my body saw the huge bed, it was done listening to my head. I climbed in and lay down, staring at the ceiling.

Maybe Linc wasn't that dangerous. He saved me and

then brought me here. The image of his face from earlier tonight, when he threatened Jake, flashed through my mind. It was the most intimidating and gorgeous face I'd ever seen.

I should be afraid, but maybe tonight's events weren't registering yet.

When my trembling body finally relaxed, I drifted off.

Chapter 12

Light pressed against my eyelids, and I blinked once, twice. I went to turn over and realized I couldn't. Within milliseconds, my heart rate tripled. Something huge and solid kept me from getting up. It was warm. I turned the opposite way and almost smacked my face into Linc. His arm was draped over my upper body, his entire body leaning on me, and one of his knees was in-between my legs. Not okay.

As quietly and gently as I could, I picked up his heavy arm and set it aside and then squeezed out from under him. Grabbing my dirty shorts from the floor, I began sneaking out of his room. I looked back. Linc. He was gorgeous. I still wanted him, but there was no way this would work. Tears pricked my eyes as I closed the door behind me.

I peeked over the balcony to see if anyone else was up. Standing there for a minute, I listened but heard no sounds. Convinced no one was awake, I hobbled downstairs, grabbed my keys from the table by the entrance, and slipped out. I ran to my car, yanked open the door, and hit the gas pedal. I never wanted to see or talk to them again. They could hurt me. Hell, they might be the reason Jake attacked me. They were probably the reason I was attacked at the last party.

My heart started racing again. *Deep breaths, keep taking deep breaths, you're almost home.* I repeated the silent mantra the entire twenty minutes back to my house. I drove cautiously up the driveway and was relieved to find Jake and Todd gone. The blood left around the house, had to be mine. I quivered and unlocked my door. Once inside my safe place, I fell to the floor, and just let the water works go.

I cried, heaved, coughed, and shook for a while. When I finally started to pull it together, there was a light knock on my door. Throwing myself backward, I hit the side of couch opposite the door. Holding my hand over my mouth, I kept my fear silent.

The knock came again. A sob, just a slight one, escaped me. As if that was some sort of signal, the door was kicked in. The doorframe was barely big enough for Linc's body. His brown eyes held me frozen. When he realized I was alone, his stare lost its intensity. I shook under his stare and recoiled back into the couch.

"Maisy?" His voice was soft as he knelt next to me. He reached out and touched my shoulder.

"Don't touch me!" It came out as a shriek as I attempted to back up again, but I was already against the couch.

He raised both hands in the air, backing off.

"Please go, please just go, Linc. I—I can't do this, I don't want you here." I tried to bury my head in my knees.

"Maisy, don't, please."

I felt a feather-light touch drift over my back and shrank away. "Get out, Linc," I bit out, trying to sound mad or scary, something not terrified.

My body had been wracked by so many fight or flight moments within the last month that I didn't think it knew what to do, except freeze.

"Talk to me, let me explain. I know this has to be hard for you. I wish I could take it back, but I can't. I need you to listen to me. I won't hurt you, I could never hurt you."

His voice was panicked, and I was surprised by my need to comfort him. *Go figure.* "You have no clue how hard this is for me. I don't want you here, Linc. I'm scared to death of you, of everything. My body feels like it got hit by a truck, and my mental state is in shambles. I don't know what to do, or how to process anything right now. You're not supposed to be able to manipulate water. Are—are you even a fucking human being? Did I almost fuck a goddamned alien? Goddammit, Linc, just leave." I needed him away from me.

I peeked to find he had risen to his feet and was looking at me, his somber face morphing into a different emotion. I didn't think pissed was the right word. It was beyond that. Wonderful, I managed to hit a nerve and offend him.

"Fine, Maisy, have it your way, but, for what it's worth, I am human, just a different strain," Then he was gone.

I lay on the floor of my hallway for hours, thinking through everything. I was torn. He came to check on me, which meant he couldn't be all bad, right? He—he—oh my god, I was crazy.

⟜⟞⟜

The next few weeks were torturous. I dropped out of the classes I shared with Linc and avoided him, at all costs. This meant I had an extra semester of school to complete, which meant staying here over summer. Not an ideal solution, but I couldn't deal with whatever the hell was going on. There were no signs of Jake or Todd.

Thank god, because I just realized Todd had a key to our house, but Todd told Sarah they were dropping out of school to deal with family issues back home and would be back in a month. She was super depressed and even offered to go with him, for support. Funny, I could've sworn Jake had told me he was from here. What a liar. Was everything he told me lies? There was no way Sarah knew about their...crap. I didn't even know what to call it.

Linc texted me a couple of times, trying see me or talk. I hit delete as soon as I received them. Tommy called once, and I hit ignore immediately. Since his sister had waterpower, it was safe to guess he did, too. No, thank you. I saw Eva once last week, and she just about chased me half way across campus. Once I got to my classroom, she stopped. I thought about going home to LA, but I couldn't leave Sarah.

To explain my battered body, I told everyone I fell into the creek where I ran. Everyone seemed to believe that story because me falling wasn't out of the ordinary at all. I was clumsy. I could definitely make an art out of it. Hell, I could teach a damn class.

It was Friday, and I was working the night shift, which I was grateful for, since it would be busy and keep me distracted. I was having nightmares. Sometimes Sarah came running into my room. I wrote them off as cramps in my legs or just bad dreams. She didn't seem to believe me but took my crap anyway.

I checked my clock and saw it was time to start getting ready for work. I grabbed my cutoffs and a cute, see-through, flowery tank and went to the bathroom. The reflection in the mirror showed fading bruises and scrapes. I sighed.

The only thing left was the black welt on my arm. I told most people it was a birthmark, and for those who knew better, I said I didn't know what it was, but the doctor said it was fine.

After putting on my makeup, I pulled on my clothes, grabbed my boots, and exited my house. I locked the door behind me and turned to walk to my car. Linc was leaning up against it. My stomach dropped. I turned back to unlock my door and get inside as fast as I could.

He had his hand over mine before the lock was even turned.

"Maisy, we need to talk," he said in a soft voice.

Absently, I wondered if it was hard for a deep voice to be considered soft, low, maybe. "No." I tried to unlock the door again, but his hand didn't move. My body began to tense, wanting to shake with fear or anger, though I wasn't sure which.

"I'm not going to hurt you, I could never do that," he repeated from that night, but I still didn't turn around.

I closed my eyes. "Please just go away, please, Linc. I can't do this," I begged.

"Just hear me out, okay? I'm not fully human if—"

"No shit, Sherlock," I interjected.

He grunted, and I shut up.

"I'm a Veden, which is a type of human, I guess. My body functions the same way yours does, just more efficiently, and I can manipulate water, as you know."

A what? I'm pretty sure he was making up words.

"Why are you explaining this to me? If you're afraid of me telling people, I won't. I've basically convinced myself that I made it up, and I'm a nut case."

"You're not crazy, Mais. You're smart, you know what you saw. I—I need to explain this to you, I need you to understand."

I turned to face him and stopped breathing all together. He was so close. We were basically breathing the same air, His exhales drifted against my nose. My stomach dropped again, but not out of fear. The feeling went lower. *Traitor.*

I didn't look at him. "Why?"

"Why, what?"

"Why do you need to explain?" My voice was so low, I could barely hear myself.

He didn't say anything for what felt like forever, so I looked up and met those gorgeous pools of brown. His eyes were the only feature that revealed what he was thinking. They truly were windows to a person soul, or however that saying went. There was a raging war behind his eyes. His face softened, and he brought his hand up to cup my cheek. I let him touch me for a second before breaking eye contact.

"I need to get to work, so I'm just going to leave." I side stepped him and walked to my car, trying to put distance between us.

"You really want me to say it?" he huffed.

Yes. I threw him an annoyed look. "Say what, Linc?"

He stomped over to me, stopping just short of my body. "I like you. That's why I need you to understand. I never wanted you to find out about any of this. When we first got stuck together, yeah, you looked like a good time. Now I know you're a good time, but you're so much more than that. You're nothing like anyone I've ever met. You're fun and awkward and clumsy. You're cute. I'm sorry I was such an asshole before. I haven't felt like this before, and you're human." He looked down at the ground, biting his lip. It was the most vulnerable I've ever seen him look. "But I'm not done with you," he said. "I don't think I ever want to be done."

Say what? Not exactly what I was looking for. I just stared at him. What was I supposed to say to that? I didn't know if I could handle what he was, or what had happened to me. I didn't know if I wanted to deal with it, but my curious ass wanted more information about his world.

My stomach was doing flips. "I'll talk to you after work, Linc, okay? I get off at two."

His face fell. Did he really expect me to tell him I wanted to be with him right now? He lied, kept a huge part of himself from me, a part of him I had a right to know, since I almost got down and dirty with him against a tree and in his family room.

Getting into my car, I drove away, trying as hard as possible to not look back in the rearview mirror. I didn't want to, but of course, my self-control sucked when it came to him. I looked back, and he just stood there. My heart ached for him, my body wanted him, and my head was the only sane organ telling me to stay the hell away. I couldn't have him until I knew what was going on.

My work shift passed in a fog. I took drink orders, brought food, but didn't really interact with the customers. Cindy worked with me, but since I wasn't in a talkative mood, she left me alone. When she tried to start up a conversation, I made an excuse to go check on another table or to go check my phone, anything. I kept replaying what Linc said earlier, and not the part I should focus on. The information that he wasn't fully human, or was a different type of human wasn't fazing me like it should. Him wanting me, that was what I kept getting hung up on.

Taking out a towel, I started to wipe down the bar. Stupid man, with his stupid muscles, and his stupid watery powers. Ugh. I needed to go home. Immediate butterflies erupted when I remembered I would see him there. I needed psychiatric help, ugh.

"Mais? You okay, love?" Cindy chirped, her red curls bouncing with her movements.

"Yeah, why?"

She raised an eyebrow and stared at my hand. "You've been scrubbing the same spot—with rigorous force, I might add—for the last ten minutes."

I turned bright red. "Oh. Um….there was a stain."

"Uh huh. So, how's Linc been? I haven't seen him in here lately."

I wanted to cringe at the sound of his name, but nope. When everything happened, my reactions were pretty normal—shaking, crying, confusion. Now, after seeing him, my body wanted to get up close and personal with his. "He's good. I haven't really seen him lately, but I'm meeting him after my shift. How's Craig doing?"

She gave me a huge grin. "I left him real happy earlier."

This time, I did shudder. She had no clue about what they could do. Honestly, I envied her ignorance. If Jake had kept his hands to himself, I wouldn't know about Linc, and we would have had sex by now. Actually, no—finding out was good.

I nodded, and then I heard Seth yelling profanities from the back room. Cindy and I hurried around and realized he wasn't in the back room. He was outside in the back. He stood there with a baseball bat.

"Are you okay, Seth?" I yelled.

"Stay there, both of you," he shouted.

Cindy stopped instantly. I, on the other hand, peeked outside the door to find my car window was smashed, with *SLUT* spray-painted over the hood.

"Maisy, I told you to stay there," he yelled and took out his phone.

I heard some of his conversation as he called the cops. I didn't think the cops were equipped to deal with whatever Jake and Todd were. They had to be behind this, and the initial attack at the party on me. There was no one else who would want to hurt me, was there?

Cindy went back to the bar to deal with customers while Seth and I stayed out back.

"Do you know who could have done this?" he demanded

"No. I don't think I've ever pissed someone off that much. I mean, what the heck?" I stared at my little cute car. *Poor thing.*

He looked over at me. "This is serious, Mais."

I sighed as a police car pulled up behind the bar, and then the twenty questions began.

Chapter 13

Cops were annoying. Seriously, it was the only way to describe my experience. They weren't helpful, they were judgmental, and when they asked to hear my side of what happened, they kept looking at Seth to confirm what I said. They asked if anything weird had happened, why someone would do that to me, and if it could be the wrong car. I doubted it. They ended up giving me one of their cards and telling me to call if I could think of anything else they might have missed or overlooked. They also asked me if I needed a ride home, or if I could find one from someone else. Definitely could find one. I'd rather walk than get into the car with the cops helping me.

I stomped over to my car and looked inside, checking to see if anything was missing. It didn't look like it. My laptop was still in my school bag on the passenger seat and the five-dollar bill tucked in the cup holder was still there. So robbery wasn't the motive, but that was sort of obvious with the huge *SLUT* spray-painted in orange across the hood.

It had been s several weeks since Todd and Jake disappeared, and it didn't make sense for them to come back just to make my life difficult. Not that it was hard, but it definitely wasn't normal.

Standing there, staring at my poor car, I heard footsteps behind me.

Seth put his massive hand on my shoulder. "How are you doing, Maisy?"

I wanted to cringe away, but I stayed still. I didn't want pity. I could deal with this, and I would. "Fine. Do you think I could get a ride?" I turned back to him and found his face was blank. He nodded. "Thanks," I said. "I'm going to grab my stuff and put it in your office until my shift is over."

"I could take you home now, if you want. It's not a problem." His hazel eyes stared at my car.

"It's okay, I'll stay." I turned around before he could push me to go home. I didn't want to be home by myself right now. I needed the distraction and, suddenly, didn't want to see Linc. Considering his reaction to my mark, a wild hunch told me he wouldn't be happy about this. This incident was a reminder that I had a crazy sauce mate, trying to make my life a living hell.

Grabbing my bag, money, and anything else of value, I walked back to the bar and into Seth's office to put my stuff in the back left corner. I stared at my meager belongings for a moment, wanting to cry, but I wouldn't. It wasn't that big of a deal, just some busted window that I would have to pay a fortune to replace. Everything would be fine.

My shift finally picked up, and I welcomed the drunken distractions. The entire baseball team was back, along with every person each of them had ever talked to in their life. Woody's was the busiest I had ever seen it. The room was packed.

I was sure this many the people were a fire hazard, because there was way more than our maximum occupancy of a hundred and fifty.

My shift felt like one of my workouts, as I sprinted

from one end of the bar to the other, while carrying three plus pitchers of beer at a time.

The bar never wound down like it should have, and Seth ended up kicking a bunch of people out at two-thirty in the morning, because no one was leaving. I got a text from Linc around two-fifteen telling me he was at the house and waiting. I told him where the spare key was and to go in, since I probably wouldn't be home till three anyway. Sarah was staying at Jake and Todd's house still, so she wouldn't be there. It made me sick to think of her staying there, but, apparently, they weren't around at the moment, so I was okay with that arrangement for now. Once I figured everything out, I'd say something to her.

Cindy helped me fill the saltshakers, stock the bar, and wipe down all the tables while Seth counted the money and went over the books.

"Why is Linc coming over this late?" Cindy broke our silence.

"He wanted too, I guess." I didn't look at her.

"Have you guys been spending nights together?"

I focused on wiping down a table. "Nope, never have. He wants to come over and talk about us."

She gave me a half smile. "Isn't that your line?"

I laughed and changed the subject. "Have you been spending lots of time with Craig?"

"Yeah, he's a good guy, and lord knows, I needed to find one of those."

I shot her a smile. "So you're exclusive now?"

"I think so. We've never really talked about it, but he's been spending every waking moment with me. His choice, of course, and I really don't think he has time to go somewhere else."

"Is that how it works?" My question was completely serious. She stared at me for a moment as if she didn't understand. "When you hook up with someone for a while, you have to talk about being exclusive, like it's not already implied?" I elaborated.

She gave me a blank stare.

"Don't give me that look. I haven't had a boyfriend since high school. I don't know how these things work."

"So, you've been having just causal sex since then?" she asked blatantly, her pretty green eyes bugging out. "Because you've been out of high school for what? Four years, now? Please tell me you've hooked up with people because, if you haven't, I can set you up."

"No need, I've had sex since high school. Dork." I chuckled. "But thanks for caring about my sex life."

"If you don't, someone has too." She grinned, and we both started laughing quietly.

"You girls ready to go home?" Seth's booming voice filled the room, and I jumped.

"Yes, sir!" we said simultaneously.

We cleaned up and threw our rags into a bin in the back as we walked out of the bar. Cindy sucked in a breath when she saw my car, but didn't say anything. She really might know me better than I thought. I gave her a thankful smile.

We said our goodbyes as Seth and I watched her get into her car.

"Ready?" he asked, walking around his car to the driver's side.

"Yup, thanks for taking me home again. I really appreciate it."

"It's not a big deal. You needed a ride, and I have a car." I heard the car lock unlock as he fumbled with his keys "Plus, your house is on the way."

"True." I slid into his passenger seat.

Seth drove a black Dodge Charger, with limo window tinting. It fit him perfectly, rugged, badass, and mysterious. I liked it.

He handed me his iPod. "You can be DJ."

"Sweet!" I scrolled through his song selection, which was a shit ton of every type of music possible. From Luke Bryan to Artic Monkeys and everything in between. I was actually impressed and extremely surprised that Seth, of all people, had a taste for all types of music. I was scrolling through when I stopped in my tracks. No freakin' way. My smile grew to epic proportions as I hit play.

"Tell me what you want, what you really, really want!" started blaring through his speakers and his face went from a nice golden brown to tomato red in a matter of milliseconds. I started laughing.

He reached over and grabbed the iPod. "You're fired."

"Please tell me that you love the Spice Girls, because their music is pure art." I was almost to the point of crying.

"Fuck off, Mais, the redhead was hot, and my sister and I share the same iTunes account," he said, smiling, the redness still visible on his face.

"That seriously made my day. Actually no, that made my frickin' week." I laughed so hard I practically snorted the entire sentence.

He switched the song to a rock song I didn't know and, by the end of it, we were turning into my drive way. As we approached, I saw Linc look out my front window and then the front door opened. He leaned casually against the doorjamb, wearing low-slung jeans and a plain black T-shirt. He looked good, scrumptious. My reaction meant I would probably buy into whatever he told me about what was going on with him and Jake. I didn't want to admit it, but I would. I liked the damn guy too much. Or I just needed to get laid so I could think straight.

Seth slowed the car and put it into Park. "Boy-friend?"

"I'm not really sure yet." I grimaced, and then im-mediately scolded myself. *Bad Maisy*.

Seth and I got out of the car, as Linc walked over.

"What happened to your car?" Linc asked concerned, his eyebrows furrowed.

"Umm, someone bashed in the windows at work, Seth called the police, and yeah, it's still at the bar."

He gave me a look, demanding further explanation on what happened in vivid detail later. Turning to Seth, Linc held out his hand. "Thanks for driving her home. Linc."

Seth shook his hand. "Seth. And not a problem."

I thanked Seth again, and we all said goodbye. We watched as Seth backed out and drove down the drive-way. We didn't move until his taillights disappeared.

I could feel Linc's gaze on me, and, suddenly, my palms started sweating, and my stomach recaptured those damn butterflies. I didn't want to turn around. In fact, I almost didn't want to know what happened or what was going on. I just wanted to act like a normal couple. Hell, I'd settle for just a hook up. At this point, I wasn't picky.

Linc's fingers laced with mine. "Come on." He tugged lightly but never dropped our hands. He took me inside my house and set me down on the couch. "Do you want water or anything else you have in your kitchen?"

"Wine, I'm pretty sure I need wine."

He nodded his head and walked over to the kitchen, behind the island.

"There's a bottle of white in the fridge already, in the door. The glasses are in the cupboard right next to the fridge, on the top shelf."

He rustled around my kitchen, and I put my elbows on my knees and my face in my hands.

I didn't want to do this right now. It was three in the morning, and I needed to be sharp. I didn't have the emotional capacity to deal with everything.

A light touch on my knee brought my head up. Linc knelt in front of me with two glasses of wine in one hand. "Hey." He smiled, but still looked concerned. His expressive eyes gave him away.

"Hey back," I said.

He handed me the glass of wine. "How are you feeling?"

"Tired, pissed, stressed, confused, the list could go on," I admitted.

"How 'bout we drink the wine, you tell me about your work shift, minus the what happened to your car, and then we can go to bed. I'll sleep on the couch, since you'd probably have a hard time having me with you. We know your self-control is lacking." The corner of his lips picked up.

"You're a jerk, but I agree to the wine and then bed." I took a small sip as my eyes fluttered over the glass to stare at the arrogant ass.

When he got up and sat next to me, he clinked our glasses together. We both took a sip...well, he sipped. I basically gulped the entire glass whole and set it on the side table. Whoops.

He nudged my knee. "So work?"

I ran my fingers through my hair. "It was busy. I think the entire baseball team was there, plus their friends. Lots of people, lots of beer."

"Is that good?"

"Definitely, I needed the distraction." The last part slipped through, and I cringed inside.

"Distraction from what?" His question bordered an accusation.

"What do you think? I've been attacked twice in the

last two months, I found out you and your friends are…whatever you are…and someone decided it would be a good idea to bash in my windows and scribble 'slut' on the hood. I think I deserved a distraction."

His jaw clenched and worked, but he nodded and, for a moment, there was complete silence.

"I didn't intend for you to find out about anything. I—I didn't want you to have to go through this. I'd rather you not need the distraction, or at the very least, be using me as a distraction."

He added the last part I guessed to get a rise out of me. He did. I smacked his bicep with a huff.

"You should have told me, since you were so intent on forming a relationship with me." I looked at him, and he gave me a questioning look. I instantly regretted using the word relationship. Shit. I tried retracting what came out of my mouth. "Not relationship, since you just want-ed to screw me—not relationship."

"You were right the first time."

"Really?" If I was a dog, my ears would have perked up.

"Have I given you any reason to question my inten-tions with you?"

"Umm, have you met you?" I shook my head and chuckled. "Seriously? You're like the moodiest guy I know. The only intentions I was sure of was that you wanted to screw me against a tree."

"So, my intentions were at clear about one thing. I told you earlier I liked you, and I wanted to spend time with you without trying to screw your brains out. We went running. Plus, I'm pretty sure my attitude is a turn on to you."

My smile widened as I remembered what our run turned into, and then I got serious. "Linc, I can't be in a relationship with you. And yes, while I do find your attitude attractive, it seriously gives me whiplash sometimes. Besides that, I need to know what's going on. I'm not sure I can handle it."

He nodded and then pulled me into his arms. He held me for what seemed like forever. "If you don't want me after I explain everything and after we figure out who is after you, I'll leave you alone." He kissed the top of my head, squeezing tighter.

I never wanted him to let go, and I didn't want to know everything. I was content to stay right here for the rest of my life. Looking at my hands, I realized I was gripping his shirt as tight as I could. *Oh, boy.*

I pulled back as he watched me, his brown eyes turning darker, hazier. He pulled me closer and pressed the lightest touch of his lips to my forehead. I angled my face up, trying to tell him what I wanted. He lightly kissed me on the lips once, twice, and my blood boiled. I didn't want any of this light crap. I grabbed his shirt and pulled him to me. He got the message.

His perfect lips crushed mine, my eyes closed immediately as I started sliding backwards on the couch, dragging him with me. His hands burned my skin as they dug into my hips. Our tongues swirled and licked. My breaths were coming out short as I gently let go of his shirt and flattened my hands to his taut pecs before sliding them down. I stopped at his abs. Gosh, he had a great body.

From there, my hands slid farther down so I could feel the sexy V of his hips, and his body tensed just a little bit, but he didn't break the kiss. I slowly moved from the V outward until my hands slid across his hips to his ass. I gave him a little squeeze.

He chuckled into my mouth, reached back, grabbed my hands from his perfectly chiseled ass, and stretched them up over my head. He finally broke the kiss and moved his lips to the outside of my jaw and then down my neck. My head swam, and the dizziness caused my body to arch up. I'd never felt this much pleasure from a guy before, and all we were doing was kissing. Ridiculous.

He kissed me from one side of my collarbone to the other, and then he stopped, still holding my hands above my head. His eyes clashed with mine. We were both breathing heavy. Good to know he was as affected as I was.

"Ready for bed?"

I answered by arching up into his body and he shuddered. I loved it. I wanted to roll my hips into his again, but he sat up, bringing me with him. He placed our hands in my lap.

"As in sleeping. Seriously, babe, you're killing me here," he corrected, pushing my hips back down into the cushions. "You need to know more about me before we go there. You told me that, and I'm not going to take advantage of you. I don't want you to regret it in the morning."

I wanted to sock him or slap myself. He was right, but he should frickin' look so damn tasty.

He pulled me up, and I followed him to my bedroom.

"I'm going to shower. Sleep tight," He pecked me on the lips and turned around.

"Night," I whispered and watched him walk into the bathroom and shut the door behind him.

Once in my room, I closed the door, half tempted to go into the bathroom and throw myself at him, but that would be embarrassing.

If I couldn't handle whatever he told me tomorrow, he was right, I would regret it. So far, he'd been an absolute roller-coaster ride. I'd never experienced so many emotions in such a short period of time. Everyone had their quirks. I got that. But Linc seemed to have just so much baggage that I hoped it was worth it. We hadn't known each other very long, but no one had ever made my body hum like he did.

I stood in my room for what felt like an eternity before my horny body finally calmed down and I was able to undress without making a run for it. I put on a pair of pajama shorts and a tank and crawled into bed. I lay awake, listening to the water in the bathroom for a while before gently drifting into a deep sleep.

Chapter 14

I woke up with a heavy arm thrown over my waist. What the hell? Linc should've been sleeping on the couch. I tried to wiggle my way out of his grasp, but he pulled me back, so my back was lined against his front. Spooning, adorable. His face pressed into my hair and the back of my neck tingled from his warm breath.

Round two. I wiggled again and threw my legs over the side of the bed, in an attempt to sit up. Instantly I was pulled back against a rumbling chest. I huffed and tried to shove my elbow into his gut.

"You keep wiggling, and I won't be responsible for my body's reaction." His voice was thick with sleep.

I turned, and his hand fell to my hip. "What happened to the couch?"

"I swear I was out there most of the night, but you started screaming and didn't wake. Freaked me the fuck out. I came in to lay down with you until you calmed, must have fallen asleep." He cleared his throat, and I noticed the dark circles underneath his eyes. He must've not slept very much. "How long have you been doing that?"

Shit, usually I woke up. Sarah never said anything, but a couple of times she ran into my room. I looked away to avoid his gaze. Awkward. "Umm, since the night of the party."

His body tensed slightly, but he didn't say anything. When I looked up, his face had gone from sleepy to hard and pained. I guess now was as good a time as any to start questioning him. I doubted it would get any easier the longer we put it off.

"Who was that, Linc? Was it Jake or Todd who attacked me?"

"I don't know. Jake and Todd are Fiskares. They hunt my kind, Vedens. They do not hunt humans, which rules them out. Vedens can manipulate water, so the person who attacked you was definitely a Veden, and they were strong."

Oh god, maybe the ass crack of dawn wasn't the best time to figure this out since. I took a deep breathe, deciding I was going to ask about him first. "What are Vedens, exactly?" My voice sounded tiny.

"Exactly? We're humans, just a different branch I guess. Have you ever heard of Atlanis?" I nodded. "Well," he continued, "that's where we originated. We can manipulate water, some of us with more control than others, and some with no control at all. The ones who can't control it well have a hard time adjusting to society. They're more loose cannons. We're also slightly stronger than humans and heal freaky fast." His brown eyes locked with mine, and, feeling uncomfortable, I diverted my gaze.

"Do regular humans know about you? I mean, obviously not mainstream society, but like the government, or...I don't know...anyone?" It was awkward talking to his bare chest.

"Some governments in Europe are run by Vedens, but I don't think the US knows. We don't share that we can manipulate water. It wouldn't be the best idea."

I nodded as millions of questions swirled in my head. Where did I start? Sitting up in front of him, I put some much-needed space between us. I hadn't gone into shock or started questioning my mental stability yet, so that was good news, right?

I gathered my hair into a low ponytail. "So, Atlantis, where exactly is that at?"

His lips tipped up. "We came from the Scandinavian Peninsula. Originally, Norway, Sweden, Finland, when they were all one country."

"Like Vikings?" I could feel my eyes widening but blinked rapidly to hide my shock.

"Yeah, like Vikings," he replied after a minute, grabbing my clenched hands.

I studied our interlocked hands. "And the Fiskares?"

"I don't really know where they were from. They appeared in our history at random and grew rapidly." He shrugged, not seeming worried that a specific group of people appeared out of thin air to hunt his people. "We're taught that, in nature, there has to be a balance, so they exist to keep our numbers in check. But I've heard crazy stories that a Veden Queen slept with a Fiskare servant, which doesn't make sense. We never imprisoned Fiskares."

I guess he felt the need for further explanation when he saw my confused expression.

"I've asked my dad about it, and he denied it. Said it was nuts and left it at that."

"Okay, so if its nature, can't only one group be the predator and one be the prey?"

"Depends. Some of us are pretty evenly matched, but if a weaker Fiskare ran into a stronger Veden, it would be bad news for the Fiskare, and vice versa."

"So it all comes down to luck or timing?"

"Not that simple, but maybe."

I raised my eyebrow. He was being purposely vague, but at least he was talking. He could have kept quiet and blocked me out completely. Even though I attempted the same with him, now I was grateful he didn't try.

"How strong are you?" I asked. He'd taken on two Fiskares, basically kicking Todd and Jake's asses, which was impressive.

He turned onto his back, so his was now staring at the ceiling instead of me. "Strong enough."

"Not a good enough answer." I plucked at the sheet between us. "Is it like a rank? What would you rank against the average Veden? One being the strongest, and ten being the weakest."

"Mais…I don't know…maybe a three?" he huffed.

"So you've met people stronger than you?" I asked, tilting my head to the side

A grin started tugging at the corners of his lips. "Not anyone my age. Hell, not anyone except maybe my dad, and that's a huge maybe."

I tried to keep my heart rate in check and my face neutral, even though I was freaking the hell out. I raised my eyebrows. "So you'd set the bar for strongest?"

He pushed up on his elbows. "I was trying to be modest."

I chuckled. "We both know you don't do modesty very well."

"Maybe not." He rubbed the back of his neck, his left bicep bulging at the movement. The octopus was in full motion.

My mouth instantly watered as I realized where we were, in my room, in my bed, basically naked with my barely there shorts and tank, alone. *Focus, Mais!* I tried to ignore the lust currently rolling through me. "What can you do? Can all Vedens do the same things?"

"Depends on the person. Tommy can freeze water in seconds flat, for some people it can take a little to a lot longer. Eva can easily pull water from vegetation, but that trick took me forever to get down. When I tried, I usually brought the entire plant with me. I could feel the water, I just couldn't pull it out."

I was tempted to say "that's what he said" but stopped myself. It wasn't the time for that, no matter how rattled my nerves were.

"Craig doesn't really have a specialty," he continued, oblivious to my inner turmoil. "He can control water and throw it around, make high and low pressure, but nothing any other pure Veden can't do."

"We'll get back to the 'pure' thing later, but you said you could feel water?"

"We can sense water, feel it. It…" He paused for a minute. "I've never really explained it before. I don't know if I can. It's a part of me. It hums, I guess, when I connect with it. Once I'm connected, the water becomes an extension of myself. Make any sense?"

Not really. "Maybe?" I offered and shrugged.

"I'm sorry, Mais, I've never tried to explain this to anyone, ever. Most of the people I hang with are Vedens. I don't share this with regular humans, and I'm not a good teacher. It's like me asking you why and how you breathe, what it feels like, and why you need it."

I just nodded because, if I needed to, I was pretty sure I could explain breathing to someone who couldn't. "You've told me about everyone else but haven't explained what you can do."

He smirked. "Luckily, I'm good at everything, good genes I guess. I never had a hard time with any of the skills."

I shook my head as I looked at my hands in my lap. Of course, he was good at everything. "What about your difficulty pulling water from plants?"

"Yeah, it took me a couple hours to get that down." His smile got cheeky.

"How long does it take most people?" His gigantic ego was getting annoying. I swore I could feel it filling my small room.

"If you don't have a knack for it, like Eva? Years. It took Eva a couple months to be as good as she is."

"What do they do to find out what you're good at it? Do they just throw you into random situations, or in schools, and test everything on you?"

"Not really. When we go through puberty, we discover our specialty. We get stronger, faster, and some of us thankfully get more control over our abilities. Hell, when I was a child, I used to blow up the pipes in the bathroom by accident."

My mouth gaped. This was flippin' crazy, I was having a conversation with a guy who claimed to be a different strain of unknown human who could control water, and...what? I was acting like we were just talking about the rules of soccer? "What did you do to Jake? You forced him onto his knees. It was like you were controlling him. I thought you could only control water?" I looked down at my hands, remembering that night.

I felt his body tense. "You cannot tell anyone about that. Okay? I know you don't understand why, and I can't explain, but you cannot repeat that. Ever."

My head snapped up "Linc, what did you do?"

"Ask something else." He broke eye contact.

"Linc, I—"

"Next question Maisy," he ordered, cutting me off.

Shit, fine. I gave him a look promising the conversation wasn't over. I would get an answer eventually. "You mentioned 'pure' before, and I'm guessing that has to do with Vedens not mixing with regular humans?"

"You guessed right. It's not looked down on, and some do it, but their kids usually don't have any abilities at all. If we want to reproduce, it's an option, just not ideal, but our population has shrunk."

Okay, so they could mix with humans. Awesome. Not that I cared, I mean, I didn't want to have babies anytime soon, but would totally be on board for a couple trial runs with him.

He gave my hand a gentle squeeze. "How are you handling all this?"

Studying our hands, with our fingers tangled, I drew in a deep breath and then exhaled. How *was* I handling this? Pretty damn good, considering I ran for the hills before. With him explaining—err sort of explaining—things, I was doing better, even if I felt I was out of my frickin' mind.

Ignoring his question, I asked a few of mine. "Why did you feel I needed to know this about you? I know you said it's because you liked me, but we've only known each other for a little over three months. Why trust me with all of this?" When he didn't answer right away, I continued. "I mean, I even dropped the classes we had together, ignored you, and you still didn't stop."

"You're interesting. You're gorgeous, and you're funny when you don't try to be. It's entertaining. You seem like a good girl, one I seriously wanted to get to know better. It's better you know about me, even if I didn't plan on sharing this part, at least not yet."

I blushed, completely embarrassed that the only thing I got out of his answer was he thought I was attractive. As shallow as it sounded, it made my entire body tingle. Guys like him didn't go for girls like me. I was average, not super thin, didn't wear name brand clothes, and my style was more jeans and T-shirts. Still, he seemed to like me.

I turned my head away from him because I'm sure the redness went all the way to my toes. The black-welted mark taking up half of my forearm caught my attention. Well, guess my next question would ruin the mood.

"What did Jake do to me?" I unlaced our fingers and covered the mark with my hand as if hiding it.

His eyes flashed with rising anger making them darken a bit. "I swear I'm going to get that fucking mark off of you," he bit out, now sitting up with the blanket pooled at his waist.

I started to forget what we were talking about. "What is it, though?"

"I'm not really good with all of their shit, but all of the wives of Fiskares have some type of mark on their bodies. It's some kind of possession mark. It means you belong to Jake," he growled.

"I don't belong to Jake," I whispered, more to myself than him.

"Damn right, you don't. Like I said, I'll get it off of you. Don't worry about it."

"How?"

His shoulders fell as he looked at my door. "Honestly, I don't know. I'll ask around though, I'll call my dad tonight or tomorrow and see if he knows of anyone or anything that can get it off."

All I did was nod because it was obviously bugging him. His eyes wouldn't meet mine. I figured that was enough questions for the day. I still had a ton of unanswered ones, starting with which Veden attacked me?

"Hey, want go get some breakfast? I'm starving," I asked trying to distract him as I patted his forearm.

He pulled on my hands so that our foreheads rested against each other, making my breath stall. "Breakfast sounds good, what did you have in mind?" he replied as his breath danced across my mouth.

"Want to go get some pancakes?" I loved pancakes.

"Anything you want." He closed the gap between our

mouths, but it was just for a split second. Way too short, in my opinion.

"Anything?" I countered.

He chuckled and moved his mouth to mine again, his tongue touching my lips, wheedling them apart. My head spun and my eyes closed. The man could kiss, and I was sure he could do other things perfectly too.

My hands inched across his chest until they were around his neck. I pushed up against him, straddling his lap and a growl escaped his mouth, which made me crash my lips harder against his, and my heart rate spiked. His hands were on my waist as he tugged me closer until I could feel him against me.

It was a fabulous moment until my stomach decided to make the most ginormous growling, gurgling noise in the history of forever. *Are you fucking kidding me*?

He chuckled and slowly reached over his head to unhook my arms. "Let's get some food in you, babe."

I pouted but nodded. Seriously, this was getting ridiculous. Every time we settled down to business, something happened, or he stopped.

"Fine." I scooted off of him and grabbed my jeans and a T-shirt. "But we're picking up where we left off, afterward."

I heard him laugh as I stomped out of my room to the bathroom.

Chapter 15

The next couple weeks flew by, and I spent most of my free time with Linc. He had one of his friends fix my car windows for close to nothing. He offered to pay, but that definitely wasn't happening. My car, my problem. He didn't like it, mumbling about how I needed to let him take care of it because it was more than likely an attack on him than having anything to do with me. Blah, blah, blah…

Speaking of problems, despite dating the guy—at least I thought I was—we hadn't had wild, monkey, lust-driven sex yet. Not from lack of trying on my part. Every time we got close, he ended it—his phone rang, he forgot to pick up Craig—anything and everything became an excuse to stop. It was driving me crazy.

At first, I thought it was because he wanted to take things slow after sharing what he was. He hadn't manipulated water in front of me for a while now and actually functioned like everyone else. Well, except he would do little thing here and there so fast that it startled me. He had told me that he was slightly faster than humans. Complete lie, his speed was faster than anything I'd ever seen.

There were a few times I dropped a glass of water, on purpose, which he wasn't aware of, but his cat-like reflexes stopped the water in mid-air and guided the glass back to my hand.

Still, the Veden wouldn't do me. I seriously considered stripping in front of him and standing there, but was terrified he would turn around and run out of my house. I'd even gone so far as trying to climb on top of him, but that never lasted long. As soon as I got comfortable, he would flip me over and run his soft lips over my neck.

Before his big reveal, we'd almost done it on his couch in his living room. Nothing stopped him until he saw the mark. Was it because of the mark? Since he never brought up the big black welt on my forearm, I wondered. He ran his thumb over it once and stared at it, as if he hoped it would disintegrate under his stare. It didn't.

Lying on my pink and green floral print comforter, I studied my ceiling, trying to figure out what was going on with him. My phone vibrated.

Wanna double tonight? Since we're both off??

Cindy. She'd been dating Craig for the last four months, and they were doing good. She, of course, didn't know a thing about what Craig really was, but they both seemed happy.

I'm in, I'll ask Linc right now, I replied and then dialed Linc's number.

"Hello?" He answered on the first ring, sounding sleepy. He went out last night with Tommy and Craig, so who knew what time he got home? He never called or texted after he told me he was going out, which was sort of weird, because he usually did, but no big deal.

"Hey, you," I said cheerfully.

"Everything okay?"

He asked that every time I called, and it was starting to annoy me. Did something have to be wrong for me to call?

Or did he expect something to happen to me? Because if that was the case, he needed to tell me, like yesterday. "Yeah, why?"

"It's early," he replied gruffly.

"It's ten in the morning."

"Ya, early."

"Well, Cindy and Craig want to go out tonight. Would you want to?"

"Whatever you want to do, babe, is fine by me."

I wanted to ask if he was sure, because all I wanted to do was him, and he kept shutting me down which, obviously, wasn't fine.

"Sounds like fun, right?" I tried to get him to make a decision.

"Let's go then. I'll be at your place around noon."

"Okay, see you soon!"

"See ya."

We're in, I texted Cindy back.

Sweet! We're going to go to dinner and then some bar down by the school.

Perfect.

For the next hour, I ran around the house, picking it up, sweeping the floor, and throwing laundry into the washing machine. I hadn't planned on doing laundry, but my skinny jeans were in there. We were actually going out, so I wanted to look cute, which required the skinny jeans.

At a quarter to eleven, there was a light knock on my door. I turned to go answer and ran into a wall that happened to be warm and smelled like the outdoors, all grass and sunshine. Mmm. I brought my arms around Linc's narrow waist and put my hands in his back pockets.

"I wish you wouldn't do that," I murmured before looking up into his deep brown eyes that were pouring into mine.

"You'd miss it."

"Not really." I sighed and let go, hitting him in the stomach. When my hand made contact with his stomach, he flexed, and I got a handful of hard muscle. "So, I guess we're going to dinner with them around six. What do you want to do till then?"

He tucked a strand of hair behind my right ear. "Anything you want to do,"

If only that were the truth. I wanted to do him. Now. In his faded jeans and a red T-shirt, his lean, chiseled arms stood out. A tentacle wrapped around his left bicep and stuck out of the bottom of his sleeve. His dark brown hair fell over his forehead.

Goodness, it should be illegal to look like that. Panties went wet instantly. No doubt about it, I was going to throw myself at him again.

"You're so full of shit." I turned and walked down the hallway to my bedroom.

"How?" There was a curious note in his voice.

"You never want to do what I want to do," I told him once we were in my room.

"Untrue," he argued.

I turned to see him grabbing a bouncy ball from my dresser.

I watched as he shut my door. My right eyebrow inched up as he stalked forward. "True," I tried to sound authoritative, but my voice faltered.

He reached out and grabbed my hips, lifting me easily, and depositing me on the bed. "How?" he asked again, easing my legs apart.

"Don't you start. You know exactly how. You do this, and then you stop before we actually get anywhere. And wipe that stupid, smug smile off your damn face."

A deep rumbling laugh came from his throat. "You want this to go somewhere?"

"Yes damn it." I grabbed his shirt and pulled him

down to my level. I rubbed the tip of my nose across his. "Please, Linc."

He pulled away from me and ripped off his shirt. "You don't have to beg."

I was about to say, *obviously I did*, but I got hung up, from the shirt being gone and how he crashed our lips together in the next second. I fell back on the bed as he rested some of his weight on top of me. His hand was tangled in my hair. He tugged on it, which brought my head back, exposing my neck. His tongue traced the pulse under my jaw, and my body jerked.

I felt him smile against my neck and then he slowly leaned up, bringing his knees between my legs. His hand went under my waist as he gently tugged my shirt off. He slid his hands up my spine until his fingers met my black, lacy bra strap. A beat later, my bra found its way to the pile of clothes on the floor. Perfect.

His lips left my body and came back to my mouth as he kissed me. Hard. His tongue stormed in, demanding entrance, and when I gave it, his tongue took full advantage. My moan escaped as he lowered himself onto me. I could feel him through his jeans and my hands instantly slid between us trying to get to the button. When I finally got to the warm metal, I tried to flick it with one hand, which didn't work, and Linc smiled. He sat up once more, tugged my shorts and black thong off, and stared down at me.

"God, you're perfect."

Embarrassment sparked, and I suppressed the need to cover myself. I reached out and pulled at his jeans. He got the hint, reached into his pocket, and took out a foil packet, then proceeded to pull his jeans off, taking his boxers with them. I stared at him in complete awe. I was pretty sure my jaw was about to drop.

The half-smile that I loved oh so much appeared on

his face as he looked down at himself. "Yeah, I know."

I threw a pillow at him. The asshat decided it was a good time to talk, and that's what came out of his mouth? He moved the pillow, which joined our clothes. Chuckling, he pushed me back on the bed and grabbed the back of my thighs to drag my body to his.

"You sure?" His tone went serious.

I exhaled, staring up at him. "God, yes."

My body shook with need as he lowered down. He kissed my lips softer than before, and I felt him against my inner thigh. He was huge, and my body reacted positively to the new information. I arched, exposing my neck and pressing my hips into his.

His reaction was a caveman growl, which I thought was flippin' sexy. He removed his lips from mine and trailed them down my body. He kissed, nipped, and licked all the way down to the inner part of my right thigh. My stomach dropped as his breath fell on me, and my blood started boiling. He stilled, and I almost told him to do something because I was wound so tight.

He dipped his head, and my body convulsed. It was slightly embarrassing, but, at the moment, I couldn't have cared less. I floated in supreme, raw sensations.

"Linc," I finally got out, as my breaths grew quicker and my muscles tightened.

He stopped. That fucker. He rose from the end of the bed. My eyes searched his, pleading for him to do something, anything.

He raised one of his eyebrows. "I'm going to go out on a limb here, and say that was good?"

Still breathing heavily, my body was still pissed it didn't get its release. "Ehh," I said, giving him my best poker face.

He grabbed my hips, picked me up, and turned me long ways on the bed. He settled his knees between mine once more. His eyes bored into mine as he ripped the foil package and slipped it over him.

He kissed me, and I felt him up against me, brushing my entrance.

"Linc, please," I whimpered.

When he finally pushed inside of me, my body relaxed. His rhythm started slow, but it didn't last long.

He removed his mouth from mine and trailed kisses down my neck. "You feel fucking amazing," he said, making me shiver as his hot breath tickled my neck.

The feeling was sensational. With each thrust, the sensations built. Our bodies were definitely in sync, because he started slamming into me faster as I reached my climax. He followed, and then my muscles turned to jelly. Completely relaxed, I felt more than satisfied.

I'd waited for this for what felt like forever, and it was perfect. I'd never felt like this after sex. Usually, I was "okay, thanks, bye!" and running out of the guy's room before the last moan drifted away. But with him, I wanted to stay there, wrapped up in him. My body tingled, and I loved it.

We laid there for what felt like an eternity and yet was way too short. His breathing started to even out until he finally rolled off me. He stretched out to the side and then turned to face me.

His expression was smug, something that was definitely earned.

"I'm guessing that was just 'ehh' also."

I giggled as I crawled off the bed. He didn't need me to tell him how incredible that was, I'm pretty sure I was moaning like a damn ghost. I pulled my sheet along as I got up.

He slapped my ass. "Where you going?"

"Shower?"

One second I was standing in all my naked gloriousness, the next I was scooped up and in the shower. His speed really came in handy sometimes.

ತಾಣಲ

We ran a little behind to meet Craig and Cindy at the restaurant. I honestly didn't even remember what type of restaurant she said it was on the phone.

"Where are we going again?" I played with the end of my black, tight skirt that I paired with a low cut, blue silk top.

"Italian place. It's supposed to be really good." He reached over and laid his hand on my upper thigh.

"Not to be awkward, but what are we doing?" We hadn't talked about us or where we were going, but it had been bugging me for a while. Especially when people asked who he was to me. My standard answer was "a friend" because until earlier, he kept withholding sex. Honestly, I didn't know if this was casual or not. Did he want to see other people, or—and this made me nauseous—*was* he seeing other people? My stomach churned as I reconsidered having this conversation now when it should have happened earlier.

He glanced over at me, looking a little confused. "Going to dinner and then the sports bar by the school."

"No, I mean with this, us." I waved my hand between us.

"What do you want to happen?"

"Umm, I don't know. I obviously like you, and I sort of don't want to be with anyone else, but I don't know if you feel the same. So, I was just wondering."

"I don't feel the same," he said seriously.

Ouch. My face fell a little bit as I looked down at my hands. My fingers twisted together. Great, so I *was* just another notch in his bedpost. Bright side, the sex was amazing, but now my stomach was knotted. Feeling used, I didn't want to go to dinner anymore. Which was irrational. I was the one throwing myself at him.

At that moment, we pulled into the parking lot. Linc parked the car, turned it off, unbuckled, and got out of the car without a single word. Fine. I sat there dumbfounded by what just happened. I guess I couldn't really be mad, but it still sucked.

My car door flew open, and Linc stood there, waiting for me. "What are you doing, Mais?" Irritation was clear in his voice.

"Getting out?" I offered, unbuckling my seatbelt.

"What was with the question?" he huffed, running his hands through his light brown hair.

"Nothing, forget I even asked. Let's just go eat." I hopped out of the car and went to walk past him when he grabbed my wrist and pulled me around until my back hit his car. He leaned until he was pressed against me, and I could feel his warm breath against the top of my ear.

"I don't feel the same because I don't 'sort of' not want to be with anyone else. I *definitely* don't want to be with anyone else. If I wanted to be with other people, I would be. I didn't realize I left you with the impression that this was casual. It's not."

In my stomach, butterflies replaced the knots, as he leaned in so his lips met mine. I smiled against his mouth and then giggled as he smiled back. He pressed another quick kiss to my lips then took my hand.

"Why didn't you say something sooner? I was sitting there pissed that I was dumb enough to think it would be a sure thing. I know I didn't have the right to be pissed, but still…" I swung our hands into his hard abs. He didn't even flinch.

"You're the one who questioned it. I thought I showed you I wanted to be with you this afternoon."

Remembering earlier, I blushed and bit my lip.

His eyes roamed over me. "Keep biting your lip, and I'm taking you back home."

I called his bluff. "Deal."

"Oh, you think I'm kidding?" He turned and threw me over his shoulder before I even knew what was happening.

"Linc!" I squealed. "I'm in a skirt put me down, jerk face!"

"Maisy! Linc!" we heard from behind us. Cindy. "We haven't even had dinner yet, Linc. Put her down, you can have her later," she scolded as she and Craig walked up.

Linc set me on my feet with a grunt. I pulled my skirt down, and my face felt redder than a tomato. I met Cindy's eyes, and she gave me a small wink. She looked good. Her red hair was pulled back in a high ponytail, and she wore a similar black skirt, but with a tight white and black striped tube top.

Craig punched Linc in the shoulder, and they started talking about work. Something about some grass, digging…I didn't know. Guys were weird.

"So how are you?" Cindy asked, pulling me in for a hug.

"Um, good." I stared at her black heels. Gosh, I was surprised she was still shorter than Craig. The heels were at least five inches.

"How good?" she drawled, her smile widening.

"How'd you know?" I didn't even try holding my surprise back.

"I can see it all over your face. That, and Linc has never tried to haul you off before." She grabbed my hand. "Wild guess why."

"Whatever," I said, matching her Cheshire Cat smile.

"That good?"

I nodded. "Oh yeah."

We stood there giggling like little schoolgirls, while the boys put our names in at the counter. Minutes later, when they called our name, we walked into a modest Italian restaurant. The brick walls were decorated with paintings of Italy and lined with various size booths. The remaining space was filled with sporadically placed tables.

Our hostess led us to one in the very back corner. Cindy and I scooted across the booth to the walls, so we were sitting across from each other, and then Linc and Craig slid in.

"Here y'all go. Any drinks I can get started for ya?" the hostess asked.

Yup, totally an authentic Italian. I smiled to myself. There wasn't a whole lot of diversity in Alabama, compared to California.

"Water for now?" Linc looked around our table and got three nods.

"I'll be right back with those."

"I was thinking we could all go to dinner at mom and dad's next week," Craig announced, looking straight at Linc with a mischievous smile.

My belly flopped. I wasn't ready to meet his parents yet. Too soon. Way too soon.

Linc studied the menu, barely acknowledging Craig. "I think we're busy."

"What are you doing?" Craig seemed to egg him on.

"Swimming." Linc still didn't bother to look at Craig.

"You can do that anytime. Come on, I'm sure mom and dad want to meet her." He gestured at me.

"Fuck off, Craig. You know I can't bring her," Linc barked out.

Ouch. I glanced away from him, looking at other tables. What the hell was that for? Was I not good enough to meet the parents? Knots replaced the butterflies in my stomach. Granted, I was totally on board with not meeting the parents next week, but to say things like that? Why couldn't he bring me?

Do. Not. Cry. Get pissed. Pissed was better. Under the table, a leg kicked me, and I lifted my head to see Cindy looking at me with in silent question. I nodded. I was fine.

The table got real quiet. I snuck a peek at Linc who was concentrating on the menu like it was a study guide for the biggest test of his life.

"I'm going to go to the bathroom." I gave Linc a little push to his side. He started sliding out of the booth.

"Me too!" Cindy yelled, pushing Craig out of the way.

I waited for Cindy to get out, and Linc grabbed my hand. I let him hold it for a minute, then I thought about what he said minutes before. *Umm, no thank you.* I removed my hand from his. His expression changed to one of shock, as if I'd thrown his cat into traffic. It made no sense. He started it.

Cindy and I walked across the restaurant and hit the restrooms, breezing through a big green, vintage looking door.

She spun me around. "You okay?"

I tried stepping around her. "Yeah, why wouldn't I be?"

She moved in front of me. "Don't deflect. You know why."

"Yeah, I'll get over it. I thought it was too soon, so it didn't surprise me until he made it clear I'm not acceptable enough." I pushed her aside and went to the sink, running cool water over my hands as I looked at myself in the mirror.

Cindy came up and stood next to me. "He technically didn't say that."

I watched her through the mirror. "Why else would I not be able to meet his parents?"

She shrugged.

"Have you met them?" I asked.

"Yeah, and they're great. I don't understand why he doesn't want you to meet them. They're warm, welcoming, and just all around great people."

Well, I didn't understand either. Maybe it was because I wasn't a Veden. But Cindy wasn't one, either, which blew that theory. Maybe he didn't see this going anywhere, despite what he said in the parking lot. If that was the case, why should I bother?

We finished up and went back out to our table. I refused to meet Linc's gaze but could feel him watching me the entire time.

"Did you guys already order?" Cindy asked Craig.

Craig put his arm around Cindy's shoulders. "Nope, we got you guys wine, though. White okay?"

Cindy melted against Craig's side. "Yeah."

Now that this double date was a lot of awkward, I wanted to go home.

"Linc!" a feminine voice shrieked.

Linc's head flew in the direction of the voice, and he stood up. A girl basically flung herself into his arms, and they embraced for an inappropriate amount of time. Or maybe that was just me. The chick had dark brown hair, fair white skin, and the brightest green eyes I had ever seen. She was easily five feet, nine inches, and her legs went on forever. Even more unfair, she had a full chest. You should only be blessed with one, not both.

"Hi, Craig!" She wiggled her fingers at Craig, ignoring Cindy. "What are you guys doing here?" she asked playing with the end of her side braid.

Obviously, we came here to eat, my snarky mental voice piped up. An unexpected pang of jealousy zipped through my chest. This is why I had a hard time believing he actually wanted to be with me. She matched his appearance more than I did.

"Craig suggested the place, said it was good," Linc said, sounding uninterested.

"Oh, yay! I'm going to be your server. How have you been lately?" She gave a little pout and rubbed his forearm. "I haven't heard from you in what feels like months."

Okay, so they shared a history, probably an intimate one, considering. My jealousy began to turn pissed, even knowing it wasn't allowed since she came before us. An "us" which had only been established officially an hour ago.

"Been busy." His voice changed from light and friendly to cold...or embarrassed? Maybe.

The girl looked around, zeroing in on me. Her knowing smile insinuated I wasn't a threat. Not up for confrontation, I looked away first Whatever. I was not jealous or territorial. *Knock it off, Mais.*

"This is Maisy, my girlfriend," he finally said. "Mais, this is Caroline."

I gave a small wave and a smile, but she didn't give me a second glance.

"We should do something sometime," she said to Linc, her hand still on his forearm.

"Yeah, maybe," he replied.

Maybe? He better be saying that to get her to leave. If not, we were going to have another problem on top of what he said earlier. Gosh, this was why I hated relationships and had avoided them my entire college career. They were messy and contained too many emotions.

She flashed a big smile that revealed perfect teeth.

She could be a goddamn model. Everything about her added fuel to my doubts. Why was he even with me? He was beautiful, and caring once you got to know him. Based on looks alone, they made a good couple. They matched each other on the good-looks scale. Unlike him and me—the clumsy, insecure human.

When Linc sat back down, she finally addressed the rest of the table. "So, what can I get for y'all?"

We all ordered our food. I opted for regular spaghetti, praying spit wouldn't be added to it. Under the table, Linc's hand found mine and squeezed lightly. I ignored him and kept chatting with Cindy. Thankfully, she kept the conversation going, because I felt like an inadequate piece of crap right then.

Caroline came back with our food, and we ate it fast. It was really good, wonderful even. I tried not to wonder if she spit in mine. Linc and Craig split the bill, and then we were on our way and outside the restaurant.

"Okay, so y'all know where we are going?" Cindy asked Craig and Linc.

"Yeah, babe." Craig pulled Cindy into him and kissed the top of her head. It was adorable how he treated her. I was glad she was happy, even if she didn't know what he really was.

I followed Linc to his massive truck. He bent down to grab me in preparation to deposit me in his cab.

"I got it." I hoisted myself up on the step and then into the seat. Perfect, I did it without falling on my face. Mental high five.

Silently, Linc got in and started the car. We were on the road when he asked, "What's wrong with you?" It sounded more accusing than anything.

"Nothing, why?"

"Really, Maisy? Because after Craig said something about going to meet my folks, you shut up pretty quick."

My mouth opened in shock. Was he really that daft? "You said 'you know she can't meet them' or whatever. How the heck was I supposed to take that?" What the fuck did he expect? "And then Brunette Barbie comes over and wraps around you like you're not there with a date, and you let her. Not only did she completely ignore me, but you let her think you guys would be hanging out sometime! You're too attractive to not know she planned on doing lots of other things besides hanging out. How do you think that made me feel?"

"We'll get back to my parents in a minute, but what did you want me to do? Throw her off? I said that so she would leave."

Sounded better than what happened. "Don't be a frickin' jerk! All you had to do was move away when she touched you. How would you like it if one of my old boy-friends got all up on me?"

"Don't assume what you don't know," he said through clenched teeth.

"Am I wrong?" I challenged. No way would I back down on this.

There was no answer from him.

"Exactly. So, let me be mad. Next time, don't be a clueless idiot," I huffed. There, I was done. I pushed my hair back out of my face.

We sat in silence for the rest of the car ride.

He pulled into a parking spot a couple stores down from the bar.

"I'm sorry, okay? I didn't mean for you to feel like that. If you want to meet them, we'll go next week."

"No, it's fine," I huffed. "But why are you so uncom-fortable with me meeting them?"

"It's not that I don't want you to. I thought I'd have more than a week to get them prepared to meet you," he said in defeat.

I gave him a quizzical look. "Prepared? Linc, we've been seeing each other for more than a week. Did you honestly not see this going anywhere before we had sex?"

"Stop being dramatic. I did too see this going somewhere." He sighed running a hand through his thick locks. "Okay, don't freak out."

What a perfectly stomach-lurching way to start a sentence.

"I don't think there's anything more that could come out of your mouth that will make me freak out. I took you not being fully human pretty well, considering."

He gave me that half smile I absolutely loved. "This is a little bit different." He looked down at his steering wheel. I was so not prepared for what came out of his mouth next. "I'm sort of the next in line to be king."

Chapter 16

I was pretty sure my jaw dropped. King? Societies still had those? "Come again?"

"My dad's king," he said, giving me a tight-lipped smile, showing how uncomfortable he was.

"Of…"

"Vedens." His answer was totally monotone.

"And by king, do you mean that in a sense of him actually ruling, like back in the eighteen hundreds? Or more as a public figure, celebrity status?" I couldn't wrap my mind around him being royalty.

And that was the moment Craig picked to knock on Linc's window.

"We'll talk later," Linc said.

I gave him my best pout. "Fine."

Linc's door was almost ripped off.

"Dude the door was locked!" Linc snarled at his brother.

Craig looked at the door and back at him. "It didn't feel like it was."

Linc jumped out and hit Craig on the arm, hard.

I opened my door and met the two boys on the other side.

"Where's Cindy?"

"She's inside. Tommy and Eva are here too, she's with them."

Sweet! After showing our IDs, we walked inside. Linc took my hand and I followed him to the upstairs bar. He ordered two beers and a cranberry vodka. Hopefully, the last one was for me.

He handed Craig the beer and me the glass with the light pink liquid. Perfect, strong. We walked over to where the other three stood.

"Maisy!" Eva hugged me tightly.

"Hey!" I returned the hug. She was wearing a maroon open back dress.

Tommy grabbed me, gave me a hug, and then a kiss on the cheek. During the hug, he asked, "How've you been?"

"Good!" I yelled over the music. "What about you?"

"Same old shit." He grinned and then went back to talking to a pretty blonde girl who smiled in my direction.

Cindy grabbed Eva and me, pulling us toward the stairs leading to the dance floor. "Let's go dance!" she yelled. We followed her as I tried to find Linc. It was a lost cause. He'd figure out where I went.

The dance floor looked small, but wasn't, just packed with people. Cindy started grinding against me playfully with her hands in the air. Eva danced behind me.

After a few songs, I got into it. My hips moved, hitting the pulsating beats of the music. Laughing and dancing with the other two girls was fun. Cindy was a really good dancer and could roll her hips perfectly. Eva managed any dance move perfectly, maybe because of what she was, or else she was just that awesome. I, on the other hand, was pretty self-conscious about my dancing skills until the alcohol kicked in and settled my nerves.

We were out there a good hour or so, and I started

wondering where Linc had gone off to. I tried to scan the upstairs loft that held bar as my hips moved with the beat of Eva's. Her hands met my waist and skimmed up my body and back to my hips. Well, then.

My gaze finally met deep warm brown eyes. I smiled. It was not returned. Instead, I got an indignant scowl. Then he disappeared. *What just happened?*

Eva's hands were on the move again and she grazed my boob. Umm, I was okay with that, but it was a little weird, considering I didn't know her very well.

I turned and came face to chest with a chest that sure as hell wasn't Eva's. A guy around my age with straight, light brown hair gave me a big toothy grin.

"Hey darlin', what's your name?" He shouted to be heard over the music.

"Maisy." I tried to walk away, but his hands tightened around my upper arms—not hard, though.

"Where ya going, Maisy?" He was friendly and non-confrontational.

"Back to my friends. See, I thought you were one of them, and you weren't, so I'm gonna go find them." Rambling. Perfect. I gave myself a mental slap.

"Wanna get a drink? Maybe go outside and talk for a little bit? Cool off?" He still held my upper arm.

"Oh, no, that's okay. I have a—"

"Boyfriend," Linc's voice snarled out, his eyes glaring at where the guy touched me.

Both boys were equal in height, but Linc exhibited a more badass vibe. If it got physical, my money was on him. Not that I was biased or anything. I scooted over to stand by Linc, and the other guy's hand dropped away from. *Good thinking, dude.*

"We were just dancin'," the idiot said, not helping.

"Come on, Linc, it's fine." I pulled him away from the dance floor. Thank goodness, he decided to follow.

The guy didn't mean anything by it, and honestly he seemed harmless.

I turned, my right eyebrow arching. "Was there a problem?"

"Huge problem," he grunted and took a swig of his beer. "He was touching you, and I didn't like it."

I smiled to myself because it was hot how protective he was, but it wasn't okay. "I was fine, there was no need to say anything. The guy was harmless."

"I'll try to remember that."

There was no promise in his voice. We stared each other down.

"There you guys are!" Cindy flew toward me, and I grabbed her before she plummeted into the bar. She was drunk.

I pulled her back to her feet. "Hey, honey, want some water?"

"Hell no. I'm fine, good," she slurred, trying to regain her composure. She looked a little green. "Actually, a bathroom might be a good idea."

"Okay, let's go. Come on." I tried dragging her as fast as I could to the bathroom.

Once inside, we went into the handicapped stall. We didn't fully make it before she ran for the toilet. What came up was blue. I was never drinking anything blue again. Ever.

A couple of gagging and coughing noises later, she was done and feeling a tad better. At least, she could walk without me now.

She cleaned up at the sink. "Thanks, girly, I feel so much better." She offered an apologetic smile. "Those drinks just snuck up on me."

I shot her a smile. "You owe me,"

"Deal."

We stumbled out to of the bathroom and back to our

group. Eva sat close to a guy who looked as if he was in the army. I wondered if he was a Veden? But from what Linc and Craig showed, it didn't really matter.

Linc smiled down at me, grabbed me from behind the neck, and pulled me to him. I went willingly, wrapping my arms around his narrow waist and breathed him in. I ran my hands back toward his front, stopping on his sides. His body was the best I'd ever seen in real life, and since I was from California where clothes seemed optional, that was saying something. He, for the moment at least, was mine. I hid my satisfied smile in his shirt.

"You almost ready?' he whispered against my hair.

Looking up and meeting his gaze, I nodded. I was ready, I wanted to go and do some more of what we were doing earlier.

"Maisy!" Cindy squeaked.

"Hmm?" I asked her lazily turning around.

She shoved a drink in my hand.

"Here, I know how alcohol gets you horny. Have more.

My face heated instantly. Did she really just say that? I didn't know what to say, because it was true, but still…

"Trust me, I really don't need the alcohol for this one," I told her.

Granted I had been wound tighter than a shoestring these last few months, but now that he finally let me indulge, that shoestring was untangling quick.

"Good to know," his deep voice said from behind me, as strong arms circled my waist.

I finished my fourth cranberry vodka of the night, and felt good, really good.

He looked toward the door. "You ready, babe?"

I swayed, a little off balance. "Yes, sir."

We said our good byes, while Cindy added, "Get some!" as we walked away.

I planned on it. We walked out, our hands laced as he led me to the truck. He picked me up and deposited me inside, with an unattractive 'oomph' from me. I was more drunk than I originally thought. Oh, well.

The first half of the car ride was quiet.

"So, I told Craig to set it up with our parents. We might as well get it over with."

"Get it over with? Thanks, asshole," I teased. He never finished telling me why he needed to prepare them for me.

"Not like that. Remember how I told you I was the next king?" It was clear from the reluctance in his voice he really didn't wanted to talk about it.

I nodded quietly, and my head swam. Maybe I was drunk, which meant this was not the time to be having this conversation. Shit.

"Well, if I marry someone, and we had kids, the first born would be next in line for king or queen after."

"Sorta old school if you ask me," I offered.

"Yeah, it's fucking stupid, but my offspring would have to be—*What the fuck!*" he roared.

I jerked up and banged my head on the roof of the car. Giving him a puzzled look, I saw he wasn't looking at me, but was staring straight ahead. I hadn't even real-ized we were at my house. There was a strange figure standing on my porch, and my front door was wide open.

"Linc? Who's that?" I asked in a whisper. Why I whispered, I had no clue. We were in the truck and who-ever was out there was at least thirty yards away.

"I don't know, but sure as hell they aren't supposed to be fucking here." He took off his seatbelt and opened the car door. "Stay here," he grunted before rounding the front of the car. "Can I help you?" Linc's voice was low and deadly.

The hooded figure didn't say anything and tried to retreat around the side of the house.

Linc's arm shot out, his fist clenching, as water came from the grass he stood on, flowing from the ground. Holy shit, he was pulling the water out of grass—water that was pebbling in the air and turning in to small clumps of ice bullets.

"I asked you a question, fuck face," he growled, and then threw his fist forward, shooting the small pellets in the direction of the fleeing intruder.

Honestly, I barely saw the ice move. Instead, it was as if ice froze in the air around Linc's body and then disappeared.

The person turned, with a palm up, fingers splayed out just in time. The ice pellets stopped inches from their fingers. Great, another Veden.

I heard Linc laugh, but it wasn't the type of laugh I was used to. It was scary, almost cruel. Then his hands went out to his sides as if he was grabbing something with both hands and bringing it to the center of his chest. Standing just outside the car, I couldn't miss when the ground rumbled, and two trees came flying out of the woods next to the house to hover right behind Linc.

Did he flippin' just uproot trees? A gasp escaped me, and my eyes bulged as I watched him wield so much power.

The person must have realized the exact same thing, because they took off running—fast, using inhuman speed. Linc threw his hands forward, and the trees followed, flying toward the person.

The intruder dodged them and kept on running, not looking back. I definitely didn't blame them. Anyone who could uproot trees was probably not someone to mess with. I made a mental note to not piss Linc off.

I inched away from the car carefully and walked over to Linc, who was still staring in the direction of the woods where the intruder disappeared. He was huffing as if finishing a marathon.

"Linc?" My voice was soft, barely a whisper. I put my hand on his shoulder and gave a little tug in my direction.

He turned around, but his expression was so dark and cold. His eyes were so fierce that I took an unconscious step back.

"You good?" His voice was gruff.

"Yeah, fine, are you okay?"

"Yeah." He shrugged off my hand and headed for the front door. I followed a couple steps behind, unable to keep up. Once we got to the door, he stuck his hand out, cutting me off, and I stopped. He inched into the house and flicked on the light. I tried peering around him, but his massive frame took up the whole damn door.

"Mais, go pack a bag. You're not staying here alone anymore."

That was not his call.

I finally got around him and took in what was left of my living room. The couch was tipped over, all the DVDs and other contents of my entertainment center were strewn around the room. His hand caressed mine in an effort to get me to stop staring. Forgetting he just ordered me around, I thought about Sarah. "Linc, I need to call Sarah."

"Later." He still looked around the house.

"No, now. Just in case she decides to come home or something. I need to warn her, please."

Sarah had been staying at Todd and Jake's place off and on, house sitting for them, while they were "out of town." So I was praying that was where she was.

He reached into his pocket, took out his cell, and handed it over. I dialed way too fast, and my fingers pushed the wrong buttons. I felt completely sober, but my hands trembled. *Fucking phone, just dial the damn number.*

Linc's hands cupped mine, as he slid the phone away and dialed the number for me after I recited it to him.

"Hello?" said a very sleepy Sarah. It was almost two in the morning.

"Hey hon, don't come home, okay? For anything, just stay there until Todd gets home." I knew he wouldn't be coming back for a while, and if he did, I'd figure out how to get her away from him once he returned.

"What?"

"Don't come home," I repeated.

"Are you okay?" Her voice instantly became alert after as my words finally registered.

"Yeah fine. Just—someone broke into the house, and I don't want you to come home without someone with you. Just don't do it."

"Do you need me to come get you? Is Linc there?" She sounded panicked.

"Yeah, he's here, I'm fine, and everyone's fine. I just wanted to let you know," I squeaked.

"Yeah, okay, be safe, Mais, and I miss your face. I need to get some clothes, though. I don't have a lot stocked up here."

"Okay, maybe tomorrow morning we can meet here? I miss you too."

"Can't. I have class. I'll ask Seth to come with me after my shift tomorrow. I'll call you later." The line on the other end of the phone went dead.

Knowing she was okay and wouldn't come home without someone with her, I was able to breathe. I followed Linc to my bedroom and packed a small bag with the essentials, a couple pairs of clothes, shoes, tooth-brush, and toiletries.

Linc grabbed my small cheetah-print bag as we walked back out of the house. I locked the door behind me, not that it would do any good now, seeing that some-one actually got into my house with the door locked.

Once at his house, we went inside. Everything was dark and quiet, even though Tommy and Eva's cars were both parked outside.

"Go ahead up and take a shower. I'll be there in a minute." Linc kissed the top of my head and wandered off into the dark hallway.

Sounded good to me. I climbed the stairs and passed a bedroom, probably Eva's since she went upstairs to change when I was over last time. I headed to Linc's bed-room and straight for his huge shower.

I undressed and hopped in. I turned the water to al-most boiling and stood under the burning stream. It felt so good running down my back. Today went from the being one of the wierdest dates of my entire life to being total shit. Well, not total shit because I ended up in his shower, but someone had broken into my home. Since my car was attacked, we hadn't had any problems, and that was a couple of weeks back. I wished the universe would back the hell off and let me have my happy mo-ment.

The door open and shut quietly, and I stuck my head around the stonewall acting as the shower curtain. The shower was a huge stone box you walked into, with peb-bles built into the sides. It was gorgeous, and I was jealous, since guys weren't supposed to have pretty bath-rooms.

"Want company?" Linc was already shrugging off his shirt and started undoing the buckle on his jeans.

My stomach instantly tightened at the sight of his

bare muscular chest, and the octopus tattoo dancing with his movements. My body reacted by giving me goose-bumps, and an involuntary shiver ran over me. "What if I said no? You're getting a little bit a head of yourself there, aren't ya?"

He laughed. "You can't refuse this." His hands made a motion up and down his body.

He was right. "Go away." I headed back into the shower, praying he wouldn't leave.

He didn't.

I was facing the showerhead, when his feet hit the shower floor, and his arms enveloped me. He pulled me back until I could feel his hardness against my lower back. I turned in his arms and looked up at him. His brown eyes were full of temptation.

"My hands instantly went to his chest. Didn't I tell you to go away?"

He chuckled as his wet brown hair clung to his fore-head. "We both know you didn't mean it."

I turned away, trying not to get hung up on certain parts of his perfect body. Plus I didn't want him to see my smile and the blush I was sure I was rockin'.

"Are you really saying no?" His voice faltered a little bit.

Good, he needed to be turned down once in his life, or at least question it—because, let's be honest, there was no way in hell I was really saying no.

I decided not to answer as I pressed my ass back into his hardness, which made his breath hitch. Then he backed up. I almost turned to see where the heck he went to, but he wasn't gone for long before I felt his massive, rough hand caress my ass.

He stepped forward again and, this time, he placed a hand on the middle of my back and pushed my upper body down lightly. My body listened. I bent forward, placing my hands against the wall. I thought he was going to use his hand first, but nope. I gasped when he forced himself inside me, hard. He moved fast and hard, and my arms almost gave out. When he noticed, he immediately pulled out of me. I whimpered in protest, as he spun me around to face him.

"Please don't stop," I said breathlessly. Why was I always the one begging? Once in a while, it should be the opposite.

He moved his hands to my waist and lifted me, my legs wrapping around him as he pressed me back against the shower wall.

"Wasn't planning on it," he said as his lips tipped up in a predatory smile.

In one swift move, he was back inside me. My hands fisted in his hair as my head eased back, exposing my neck and breasts. He took full advantage, his tongue licking and sucking me. My locked legs tightened as I reached my release, urging him closer, deeper. Exploding, I moaned, and he followed suit right after me. My body went limp, feeling like Jell-O.

He pressed a quick kiss to my lips and slid out of me, stepping back. He looked me over. I was sure I looked thoroughly fucked, in definitely the best way. He definitely did, with his chest moving with his fast breaths, his muscles tightening at each inhale and relaxing with each exhale. Our eyes locked, and his rich, deep eyes softened. His usually hard features melted, and he looked relaxed, content, just staring at me. One second he stood out of reach, the next he was right in front of me, so close our chest grazed.

His head dipped toward my lips, and he kissed me softly, biting my bottom lip as he pulled away. "Finish showering, I'll see you when you're done."

He rinsed off one more time and left me there, still

breathing like I had just run a marathon. That look he gave me was indescribable. It made my stomach flip and my head swim. He looked at me as if I was the best thing to ever happen to him.

Chapter 17

The next couple of days majorly sucked. Well, except for the person I got to sleep next to. I talked Linc into letting me call the cops the morning after the break in. It was ingrained in my head to call the cops when something like this happened. At first, he was super reluctant, he worried bringing in normal humans wouldn't do anything to help. He was proven right. They came out, took pictures of the house, and asked a bunch of questions, none of which I had answers to. We didn't see enough of the intruder to help with identification. The whole process was extremely irritating. Maybe I should have listened to Linc.

The next two weeks flew by. I'd been busy with work and school, Linc had been in and out of the house with his work and family obligations. I'd talked to Sarah a couple of days ago, and Todd and Jake still hadn't returned. So that made me feel better, since Sarah was still staying at their house.

I honestly didn't know which was the lesser evil, her staying at their place and having them come home unexpectedly, or having her staying at our place, which apparently wasn't safe either. I'd much rather her stay here with me and Linc but, with everything going on, I didn't want to drag her into this too. Maybe we could go in on a hotel? But that'd probably be really strange to her.

Sarah and I hadn't shared a shift at Woody's this week. Not only did I miss her, but I felt bad about the whole messed-up situation. Offering to go over and stay with her wouldn't go over very well with Linc. In fact, if I tried putting my foot down and heading over, I knew my ass would get hauled back to his house. Instead, I picked my phone and sent her a quick text. Maybe we could do breakfast. Not even a minute after hitting send, the screen lit up.

YES!!

Yay! I felt just as enthusiastic as her text sounded because she must miss me as much as I missed her. We decided to meet in half an hour at a café in town. After pulling on some jeans, a black tank, and a light green jacket, I walked out of Linc's room. Earlier that morning he left for work and promised to be back by lunch. Why he promised, I wasn't sure. I was grateful he was gone, because he'd been watching me like a hawk lately.

He made sure Tommy or Eva was home if he was at work. Constantly being babysat was getting annoying. I passed Tommy on my way to the door.

His right arm snaked out and wrapped around my waist. "Going somewhere?" His sandy blond hair fell into his face.

"I'm meeting Sarah for breakfast," I looked into his bright blue eyes—eyes I would kill to have.

"Where?"

"The Bagel Café."

He turned to a table in the hallway and grabbed his keys. "Sweet, I'll drive you."

I placed my hands on my hips. "You don't have to, Tommy, I'm perfectly capable of getting there by my-self."

"I know you are, but if I leave you alone and something happens, I'm going to be put in an early grave. I'd feel better if you let me take you. Plus, I have some errands to run anyway." He started walking toward the front door.

I followed him out. "Stop being dramatic. Linc wouldn't put you in an early grave."

He chuckled. "You haven't witnessed his temper yet. Just you wait."

The drive into town didn't take long, and Sarah was standing outside the Bagel Café when we pulled up.

"Call me when you're ready," Tommy said right before I shut the door.

I nodded.

"Linc?" Sarah asked as I walked up to her.

"He's working, Tommy was coming out, so he thought we could carpool."

She pulled me in for a hug, and I welcomed the familiar cherry scent that wrapped around me. Gosh, I'd missed her.

We walked into the café, bought our bagels, and then sat on the patio. The cafe was a cute little place, with a few tables inside and some scattered tables outside. The sun was shining, but fall was definitely here. The cool crisp wind made me shiver.

"What have you been up to?" I asked as I took a bite of my everything bagel.

She tucked strands of dark mahogany hair behind her ear. "Absolutely nothing. I have Todd and Jake's huge house to myself, and I'm bored outta my mind."

"Have you heard from them at all?" I was totally being nosy.

"Yeah, Todd's been calling me every night," she said between chews. She was one of the only people I knew who could look good while chewing and talking.

I tried for casual. "How's he doing?"

"Good, he said they should be back for winter break." She paused awkwardly, which made me look up from my food.

"What?"

"Jake asked about you, you know."

My smile faltered a bit.

Shit. I stared down at the metal table. "What'd he say?"

"First, he wanted to know if you were still going out with Linc. He didn't phrase it that nicely, but—"

"Got it. Anything else?"

"He wanted to make sure you were okay and made Todd ask when he called right before you did the night our house got broken into."

That was really strange timing. Since right before that call Linc was fighting with the intruder. "Weird. What'd you tell him?"

"That you were fine, and staying with Linc. He didn't like the sound of that. Were you and Jake still hooking up when you met Linc? Not that I thought you were, but—"

"Nope, we haven't been for a while. Not sure what Jake's problem is." *Besides the fact that his archenemy happens to be my boyfriend.*

"Maybe it's because he still's into you, and now you're unavailable, therefore more desirable?"

Ha, right. He thought it would be fun to throw me around and purposefully mark me as his mate, because that screamed "into you." "Doubt it. He was the one who didn't want a relationship when we hooked up."

"Dumb boys." Her green eyes focused on the parking lot.

"Yup. Anyway, you haven't gone to the house alone, right?"

"No, I went with Seth a couple days after the break

in. I was planning to, though, after this. Wanna join me?"

I checked my phone, thinking. Linc wouldn't like it, and Tommy would freak out if he came back and I was gone. But I didn't need a baby sitter, and it wasn't like I was going alone. Not that I wanted Sarah to get in the middle of it, but it was daylight outside, and all the attacks had been at night. We'd be fine. "Sure."

"Sweet, I'm going to a party tomorrow, and I need to grab some cute clothes, all I have at Todd's is jeans and sweatshirts. What are you doing tomorrow? Wanna go with me?" She pulled her hair back up into a ponytail, the shorter strands falling to frame her face.

"I can't, I'm going to Linc's to meet his parents." Something I was trying hard not to think about since I wasn't looking forward to it.

Her smile grew. "Really? That's awesome! It means he's serious! Why aren't you as happy as I am?" she squeaked.

"I don't think he wanted to take me. Craig's taking Cindy over and invited us to join them. Linc shut the idea down immediately."

Her forehead creased as she frowned in sympathy. "And now he's okay with taking you?"

I shrugged, not meeting her gaze. "I guess."

"Besides that, is he acting weird?"

"Nope, besides being a little over protective since the break-in."

"Then don't worry about it, I'm sure he doesn't usually take girls home. He doesn't strike me as a guy who's used to being in a relationship. I mean, if I looked that good, I wouldn't limit myself to one smoking-hot person for long." She laughed, and I smiled.

"You sound like Cindy. You've been with Todd forever, so you have limited yourself, silly."

Sarah blushed slightly. "You ready?"

"Yeah, um can you drive? Tommy's my ride."

"Of course, come on," she said, pushing back from the table.

I forgot how scary a driver Sarah was. She didn't pay attention to the road at all, sometimes not even holding onto the wheel, too busy using hand motions to explain the story she was telling. How she managed to avoid an accident was beyond me. Thankfully, we finally pulled up to the house in one piece.

As we walked up to the front door, I pushed past her. "Let me go in first." Not like I could do anything if a murdering Veden lurked on the other side, but at least I knew what I was getting into.

She moved out of the way. I slowly opened the door and checked the living room and kitchen. We walked in together and went through every room of the house to make sure there was no one around. Once we were sure no one lurked in the shadows or closets, we grabbed bags and started piling in clothes, make up, and everything else we needed.

We were in the kitchen looking through the fridge for a bottle of water when my phone started blaring out Luke Bryan. *Crap on a stick.*

I reached for it on the island where it sat and checked the name. Tommy.

"Hey, Tommy," I answered as Sarah watched.

"So, I'm at the bagel shop, and you're not. Where are you?"

Well, he didn't sound pissed.

"Umm, with Sarah," I offered.

"And that place is where, exactly?" he bit out, now sounding annoyed.

"The house," My stomach flipped for the upcoming lecture.

"My house, Todd's house, or your house?"

"Mine," I said in a small voice, knowing what was coming.

"Dammit, Maisy, I thought I told you to stay at the bagel shop. Do you want Linc to murder me?" he yelled.

"Tommy calm down. He's not gonna do anything. We're just grabbing our clothes and then heading back to town." I shook my head at Sarah as I pointed to the phone and she giggled.

"I'm already on my way over—just, for the love of god, stay the fuck there."

The line went dead. Sheesh, so melodramatic.

"Tommy's on his way," I announced still focusing on the bags we put together.

"Why?" Sarah asked.

I sighed. "Something about it not being safe."

"Okay." She extended the syllable like she thought it was strange.

"Well, I'm pretty much done. Anything else you need, Mais?"

"I don't think so," I said, looking over at her.

We walked out to the porch to wait for Tommy.

As I sat there, staring at the road and the trees lining it, I realized how gorgeous this place was. Such a shame we couldn't stay here. The sun set behind the trees, edging the leaves with an amber glow, and everything was a vibrant green. It was not like this in LA, which I didn't miss at all. It might have to do with a water manipulating, gorgeous man, but whatever. Unfortunately, I was starting to like him more than originally planned.

"Hey, Mais?" Sarah said, breaking into my train of thought.

I swept my frizzy bangs over to the side and focused on her. "Yeah?"

"What's the story with Tommy?" she asked, almost whispering.

I caught a blush rising under her skin and gave her my biggest, cheesiest smile. "Sarah Anne Thorne. You did not just ask that!"

The red on her cheeks made its way down her neck. "I think I just did."

"What about Todd?"

"He's been distant lately. He still calls me, but he won't tell me why he's down there, he never answers when I call, and ugh—" She placed her head in her hands. "This is dumb, never mind."

"No, no, please keep telling me what a giant ass your boyfriend is."

"Maisy," she scolded, peeking through her fingers.

"Nope, you can't get mad. You just asked me about another guy, which, by the way, he is awesome, super laid back, and funny as hell. I've seen him with his shirt off. Definitely better to look at than what you currently have. You guys would be so cute together!"

"Shut up!" she squealed. "I just asked about him, I didn't say I was going to explore the idea. Just wondering."

I laughed. "Fine, baby steps. I vote you break up with Todd. Like now."

She nudged me but didn't say no, which wasn't a bad sign. In fact, it would make me so happy if she left Todd. She could do better, way better. She needed to do it— maybe not with Tommy, though. I didn't want anyone to go through the situation I was in at the moment. Cindy was probably going to find out soon enough. How Craig could date her and not tell her was beyond me.

There was a huge rumble of an engine and Tommy's truck came down the drive. He parked and jumped out of it.

"Ladies." His sandy blond hair was coming free from his small ponytail.

"Tommy, you remember Sarah?" I began the introductions, and Sarah shot me a look.

He held out his hand to shake hers. "Yeah, pretty waitress with the boyfriend, right?"

She took his hand. "Nice to meet you," she offered, her voice low, completely embarrassed.

He motioned to the bags. "Is this what y'all are taking with you?"

"Yup," Sarah and I said in unison and started laughing.

Tommy grabbed two of the bags and started walking toward the parked cars.

Sarah ran after him. "Oh, those are mine!"

"Then open your car, sweetheart."

She grabbed her keys and popped her trunk. Tommy loaded her bags and came back to grab mine.

"Thanks," Sarah sounded a bit taken aback, probably not use to nice gestures.

"I got it," I told him as he reached for the bag slung over my shoulder. It wasn't that heavy. He didn't listen, taking it and dropping it in the truck bed. Great, my bag was gonna be filthy.

Tommy walked back and stood next to me. "You guys ready to go?"

"Yeah. Sarah, I'll call you later." I wiggled my eyebrows and then gave her a great big hug.

"You better not say anything," she whispered in my ear, squeezing me tight. Little did she know, Tommy could probably hear her. Everyone in his house had freakin' bat ears.

"No promises."

Tommy leaned down and wrapped his arms around Sarah, giving her a hug goodbye, too. She looked at me from over his shoulder, and I gave her a thumb's up as she rolled her pretty green eyes.

Sarah scampered to her car. "See you, guys."

Tommy and I hopped into his truck, and he immediately turned to me, worry clouding his eyes. "Linc's not gonna know about this, right?"

"Of course not. I'm not that dumb."

"Just checking." He gave me a wink. "So, what are you not supposed to say anything about?"

I just smiled at him.

"You gonna tell me?"

"I'm pretty sure Sarah wants to jump your bones." My tone was matter-of-fact as I tried to keep a straight face.

"Isn't she the one with the idiot-looking Fiskare boyfriend?"

"Yup, Todd."

"Sweet, set it up." He grinned then turned the truck around, sending dirt and rocks flying.

Chapter 18

I hung out with Tommy the rest of the day, since Linc didn't get back home until dusk. So much for "See you around lunch time."

After Tommy and I got back from grabbing my stuff, we made smoothies and watched terrible reality TV until I couldn't take the fake tans, or even more fake boobs, anymore. Tommy even went running with me, which wasn't a huge surprise, as he was supposed to be babysitting me. We ran a little farther than my usual, and, on our way up the driveway, I saw Linc's big, blue-jeans colored truck. Breaking into a sprint, I yelled, "Race ya!" as I passed Tommy.

I took off as fast as I possibly could, even knowing there was no way to win against his inhuman speed. When I stopped and turned around, I wasn't surprised that Tommy wasn't behind me. Maybe he went to the house? A quick check revealed he wasn't there either. Yelling his name a couple of times, I headed toward our starting point. If he didn't come out soon, I would start panicking. If I started panicking, guaranteed I would do something idiotic, like traipse through the woods by their house on my own to find the idiot. I scanned the front of the house once again. After a couple of seconds, I made up my mind to wander in the direction of the woods. Before I got my first step down, I was airborne. Wind whipped through my hair and across my face, as strands got caught in my open mouth. I tried stifling a scream that probably sounded like a dying cat.

Flailing is too pretty a term to describe what I did. Flailing meant I managed to get a good hit in, which didn't happen. What I did could probably fall under the lines of indecorously plummeting.

Tommy twisted in mid-air to take the brunt of it. When we landed, we were both on the ground, with me on top. I'm pretty sure I yelled "What the hell?" but laughed too hard to sound irritated.

Staring into his diamond-blue eyes that mirrored tropical oceans, I knew why he was a man whore. He was so full of life, and his eyes definitely promised a good time.

Behind us, someone cleared their throat, and my head snapped around at neck-breaking speeds, even as I sprawled over Tommy. And that was the exact position we were in when Linc walked out of the house.

Linc stood in his mud splattered white shirt, his jeans smeared by grass stains, and his untied brown work boots. He raised an eyebrow. The man was gorgeous and probably unhappy with the position his girlfriend and best friend were currently in.

"Um, hi?" Tommy offered, before I could even do or say anything.

I stared like a deer in headlights, before regaining my composure. I pushed off of Tommy's chest and stood, brushing the dirt and rocks stuck on my skin. "Hi." I ran over to Linc and threw my arms around his neck.

Thank god, he returned the hug. He wrapped his arms around my waist, crushing my body into his, kissed my temple, and set me back down on my feet. "Hey, babe, sorry I was gone all day."

I backed up a fraction of an inch. "How was your day? You're dirty," I informed him, wiping the mud from the front of my running top.

He smiled, showing off his perfectly straight white teeth. "Good. We just started a project for the college, redoing the campus's landscaping and putting more trees in."

He leaned in and pressed a soft kiss to my lips, and my insides turned to mush. The blond man standing behind me was totally forgotten as I smiled up at Linc, tugging on his shirt for him to come back down and give me more attention with his lips.

"So babysitting is done, Linc, I hope you know I'm charging twenty bucks an hour for this one." Tommy smirked at Linc, his thumb pointed in my direction. "That makes it about two hundred dollars."

Linc punched Tommy's shoulder. "You're not getting shit," he grunted as we turned to go back toward the house, his arm thrown over my shoulders.

"You're wrong. I got your girlfriend on top of me, which I guess is payment enough. I could feel her—"

And that was all Tommy got out before Linc lunged. They flew into the pebble-covered driveway. Fists pummeled on both sides, so fast I could barely see them, but their grunts as those fists connected with flesh came through loud and clear.

I walked back inside while the two grown men acted like cavemen. The front hose exploded, taking a piece of the house with it. I let out a shriek and spun around to see Linc on top of Tommy with his right arm out behind him, palm up, as the water gravitated toward his hand. His hand darted toward Tommy's face, his upper back muscles rippling beneath the shirt. Before my eyes could track it, the water hit Tommy's face. Both men blurred, and ended up on the other side of the truck.

Tommy was on his knees with both hands splayed in front of his face, stopping the attacking liquid. Linc stood twenty feet away with his right hand in Tommy's direction, directing the water. His left hand was by his side, and then he made a swiping motion with his arm as his hand curled into a fist, almost as if he was grabbing something. The water followed, gaining strength as it shot out from behind him and barreled toward Tommy. The water looped around Tommy's backside, right under his ass, and jerked forward causing him to fall on his face. Linc lowered his right hand to the ground hard. The water hit Tommy's back with such force, that should have broken his neck.

Tommy lay there for a minute, I couldn't even see the rise and fall of his chest.

When I walked over to Linc's side, I caught his big ole goofy grin. The nut was thrilled at taking out his best friend. I was sort of worried about Tommy.

"Did you—"

"Payment received." Tommy rolled over and propped his head on his hand as he lay on the ground and gave Linc a thumb's up.

After he hopped up, wearing the same stupid grin as Linc's, I settled down. Men were so weird. Tommy disappeared into his room, probably to shower because he and Linc looked as if they decided to take a mud bath together. Awkward.

Linc weaved our fingers together and pulled me up the stairs. "Come on."

Once we got to his room, I stopped in the doorway. He reached his arm behind him and lifted his shirt over his head as continued into the room. His athletic physique was apparent, but you didn't get muscles like that from hitting the gym a couple times a week. It had to be his job. My mind went to the gutter, picturing him dirty, dripping with sweat—an involuntary shiver ran through me.

He stood in nothing but his black boxer briefs, smirking, with that damn raised eyebrow, and prowled toward me. "What are you thinking about?"

You, dirty and sweaty. "Nothing."

His eyebrow lifted higher. "You were smiling about *nothing*?"

I gulped. "Yes."

"Right." He dragged the "I" sound out. "You want to go out tonight?"

I didn't quite process what he said because I was no longer staring at his face, but his stomach. Those abs—Gosh, I wanted to run my tongue down them and keep going south.

"Maisy," Linc said a little louder, and my eyes clashed with his whiskey-colored ones. They were filled with laughter.

"Huh?" *Smooth, Mais.*

"You didn't hear a word I just said, did you?"

"Umm, no."

"Maybe I should start wearing more clothes, since my stomach is too much of a distraction for you."

That would be a damn shame. "What'd you say, ass-hole?"

His grin widened, "No need for name callin'.'"

Tipping my head to the side, I gave him an una-mused look.

"I wanted to know if you wanted to go out tonight? Like on a date, since we really haven't done that."

"A date? Didn't we go out with Cindy and Craig a couple weeks ago?"

"Yeah, but that doesn't count, it was a group date, and we've been dating for…how long now? I haven't re-ally taken you out anywhere."

"Huh, I never noticed. I feel like a cheap whore."

He shook his head. "Cheap maybe, whore definitely not."

"Where'd you want to go? So I know what to wear."

"Mexican restaurant. Taco's and Margaritas."

"Yum!" I took two big steps toward him. Stretching on tiptoes, I pressed a kiss to his cheek.

Once in the bathroom, I locked the door and pressed my back against it, smiling like a dumbass. No hanky panky until after he took me out and spoiled me with tequila and tacos.

Against my back, the door handle turned.

He yelled through the door, "You know, locked doors don't really work on me."

"You break the door, and you're going by yourself on our date. I'll even sleep with Eva so you and your hand can have some alone time after."

I heard him laugh. "Hurry up. We're leaving in an hour."

We both showered and got dressed. I decided to wear dark jeans and a cute silky coral colored tank. As we headed to the car, we passed Tommy, who thanked us for the invite as we left him behind in the kitchen.

The restaurant was a hole in the wall that I had never heard of, and I was surprised, since finding that kind of "authentic" Mexican in Alabama was difficult.

I walked past Linc and stopped in the doorway. The walls were red and cream in color, the outer rim of the restaurant floor was lined with booths, and in the center was small table that could hold two to four people. Linc's hand settled on my lower back, and my stomach tightened. He gave me a slight push, urging me to the back of the restaurant.

We walked up to a corner table on the far left, it was cute and with a small candle in a red votive holder. I slid into the booth before Linc sat down. The waiter handed us water, chips, salsa, and the menus.

I studied the menu. "What's good?"

There were the regulars—burritos, enchiladas, tacos...and so on. I looked up and caught Linc's watching me.

"Linc?" I asked him in a small voice, because he was staring at me with a strange look that melted my insides and made my head fuzzy. It was the same look he gave me when he got out of the shower a couple days ago.

He snapped out of whatever trance he was in. "I usually get carne tacos. They are the shit."

"Sounds good to me." I sipped my water, dropping my gaze to the table to hide my wince since my voice came out abnormally high. The urge to smack my hand to my head was strong. Even after dating the guy for the last few months, I was still nervous. Shouldn't I feel comfortable by now? He made my insides twist and turn every time he looked at me. It made me feel like he was still not sure how to read me. Which was stupid because I was not that complicated.

"Hey." Linc reached across the table and grabbed both my hand. "Relax."

I raised an eyebrow. "I am."

"Bullshit, you're whole body just tightened, and I'm pretty sure you chewed the top of your straw off."

I blinked and looked down at the straw. *Crap*. I'd be surprised if I could get anything out of it. It was decimated.

He gave my hands a light squeeze.

"What were you thinking about?"

Nope, not going not share how I didn't feel comfortable around him. It wasn't the best thing to say to your boyfriend. It wasn't a bad uncomfortable, but every time his abs peeked through his shirt, or he lifted something, I wanted to jump his bones. Every time his eyes landed on me, or he spoke, my heart went frickin' crazy, and my head couldn't put two and two together.

"Is it about my parents' tomorrow? Because you don't have to worry about that. They'll like you." His eyebrows knitted together, he released one of my hands to move his hair out of his eyes.

Oh, now there's a good excuse. "Do they know I know?"

He glanced away. "No."

I tugged my other hand free and placed it in my lap. "When are you planning on telling them?"

"Soon, I guess. I don't think it would be a good idea to bring it up tomorrow, though. I need to share on my own schedule."

I met his eyes. "Are they going to freak out?"

"Nah, don't worry about it. Everything's gonna be fine. You'll love the house. It has a huge lake in the backyard, and everything outside is green. The house is big, but it's an okay house. It's the landscaping that's the best." His relaxed voice did not match his tense posture.

"Were ya'll ready to order?" the waiter asked. The "ya'll" really added to the authenticity.

"Two margaritas, and can I get an order of four tacos? She'll have an order of two, please." Linc said, ordering for me, which was fine.

I found the gesture hot. Waiting until the waiter left, I decided now was a good time to pry.

"Okay, I have a question," I announced and his eyes bounced to mine, his pearly white on display. "So you have these powers and half the time you don't even use them. Plus, you're a prince, so I would think you would live a more charmed life and use those abilities on a daily basis."

His smile widened. "Yeah, I don't have to use them

all the time since I'm pretty awesome on my own. Tommy, on the other hand, feels the need to use it constantly." He rolled his brown eyes at the last statement.

"Did your mom tell you that?" I challenged.

"Actually, she did."

I wrinkled my nose then broke eye contact and fiddled with my water cup. A wicked smile hit my lips. "So, what's your reaction time?"

"My reaction time?"

"Yeah, how long does it take for you to muster up whatever it is that you muster, to make the water listen to you?"

"I basically think I move my body a little to direct the flow, and it works. So, instantaneously." He shrugged not catching on to where I was going.

"Oh, that's awesome."

I looked around the tiny restaurant. There were two other couples up near the front and no workers around. Taking my cup of water, I threw it at his face. The water barely made it out of the glass. Drops dangled in mid-air for a second, then moved back into the cup, which slammed onto the table, then shot to his outstretched palm.

He winked at me. "See? Awesome."

I stared, a little put out because I hoped the water would go farther than that. "Whatever." Fine, he was awesome, but I was definitely not admitting it. "How's that humanities class going?"

"Haven't shown up since you dropped. Not as interesting without you there."

"You dropped?" I was dumbfounded.

"Yeah, I figured we totally blew our hypothesis when we started seeing each other. So much for you not wanting all this."

"I didn't. You, sir, are the one who decided it was a

good idea to devour my lips." I almost did the pointing thing my mom did when she argued.

"I've devoured more than that." His lips tipped up into a gorgeous, proud smile.

And cue my blush that almost reached my toes.

"I'm pretty sure you'd agree when I say it was a fucking excellent idea," he added.

My stomach twisted, and the tense feeling moved lower until I was crossing my legs and clenching my thighs together.

He smirked. "So whatcha thinking about now, babe?" He leaned forward. His foot brushed against the inside of my calf. He was evil.

"I have six tacos and two margaritas." The waiter put a platter in front of us, two plates, and two lime margaritas.

I jumped. I mean full on jumped, and almost knocked my water over.

Taking a sip of my drink, I watched as Linc grabbed the tacos. Whew, tequila. Silently, I thanked the bartender for the strong drink. We sat in silence as we ate. The tacos weren't bad, but it could be because I was starving. Regardless, I expected them to be whatever, but they were really good.

When we finished, Linc picked up the check, and we walked back out to the car.

I grabbed his hand and knitted my fingers with his. "Is our date over?"

"Nope." I didn't realize I was pouting, just a little bit until he added, "You can't get me into bed that easily."

"That was totally not what I was getting at! I was just curious. So, where are we going?"

"Whatever you need to tell yourself. To a lake."

"A lake?"

He didn't answer as he put me in his truck. He got in

and turned up the music, so there wasn't much conversation as we flew down the highway. I'm pretty sure my eyes bugged out when he made a random right turn. There was no road as he went through a valley, then parked at the tree line.

"Come on." He jumped out of the driver's side, and I followed.

"Where's this lake?"

"Just up ahead, I think you've already been there."

"The one that's across from the creek where I run?"

"Yeah, it's a good size, and no one comes around. It's where Tommy, Craig, and I practice techniques," he said as we walked through the trees and brush.

"Linc," I tugged on his hand until he looked at me. "How did you know I've been here?"

He didn't say anything for a few awkward seconds.

"Oh my god, were you fucking following me?" I almost shrieked. "That's not creepy or anything." I let go of his hand and crossed my arms.

"I wasn't following you. Craig and I were out here when you ran up, and we scattered. I watched you from the trees until you left, though. I could tell you liked the place."

"Yeah, it was gorgeous." I sighed and, feeling the water, knew we were close to our destination.

He snatched my hand back as we came around a bend. He helped me over a fallen tree. As we got to the lake, my breath caught in my chest. Mother nature was showing off. I liked the way the lake looked at night more than during the day. It mirrored the sky, as if diamonds floated in it. Gorgeous. The water was calm, and specks of yellow hovered above the surface. Lightening bugs.

"Okay, I'm guessing you brought me out here so you could show off? So what can you do?" I smiled up at him.

He winked and pulled me in front of him. "You ready for the upcoming awesomeness?"

My hands went to his stomach, and my fingers stretched over his rolling muscles. "You mean cockiness?" I asked, watching my hands roam.

He laughed. "I like to think of it as awesomeness, amazingness, knock-Maisy's-panties off-ness."

I unwillingly removing my hands and gestured towards the water. "Well, please, do show."

He walked forward toward the bank and right up to the water before he stopped. His back moved up and down as he took a deep breath. He stepped into the water and shot forward, the bottom of his feet barely skimming the moonlit surface. It was as if he was sliding on glass or crystal clear ice. In the lake's center, he stopped and turned around, the water barely rippling. He'd gone at least a hundred yards over the water and didn't make a sound.

I stared at him in awe. Feeling my eyes widening and my jaw clenched together, I attempted to tame my reaction since there was no need to add to his already over inflated ego.

He smiled at me. I knew because the moonlight hit off his teeth, making them shine like stars. He held out one finger and then curved it, silently telling me to come to him.

Hell, no. Was he crazy? I didn't have super freaky water powers that would allow me to walk on water. I would drown. I shook my head.

"Maisy, get your cute ass over here," he yelled, extending his arm out.

"You think I have a cute ass?" I whispered, knowing he could hear me. It was a trick that must come in handy while eaves dropping.

"Babe, your ass is what my dreams are made of. Now, come on."

I could barely see the movement his fingers.

"Oh my god, stop talking. I'm not going out there, I'll get soaked."

"Yeah, you will, just not in the way you're thinking. I promise I won't let you fall," he said, and I was thankful there weren't any homes or people around to hear our bizarre conversation.

Turning around, I started toward a rock I could sit on. I'd watch him do whatever he was going to show me. I didn't make it halfway, before water rushed by my feet. It was cold as it curled over my warm skin not covered by my sandals, and wound around my ankles, to the point I couldn't lift them because the pressure was too much. Fucker.

The water started moving, taking me with it. I was having a little problem balancing. As soon as I reached the lake's shore, the water rose up a bit and took off. My upper body flew backward, but I steadied myself. It was like body surfing, only on my feet...so maybe surfing without the surfboard? The water under me moved. It was cool and a bit scary, but such a rush.

The cold air chilled me as the water brought me closer and closer to Linc. Once I was about ten feet away, the water slowed, like way down, until I almost drifted into his waiting arms. The water under my feet swayed with the motion. It was unreal. Blinking a couple of times, I finally looked at him.

"That was rude." I punched him in the chest but was thankful for his hug. This was the most alarming and enthralling thing that ever happened to me, and I wanted to do it again.

"You didn't like it?" He sounded as if he already knew my answer.

"Whatever." I pulled my hair back into a ponytail and fastened it with a rubber band from around my wrist. "So what now? I thought you had to move your hands to guide the water or something."

"Remember how I told you I was awesome, amazing—"

"Pompous," I added to his list. "Get on with it."

He smiled wider. "As I was saying, I don't need to use my hand motions at all. I can actually think about what I would like the water to do, and it obeys. But no one caught on to that until I was in my teens. Anyway, when we were taught how to fine tune control the water, my father and others demonstrated certain techniques on how to use your body to help direct it. Moving my limbs feels natural, which is why I use my body. Plus, the look on your face was worth it. You didn't see it coming."

No shit, Captain Obvious.

I tried to take everything in. Linc didn't have to warn anyone what he planned to do. It was crazy sauce, with an extra helping of sauce. My gaze met his warm one, and I smiled. "Okay, so maybe you are sorta of awesome," I said, feeding his ego a bit.

He removed his arms from my hips and slowly raised them up. As his arms lifted, the water around us rose, going higher than our heads. From that position, he swooshed his arms toward the left and the water started spinning, rising and rising until I could no longer see the moon—or sky, for that matter. We were completely engulfed in water.

I was still looking up in awe when the water began to plummet toward us, and I pushed closer to Linc with a squeal. Having tons of water head straight toward my face, with pressure that was sure to kill me, scared the crap out of me. The water under my feet gave way, and I clutched Linc, waiting for an impact that never came.

"Maisy, open your eyes."

Linc's soft voice interrupted my thoughts of dying from drowning. I peeled one eye open, which was the one pressed against his chest, so all I saw was black. *Smart, Mais.* I slowly opened my left eye and turned. We were still standing on the water, but we were underwater. Like under the frickin' lake trapped in an air bubble underwater. The only light came from the moon and the stars, so seeing beyond our immediate area was difficult. It was so damn awesome I couldn't speak, just stare.

"Only problem," he said sort of low. "Is that I don't know how long you can be in here before you start suffocating."

"What do you mean?" My voice came out breathy. If he wanted to knock my panties off, mission accomplished.

"I don't need to breath underwater, but this air is the only air we have. Once you use up the oxygen and carbon dioxide takes over, you'll pass out, I'm guessing."

That made sense.

"So with that being said—" He trailed off and curled his arm around my waist, drawing me against his chest. Then we shot straight up.

I closed my eyes and, when I opened them, we were above the lake, still standing on the water. Like way above the lake. We were almost level with the tops of the pine trees in the distance. It was the most amazing thing I'd ever experienced.

"This isn't tiring?" I asked, worried about how much energy he was expending.

"Not yet, this stuff is small shit. When I train with Tommy or Craig, it wears me out, but that requires mental and physical work, since I have to focus not only on my next punch but where the water needs to go to help out."

"You train a lot?" I looked over the side of the water pedestal we stood on.

"Yeah."

"Do you get in fights often? With the Fiskares? Or is the training just to keep in shape?" I felt a pinch on my bottom lip from my teeth.

"This year has been the worst, mainly because someone's targeting you. But before last year, I think I could count the fights I was in on my hands. We have to be ready for the Fiskares and for rival territories trying to take control."

Alarmed, I met his whiskey colored eyes. "Rivals?"

"Rivals." The corners of his lips lifted as a particular look settled on his face.

Shit. Nothing good comes from that look.

The next thing I knew the water disappeared from beneath my feet, and I was falling—fast. I let out a scream and, just before splash down, the water erupted from the lake and snatched me. Now I was soaked.

"Really asshole?" I turned around looking for Linc.

"That mouth," came a voice from my right. Linc was back on the shore.

"You like it." I started to wring out my hair, and the water dripping into the lake. The same lake I was currently standing on again. So trippy.

"I like it better when it's around my—"

"Oh, my goodness, shut the fuck up," I yelled. "Can I come back to dry land now?"

He chuckled, and I was airborne again. This time, I was literally thrown out of the water, and Linc caught me easily. Not even a grunt, which was weird, because I wasn't the skinniest thing in the world. He set me down and put his hand palm up, fingers splayed. He closed his fingers slowly and all the water in my clothes, hair, and clinging to skin gravitated toward him.

Now I was dry. Well, that was handy. "What else have you got?"

His smile widened to exponential proportions.

Chapter 19

The next day, work went by way too fast, probably because I was meeting Linc's parents tonight. I didn't want to go back to his house to get ready. Instead, I was fine if Seth said he needed me to stay, but when I explained what was planned for the evening, he was surprised and told me to have fun. He seemed genuinely happy for me.

The drive to Linc's parents' house was just over an hour long, and the whole way there I was on the verge of shaking apart. When Craig first brought up meeting them and Linc shut it down, it hurt that he wasn't into it. Still, logically, I got it. They didn't know about me.

I hadn't wanted to bring it up again, because that was more nerve wracking. Plus, it would agitate Linc. If our relationship was finally growing, and turning out to be more than just sex, no sense in upsetting the status quo. Our date last night was so fantastic, I woke up with butterflies in my belly.

I had passed out on him when we got home, so I tried to be funny and sneak in an apology this morning. His response was, "I settled for a kiss before you passed out, but you can make it up to me now if you're really feeling that bad."

I totally took him up on the offer. Him being this super powerful water person scared the absolute living shit out of me, but here I was sitting in a car, going to meet his parents, the king and queen of the Vedens.

Worrying over tonight's meeting, I wondered if he hadn't wanted to take me because they wouldn't approve of him dating a human. But that theory was shot because Craig and Cindy had been dating for a while, and she'd met their parents on more than one occasion. What if his parents didn't like me? I wasn't the most talkative. What if I come off as snooty or something? Should I be bubblier than normal? Or what if they didn't think I was worthy? That right there was probably what I was most nervous about. Which, honestly, Linc put himself on a high enough pedestal, that if I wasn't worthy, I definitely wouldn't be here.

I felt awkward the entire drive as if I was heading into a lion's den, unprepared for the slaughter. It didn't make sense. I've never been this worried about meeting a boyfriend's parents, but Linc's initial reaction to everything left me worried.

We took two separate cars, which was weird since we were going to the same place and would've been easier to carpool. Craig suggested carpooling, but Linc shot it down. Maybe he wanted an easy escape. My hand was engulfed in his, and I realized I was squeezing the life out of it, like a python. Easing up, I took my hand away.

Linc shook his hand out and kept driving. His lips were set in a hard line, and his fingers were tapping off beat to the music. His thoughts were consuming him, which didn't help calm my nerves one bit. If he was nervous, then there was probably something scary coming.

I broke the silence. "How much farther is it?"

"About ten minutes, and we'll be there. You nervous?"

"No," I scoffed.

He peeked over at me. "Uh huh."

"Fine, I'm so frickin' nervous I'm on the verge of shaking, and it doesn't help that you really haven't talked in the last twenty minutes because your so preoccupied in that big head of yours. Makes me think you're nervous, and, if you're nervous, then I should be terrified."

He let out a shallow chuckle. "You done?"

I shot him a dirty look but nodded.

"You have nothing to be nervous about. My parents are friendly. The only reason I'm on edge is because I've only brought one other girl home before. Bringing girls home isn't something I make a habit of doing."

"Then why'd you bring me?" I suddenly realized I said that out loud and not in my head. Shit.

"Is that a serious question?"

Double shit.

"I didn't mean to say that out loud. It's fine. Never mind. I get it."

"No, I'm going to answer you, but your lack of self-confidence is annoying."

"Well, maybe it's just to balance your arrogance," I grumbled, knowing he could hear me.

He ignored that. "I like you, Maisy, a lot. Hell, more than I should. You're funny, and you get along with my friends, which is a damn miracle. You care about people more than you should, and it helps that you're beautiful."

And now the butterflies in my stomach fluttered for a whole different reason. He could be sweet when he wanted to. I looked at him. "So are we just doing dinner with your parents and then getting the heck out of there?"

He reached over and covered my hand. "I think so, but we can stay as long as you want. Or we could just say hi and leave."

"Deal." I chuckled and his laugh mixed with mine.

He raised our laced fingers to his mouth, placing a kiss on the back of my hand, and glanced over at me. I squirmed under his gaze, uncomfortable.

He turned his head back to the road and slammed on the breaks.

Tires squealed as we came to a stop, smoke smelling of burnt rubber drifting around us.

I kept a death grip on the door handle and his hand.

Wide-eyed, I turned to him. "What the heck was that for?"

"Red light." His smile got bigger as he nodded his head in the direction we were stopped. "You're distracting," he added.

I smiled back at him rolling my eyes. "Whatever."

Within minutes of the light turning green, we turned right and stopped at a gate.

"Welcome to the Flodpoikas'. State your business," said an extremely monotone voice via a call box.

"Ey, George it's me," Linc yelled back.

"Sir," was all the response he got before the gate opened.

Once we drove through the gate, there were trees with purple flowers lining the pebbled road. The driveway was about a mile long. I stared out the window of his truck in complete awe. It was gorgeous. There was so much land and water. A small river curled off to the side of the house and wrapped around to the back, where I assumed the lake was that the guys talked about earlier.

The house we pulled up to was ridiculous. It was massive, built out of logs. The roof was a dark wood with solar panels on one whole side. The huge porch was gorgeous and wrapped around the entire house.

I looked down at my jeans and sheer black tank top paired with strappy black sandals. Linc said casual, so that's what I dressed for. "I feel underdressed."

"Stop, you look beautiful." His hand squeezed mine before he untangled our fingers and jumped out of the car.

I opened my door and hopped down to where he stood.

He hooked his arm around my neck and pulled me to his chest. My arms swept around his narrow waist out of instinct.

"Stop worrying so much. This—this is going to be fine," he said into my hair.

It was the same thing he'd told me all night, and I wasn't sure why he felt the need to repeat himself, unless he was as nervous as I was. *Shit.*

A rumble came from behind us, and I turned my head to watch another truck come up the road. Craig's, I guessed. I was right because Cindy bounced out of the vehicle, her fiery red curls framing her face in wild abandon, as she grabbed me in a hug.

"Maisy, you look pale," she whispered in my ear.

"Yeah, sort of freaking the frick out."

"Stop, their parents are really sweet. They'll love you. Shoot, they liked me, so you're definitely fine."

I giggled and relaxed. Craig gave me a hug, and we all headed up the wooden stairs, across the porch, to a beautiful wooden door. It was cool, with a knocker and everything. Totally old school Southern.

We entered and, if it was possible, it was even bigger on the inside. It had a homey cabin feel—well, as much as a house that size could feel homey—but it was modern. Exposed beams lined the ceiling, and the floor was hardwood, dark, and worn. I loved it.

"Boys? Is that you?" came a soft, but clear feminine voice.

A woman appeared. She had bright blue eyes, I would kill for, and Linc's light curly hair. Her complexion was much lighter than Linc's, and she was much shorter, maybe five feet, two inches—definitely shorter than me.

"Hey, Ma," Linc said as he wrapped the gorgeous woman up in one of his bear hugs, Craig followed suit.

"Cindy, I'm so glad you came back. I thought for sure this one would run you off faster an antelope being chased by a cheetah."

"Nope, still here, Ms. Flodpoika," Cindy said as their mom wrapped her in a warm hug.

"I'm pretty sure the cheetah always gets the antelope, Ma," Craig chimed in, reaching around Cindy's waist and hauling her back. She giggled.

Gosh, they were too frickin' perfect. I stepped forward and took Linc's hand. He smiled at me.

Ms. Flodpoika's looked around her son at me. "And who's this, Linc?"

"Ma, meet Maisy, Maisy this is my mom, Annette." Linc introduced us, pulling the hand connected to me forward, and put me in front of him.

I let go of Linc and offered my hand. "Nice to meet you, Ms. Flodpoika."

"You too, dear, and call me Annette please," she said, but in a different voice than what she used with the others.

It wasn't exactly cold, but it sure as hell wasn't warm. She stared at me like I'd sprouted two heads. Great.

"Come on into the dining room. Dinner's about ready, and your dad should be home soon."

"He's working on a Saturday?" Linc asked as we followed his mom and the other two into a massive dining room with a huge harvest wood table with daisies and pink and purple tulips in the center. It was a weird combination, but it looked beautiful.

"You know your father. I apologize now, girls, if Alexander stars talking about the catfish he caught last night and whether he should take it off the ice and gut it now to eat, or wait until tomorrow."

"I vote now, your catfish is the shit," Craig said.

Cindy looked at me and crinkled her nose.

"Language, Craig, and thank you," Annette called back. "Linc, while we wait, why don't you show Maisy the rest of the house? The others can help me in the kitchen since Cindy's already seen everything."

"Sounds good." Linc stopped and pulled me back to where he stood. He took me through the downstairs at lightning speed, showing me the living room, kitchen, office, and a sitting room with a bunch of books. I pulled back into the sitting room because there were pictures scattered among the books, and I wanted to look. "You don't need to see those."

He grabbed my waist and tried pulling me back, but failed. I knew he didn't care, because he was like a bazillion times stronger than me. If he didn't want me to see them, then he would toss me over his shoulder.

Walking around the room, I gazed at the pictures of the boys growing up. Them in their teens going to prom, their senior pictures, and some when they were five and at a soccer game. They were adorable, especially the one with the curly brown hair. You could tell, even from a young age, he was gonna be a looker.

I smiled at him. "You were cute then, what the heck happened?"

"What are you talking about? I was damn good looking then and still am." He smirked. "So much so that you can't take your eyes off me every time I walk around the house shirtless. I've seen you wipe the drool off your chin."

"Modest, aren't you?"

"Always, babe," he said, coming up behind me.

We were leaving the room when a picture on a side table caught my eye. It was of Linc, probably still in high school, and he was with a tall, dark-brown-haired girl with green eyes who was wrapped around him. They were smiling big at the camera, and I couldn't help but notice that his hand wasn't exactly on her waist. It was lower. For a second, I stopped and realized it was the same girl who was our waitress at the Italian place, Caroline, I think her name was. Goody, I was right. They had a history.

"Oh, that picture's cute. Who is she?" I said, trying to playing dumb and nonchalant about the whole thing, but I was sure I was obvious.

"Just an ex. Come on, there's still more to see." He grabbed my hand and pulled me toward the stairs.

Fine, whatever. I knew he had a past, but the pang of jealousy was still there. It was awkward that his parents still had a picture of her in their house. Maybe she and Linc went out for a long while, or they just broke up. *Awesome.*

Upstairs, we walked down an olive green hallway. "That's my parents' room, Craig's room, my room, and there's this really cool game room over here with a balcony. It has a killer view of the backyard," he said, pointing out the rooms as we passed.

"Can I see your room?" I asked in the quietest voice I could muster. I was curious what it would look like. Sports trophies or cars or whatever hobby he previously loved? Maybe he was like a chick with pictures of his friends everywhere?

He gave me a weird look, though, as if he was anxious or nervous. "Sure." He took a deep breath. "Come on." He led me by the hand toward the closed door.

We walked in, and it looked like a normal boy's

room—white walls, soccer trophies, a poster with girls in bikinis, a dresser with pictures lining the top, and a small side table next to a king-sized bed.

Walking over to the dresser, I scanned the pictures, and the breath stalled in my throat. It suddenly made sense why he was so reluctant to bring me in here. Her. Most of the pictures that were on the dresser were of him and Caroline. Some had Tommy and Craig in them, but most were Linc and her, smiling, kissing, touching. I didn't want to be jealous, this was before me. But hell, if jealousy wasn't a cold hard bitch whose claws climbed right up my spine.

Shoving that emotion back down, I swallowed. "Show me that game room with the view you were talking about." My voice didn't come out as chirpy as I planned. It came out shaky. *Dammit.*

"Maisy, I'm sorry. I haven't stayed here since high school, so I never really redecorated and my parents never took anything down."

"Shhh." I covered his mouth with my fingers. "It's fine. We both have exes, and you don't have to explain."

He removed my fingers from his lips, opened my hand, and placed a delicate kiss on my palm. "Fuck, you're perfect."

He grabbed my waist and rammed it into his. I giggled. He kissed my lips hard and then led me out of the room.

"So, what is your mom making for dinner? It smells wonderful." I wasn't lying, it smelled tangy and spicy.

"Ha! My mom doesn't cook, but I think its jambalaya, my favorite."

"I'll keep that in mind. You have a cook?"

We were still walking down the long hallway, family pictures lining the walls.

"Yeah, she's cool. Her name's Helen. She's been

with the family since I can remember. She practically raised Craig and me."

I nodded, not really sure what to say to that. I was actually surprised. His mom seemed so warm and family oriented, the way she acted with the boys and Cindy. The idea of a cook didn't really fit.

The game room was massive and seriously had everything. There was an air hockey, foosball, and pool table. To the right was a comfy looking couch, that had seen better days, and a big screen TV. A table under the TV looked as if it had every game system known to man, and to the left was a fully stocked bar.

I smiled. "Looks like you and Craig had a rough childhood."

His full lips curved upward. "We did, we had to wait for the Xbox almost two weeks after it came out."

"Jeeze, how'd you guys survive?" I asked, rolling my eyes.

He laughed. "Come on, you're gonna love this."

I followed him to a huge balcony overlooking the backyard. My breath stalled. *Holy mother of frickin' nature and everything else. Wow.* The lake was huge. There was green grass everywhere, and huge oak trees I guessed lined the entire property. There were also flowers of every color surrounding the lake and then following the river that ran into it. The moon and stars reflected off the crystal water, almost as beautiful as our lake.

"This is unbelievable. You guys made this?"

"Yeah, Craig and I designed the backyard a couple years ago."

"It's beautiful," I whispered, gripping the wooden rail.

His arms encircled my waist and his warmth pressed against my back.

We stood there for a good fifteen minutes before we

heard Annette say his dad was home. My stomach immediately dropped. I was about to meet a king. He had no
idea I knew, but still…

We walked down the stairs and into the dining room,
with the harvest table I planned to steal. Everyone was
already in their seats. Cindy and Craig were down at the
end, across from each other. Next to Craig was Annette,
and next to Cindy were three open seats. At the head of
the table was a large, blond man. By large, I meant tall,
easily taller than Linc, who was six foot, four.

"Son," the blond giant said, spreading out his arms.

His facial structure matched Linc's, strong jaw, full
lips, and almond eyes. He was very handsome.

Linc and his dad hugged, stepped back, and grabbed
my hand again. "Dad, this is Maisy, Maisy this is my dad,
Alexander."

"It's a pleasure to meet you, Maisy."

He reached for my hand. I took his. He had a hard,
strong grip. But he wasn't as intimidating as I thought he
would be.

After the introductions, I took a seat between Linc
and Cindy. An older lady with frizzy white hair walked
out and placed a massive bowl of jambalaya in the center
of the table. She took a seat at the end.

We all dug in. The jambalaya was the best I'd ever
had. I had seconds and seriously contemplated having
thirds. Linc, Craig, and their dad had at least fifths. The
conversation was casual and light, mostly consisting of
the five of them talking and me sitting there listening,
which worked for me.

"So, Maisy, what is it that you do?" Annette asked.

I smiled. "I work at a bar near campus, called
Woody's."

"You're a waitress? What do you plan to do after
college?" she asked quickly, and I got the feeling she

didn't exactly approve, but I was still in school, so what did she really expect?

"I want to eventually become a teacher, preferably a high school English or history teacher, since I'm studying humanities."

"Oh, I guess that's probably the only choice you'd have with that major—" she said.

"It's a good choice," Alexander cut in. "There's a need for good English teachers, a lot of kids struggle in that area."

I smiled at him. "Yeah, a lot do."

Linc's hand found my upper thigh. He gave me a gentle squeeze, and I placed my hand on his.

Thank goodness the conversation turned away from me when Annette asked Cindy the same question. Craig cut Annette off again, saying she already knew Cindy was a nursing major, or soon to be nursing major. She wasn't even in school yet. It was as if Linc's mother was trying to make me feel inadequate. Something I didn't need help feeling since my major was rough when it came to finding a job after college. Yet, it was something I was passionate about, and I had every intention of making work.

After everyone was done eating, and the conversation died down, Linc pushed away from the table. "Craig, you want to take the girls out to the lake?"

Craig pushed off the table and stood up. "Yeah, let's go."

He met Cindy on the other side, grabbed her hand, and walked toward the sliding glass door leading to the outside patio.

Alexander pushed back from the table. "Linc, can I talk to you for a minute?" His question sounding more like an order.

"Sure." Linc turned to look at me and gave me a quick kiss. "I'll meet you out there."

I turned and saw Craig and Cindy waiting for me at the door. When I reached Cindy, she looped her arm through mine, while Craig opened the door for us.

Outside smelled like water and grass. It reminded me of Linc—earthy. We walked toward the lake. The grass was wet and stuck to our feet as we headed toward the dock that had a couple of pedal boats and a rowboat. Next to the lake was a garage that Craig explained had a speedboat and some Seadoos.

"Y'all want to get in the boats? I can go in a single?" Craig offered.

"Sounds fun," Cindy said, but I felt like I was intruding on something that would be romantic. They shouldn't have to split up.

I smiled at the cute couple. "You guys go ahead. I'll wait for Linc back on the deck."

Craig helped Cindy climb into the rowboat. "You sure?"

"Yeah go." I pushed his arm, and he smiled.

I watched him row, but he was going faster than he should be with such lazily strokes. How could Cindy not tell? But from the look on her face, she wasn't paying attention to anything around her except Craig. I was glad she was so happy, and they seemed to be on the same page, considering his expression mirrored hers.

I turned and walked up to the deck slowly, studying the grass covered in dew. The tiny droplets made the backyard look prettier, almost enchanted. I could hear voices, mainly Linc and Alexander's. He and his parents were standing in the kitchen. Taking a seat on one of the chairs by the lit fire pit, I looked at the lake and grabbed my phone.

Cindy and Craig were going at it in the boat, and it

made a pretty picture with the moonlight in the background, so I snapped a photo for Cindy.

"Why did you bring her? She seems like a sweet girl, but there's no point leading her on, son. You know better than that," a deep voice drifted from the kitchen.

"I agree with your father. You shouldn't have brought her. You know I don't approve of you doing what you do with normal humans, but to make her feel like you're serious isn't how we raised you," his mom said.

I stood up and tiptoed toward the door before I knew what I was doing.

"She's fine, we aren't even really dating. She's nothing. I brought her because Craig said something about Cindy coming and that's her best friend. After tonight, I'll probably break it off."

From where I stood in the shadows, I could see Alexander nod his head as Linc's mother took a sip of her red wine. She removed the glass from her lips. "Caroline and her family are coming over for dinner on Wednesday, I expect you to be here."

Linc ran his hand through his light brown curls. "Yeah, cool."

It was the last thing I allowed myself to hear. What the fuck? I backed up and turned, walking as fast as I could toward the dock. Tears threatened to make an appearance. I needed to get home, like right now. What the hell?

'She's nothing,' replayed over and over in my head. God, I had to get away. His rejection made a horrifying sort of sense. He was gorgeous with royal ties and wasn't even fucking human, for crying out loud. Why did I think this was turning into something more? I shouldn't have let it go further than a hook-up. Maybe I should've done the damn humanities project alone. Fuck.

Waving at the boat Craig and Cindy were in, I tried not to cry as they came toward the dock.

Catching sight of me, Cindy asked, "Mais are you okay?" Her voice was laced with concern.

"Not really, can um Craig take me home? Please?" I tried holding the tears back as long as possible.

"Yeah of course, where's Linc? What's wrong?"

"I'll tell you later, can we just go?"

"Did Linc do something? You know what? Hold on." She turned to Craig, who was tying the boat up. "Hey, love, can I just take Maisy back in your truck, and you catch a ride with Linc?"

"Yeah, whatever you want," Craig replied, digging out his keys and handing them to her after she kissed him twice. "I love you," he said, which earned him another kiss.

Chapter 20

It was exactly two minutes from when Cindy and I pulled away from the house that Linc called.

'*She's nothing.*' I hit the ignore button immediately. Watching the road, I felt silent tears roll down my cheek.

"So why'd we leave?" Cindy finally asked as we pulled through the gate and onto the main highway.

"Boys are fucking assholes," I replied, looking away, trying to keep my breathing under control.

I would not wail, but crying was a given, the minute I stepped into the safety of Craig's truck.

Cindy tucked her knee under the steering wheel as she pulled her red hair into a ponytail. "How is Linc an asshole?"

I sat there for a minute, trying to figure out how to tell her what was said, because she had no clue about them. "He told his parents that I was nothing." I hadn't realized how my body tightened and retreated as I repeated Linc's comment until now. "And that he was probably going to break up with me after tonight. He told them he only brought me along tonight because Craig was bringing you, and we were friends." More tears fell against my cheek and I huffed.

"What a fucking dickhead. Maisy, I'm so sorry,

hon." She gripped the wheel a little bit tighter, "Want me to kick him where it hurts for you?"

I let out a chuckle but winced at the sound of the laugh, "No, it's fine. Just can you take me to my house? I know all my stuff is over at his place right now." My phone started buzzing again, and I hit ignore. "I can call Tommy or Eva tomorrow to see when I can go get it."

She nodded. "Do you want me to stay with you tonight?"

"No, I'll be good. I'm sure Linc will make an appearance sometime tonight anyway. I just didn't see this coming. Last night we had a really good night, like, really good. It doesn't make sense. I…shit, I don't know." I shook my head and continued looking out the window.

"I could ask Craig if he knows anything, or to keep Linc home if you want."

I could feel her watching me. "Nah I don't want to put Craig in that situation. Plus, Linc pretty much does what he wants, if he's gonna see me, it'll happen." My phone lit up again, and this time Cindy reached over and grabbed it before I even had time to protest.

"If it's not obvious to you, let me make it obvious. Maisy does not want to talk to you, so stop blowing up her fucking phone," Cindy all but snarled.

I stared at her, mouth agape. Did she just…

I didn't even know how to react to that. Did I say thank you?

"No, you look, Linc," Cindy started then looked at me, her eyes softening just a bit. "Can I speak now? Maybe I don't get it, but neither does she." She hung up the phone, setting it back down on the middle console.

"What'd he say?" I finally squeaked after a couple very uncomfortable minutes.

"He sounded surprised by what I said and then asked what happened. Then he wanted to talk to you. Said I didn't understand what was going on with you two. That's when I looked up because he's right, I don't understand what's wrong. He sounded legitimately freaked out over the phone."

I shrugged. "I honestly don't know what's going on either, Cin, and, from what he's told me, and how he acts with me, I honestly thought I—I—" I huffed in frustration because I hadn't told anyone this, hadn't even let myself believe it, because our relationship was new, and it didn't happen that fast—

"You thought what?" Cindy asked in a low soft voice.

I looked up from my entangled fingers. "I thought we were actually falling in love with each other, as stupid and corny as that sounds. I thought we were headed there. Everything about this relationship felt different." Besides the power he possessed. "It felt real, you know?"

I realized we were stopped and sitting in front of my house. It was dark inside, no lights and definitely eerie—not unexpected since no one had been living in it for weeks.

Cindy's hand came out to rest on my mine, and she gave a squeeze. "I know exactly what you're talking about."

I looked over at her, and her cheeks had little pink spots. I remembered Craig saying those three little words almost every girl desires to here from a man. I remembered the smile she gave him.

I mustered up the best smile I could. "I'm really glad you found Craig, Cindy. You guys seem really good together." I just wished he would tell her about what he actually was.

She looked at me and smiled back her eyes almost glazing over. "Yeah, he's all right."

I let out a shaky laugh and opened the heavy truck

door. "Thanks for driving me home. I'll call you in the morning."

"You sure you don't want me to stay? It's really not a problem," she said as she started to take off her seatbelt.

"I promise, I'm good. I'm just going to fall asleep. I'll figure out what I'm going to do in the morning, if there is even something for me to do. I'll call you."

She smiled. "You better. I'll stop by in the morning with bagels."

"Sounds amazing. See ya." I closed the truck door. Pulling the spare key from under the porch, I unlocked my front door. Opening it, I turned and waved to Cindy, even though I couldn't see her since the truck windows were thickly tinted.

Flipping on the living room light, I looked around the house. Everything was exactly the way I had left it. There was still a bunch of stuff out of sorts from the break-in and us moving to the boys' houses, but the kitchen was normal. I went to the fridge and pulled out a water bottle, then downed the entire thing. I stood there leaning against the counter, staring at the stove for what felt like an hour.

'*She's nothing.*'

Two words I would never be able to unhear that would haunt me for a long time. How could he do that? Say that? I could have sworn we were on the same page, that this relationship was really working. I really liked him, and now we were over. It didn't make sense. What the hell was last night, if he was going to break up with me? There would be no frickin' point of taking me out on an amazing date and showing me all of his cool tricks. He could have saved his money and not wasted his time. Knowing him, he wanted to show off and pump up his already massive ego. Dick.

My head hurt, and it was Linc's fault because my

headache was from the heartache he caused. So I blamed him, for all the pain and my stupidity in believing I was something more than another walking vagina to him.

After checking the house and making sure no one was lurking in the shadows, I took a shower, brushed my teeth with my finger, since my toothbrush was at Linc's, and put on one of his shirts that he left here. Why? I had no clue, but it smelled like him.

I lay down on my bed and bawled, which was absurd, since crying didn't do anything to make the pain better. On top of that, it would piss me off come morning when my pillowcase was ruined from mascara marks.

My phone lit up. Twisting away from my pillow, I grabbed my phone off the small, white side table. Linc's name flashed across the screen. I stared at it, listening to the Luke Bryan ringtone. Sorry, Luke Bryan, I was definitely not feeling like shaking it at the moment.

I clicked answer.

"Maisy?" a familiar voice yelled.

"What do you want, Linc?" My voice was frigid, even though it faltered at his name.

"Why'd you leave? I walked outside, and Craig was standing out on the patio alone. He said Cindy took you home, and you were crying, but he didn't know why. I called, and you didn't answer." He took a deep breath, sounding panicked—like, really panicked.

"I—" *Breathe, Maisy.* "I heard you talking to your parents, and I figured since you were planning to break up with me after dinner, I might as well make it easy and just leave. No point in me staying where I'm not wanted."

"What?" Linc said. "I didn't—"

"Don't you dare say you fucking didn't say it, I heard you." I was surprised at how lethal my voice sounded, my anger searing away the sadness. Right now, I was glad for my temper.

"I was going to say I didn't mean it. Where are you? Cindy's? I'll pick you up in five, I'm already on my way over," he said calmly, but I could tell he was trying to keep his temper in check.

Fuck that. I held onto my anger. "I'm not at Cindy's."

"Where are you?" He enunciated each word.

"I'm home."

"I went home, and you weren't there, Maisy. I left right when I realized you were gone, so don't lie to me."

"How fucking dare you? I'm not lying, asshole. I don't live with you, Linc. I'm at *my* home." Did he actually think I considered his home my own?

In my ear, tires squealed as Linc cursed into the phone.

A sudden fear that he just crashed had me saying, "Linc?"

"Are you fucking kidding me?" he yelled into the phone, clearly pissed. "Why the fuck would you go back to that house? You know it's fucking dangerous for you to be by yourself with all the shit that's been going on," he growled, full-on caveman growled. "I'll be there in fifteen."

As if he really gave a damn. Besides, how much danger could I be in if he was planning on dumping me. "Don't bother," I hissed. "I don't want to see you right now. Just go home." My hand clenched my phone to the point my joints started hurting.

"No."

"I'm not going to open the door for you, so you better be prepared to sleep in your car." I didn't take well to being told no.

"Did you forget that locked doors don't really apply to me?"

It was the last thing I heard before I hung up.

I huffed and got out of bed to rewash my face. I didn't want him to see how messed up I was over this whole thing, how much it hurt to hear I was nothing to him. He didn't get that. I needed to act like I was either okay with the fuck-buddy arrangement or I could be pissed, but not hurt and sad. I decided to be pissed.

I rinsed my face off and looked myself over. My eyes were puffy, and my hair resembled a bird's nest. I ran a brush through it, and it achieved more volume. If I was going for full-blown male lion mane, I nailed it, but I wasn't, so I threw it into a messy bun.

I decided not to take his shirt off or put on shorts. I did change my thong out for black lacy booty shorts, though. Teasing, that's all I was going for, and he'd get one last look at what he was rejecting. I brushed my teeth and went into the kitchen to grab another bottle of water. I lifted myself up onto the counter to wait.

Staying at Cindy's had probably been the better plan, since I could at least have stood behind her while she chewed him out. Cindy was scary when pissed. I didn't have the fierceness she had. I'd been told that I looked like a hyped up chipmunk when mad. Not threatening at all. Pissed-off Maisy was just funny. Not tonight. I would be strong, I wouldn't cry, and I would make him eat his words. And if he apologized, which didn't sound likely from our phone conversation, but if it went there, I would not give in and accept it. What he said to his parents was not okay, and if he didn't mean it, then he shouldn't have said it in the first place.

A knock on the door roused me from my pep talk. I froze, my stomach plummeting and goosebumps trailing along my skin. So much for being strong and ferocious. The knock came again, this time harder. Shit. I jumped off the counter and walked slowly to the door.

Peeking through the peephole all I could see was a

black shirt on a masculine body. Since I had been up close and personal with Linc's chest, that was definitely not his. A cold sweat shot through my body, and I backed up, aiming for my counter where my phone sat. I ran over and picked it up, hitting Linc's number as I heard the door unlock. There was a mass of black hair to my right.

I turned, punching in the direction of the hair, but a small white hand grabbed my wrist. The last thing I saw was the person's perfectly manicured red nails digging into my skin before something hit my head and my world faded.

Chapter 21

I was spinning, spinning, spinning. Holy crap I was going to be sick. I gagged, fluid seeping over my lips, lips that were dry and cracked as if I slept in a windstorm. The back of my head throbbed as I spit on the ground.

"I thought you weren't going to hurt her?" an alarmed male voice yelled. "She looks like shit, and she's throwing up. What if she has a damn concussion?"

"She's fine. I only hit her hard enough to knock her out," answered a female voice that I swore I'd heard before.

I attempted to open my eyes, but my eyelids weighed more than a semi-truck. *Come on, open.*

"I'm pretty sure throwing up is a sign of a concussion. I think we should take her to a hospital, or at least call Marge," the male voice said again.

"What would we tell the hospital to possibly explain why she looks this way?" the female voice sniped. "I'll call Marge if it makes you feel better."

My eyes finally cracked open, but I couldn't see anything except colors. As if someone took paint, splotched it all over paper, and then ran a clean brush through all the colors, mixing them together.

That voice, where had I heard it before? I tried to

move my hand to my lips to wipe the slosh of spit, but couldn't move my arm. I tugged harder. A chain rumbled. Was I tied up? Forcing my eyes open took all my strength, but I managed and lifted my head.

A pale white figure stood in front of me, with long black hair and startling green eyes. Caroline. "Nice of you to join us, Maisy," she sneered.

Us? I looked around the room. There was only her and me. Where did the male voice go?

The room was small, like a spare bedroom. The walls were painted a bright yellow. There was a twin size bed in the corner with a dresser across from it. Where the hell was I? The room looked like it belonged to a young girl. Checking my right hand, I discovered I was cuffed to a bashed in wall with revealed pipes. Checking my left showed the same. Double shit. Suddenly, as if by noticing it, I could feel the metal digging hard into my wrist. I wasn't putting any weight on my knees that were on the ground beside my vomit. I stood and relieved the pressure at my wrists. Blood trickled down my forearm to my elbow and dripped on the floor.

"What do you want?" I bit out, way beyond fucking pissed. I yanked my right arm against the chain, testing how sturdy the pipes were and winced. Conclusion, pretty damn sturdy.

She laughed. "Come on, Maisy, you're smarter than that. I saw you at his house earlier today. I know you know who I am and can put two and two together."

Linc. She wanted Linc. That first attack at the party was on our first date. Then my car happened after our run turned into an R-rated escapade against a tree. My house was trashed after that, too.

"If this is about Linc, there's an easier way to get him than trying to destroy everything I own." I tried throwing my hair back off my face. What happened to my bun? *Oh, shit.* Remembering, my attention went straight down to my bare legs. Wonderful, no pants.

She stared into a mirror resting on the dresser. "There really wasn't. I tried to scare you off numerous times, warning you both. It's not my fault you guys decided to ignore me, no matter how much I stressed my point. Obviously, it was bound to come to this."

Well, the Katy Perry look alike just got off the kooky bus a couple stops before she made it to the loony bin. Funny. She didn't look murderous at the restaurant. I'm pretty sure the boys even left her a really good tip. How could Linc ever date her?

I met her gaze in the mirror. "You could have approached me the first week I met him and told me you were Linc's psycho ex and would cut me if I got near him. That probably would have sent me running for the hills."

"I'll keep that in mind, the next time someone tries to fuck my fiancé." She stood, turned, and ran a brush through her hair. Considering the strange peaceful look on her face, it calmed her.

"Fiancé?" I huffed out.

"Linc didn't tell you? I thought you would have asked why pictures of us lined his room. He proposed to me earlier this year, back in April. We were supposed to get married over summer, but by the end of May he got cold feet and told me he wasn't ready to mate and take the throne. You can imagine how completely blind-sided I was. I had my wedding dress bought and everything. A week later, he broke up with me completely."

With the new information she just gave me, I almost felt bad, almost. "I would say sorry, but you ruined my car, my home, and now I'm sure your planning to ruin my face." I shook my head. "So, I'm not."

She smiled. "You don't understand. I come from a

very powerful family within the Veden community. My family didn't understand how or why Linc got cold feet. They said it was my fault I didn't seal the deal to bind our family lineage with royalty. They disowned me. I called Linc, trying to reconcile, but he'd told me he met someone else. And he apologized." She came over and knelt in front of me, staying clear of my vomit. "Apologized, can you believe that? Like an 'I'm so sorry, but you wouldn't have been happy with me in the long run' could make up for the complete heartbreak he caused me. I lost everything. I lost the love of my life, my family, and my status. Everything. All to be replaced by some human tramp, one who is marked by a fucking Fiskare."

She ran her hand against that black mark, and I tried jerk back from her touch. My arm slammed into wood and metal behind me. The impact stung, and more of my blood hit the carpet.

"You could never really be with him, you know. He can't legitimately be with a regular human. Your babies would come out mixed blood, and the royal lineage needs to be full Veden. I don't understand what he's doing with you. Nor do I see the pull. I'm sorry, but you're very ordinary looking, blonde with gray eyes? There's a million of you Barbie types running around." She gently moved my hair out of my face.

"Trust me. He made it clear that I was nothing to him. I've never been in your way."

She nodded in agreement.

"So since we agree on that, why did you kidnap me? What are you going to do?" I tried to keep my voice even and keep the "scared shitless" out of it. Thank god, I succeeded.

Caroline stared at me as her smile widened. "I'm going to hurt Linc where it counts."

I stared as understanding filtered through. "I just told

you he said I was nothing, am nothing. If you think hurting him where it counts means me, you're wrong." I looked away, *'She's nothing.'* Tears clogged my throat, tears that should be there because of the predicament I was in now, not because some stupid man didn't want me.

"You're wrong. Linc doesn't stay with girls for more than a night. He strayed from me more times than I could count, but he's been with you for months. From what I could see, there hasn't been anyone else. Unless he's gotten sneakier within the last year, which I doubt."

My head snapped up. "You've been stalking him?" There was no hiding my disgust.

"I prefer to think of it as my job. I have to make sure no one gets close to stealing him and my title." She crossed the room and grabbed a bucket of water. Bringing it back, she set it to my side.

Shit, she's going to drown me. Or put an icicle through my skull. My heart jumped into my throat and I couldn't breathe.

"I thought you said I couldn't be with him anyway, so what does it fucking matter?" I laced my voice with as much acid as I could muster.

"Like I've said, I want Linc to feel the same heartbreak I do. I want him to experience what it feels like to lose your mind, to lose complete control of your life." She brought a finger up, and the water from the bucket followed and hovering like a snake about to strike.

"It won't work. Besides, Linc was on his way to my house when you snatched me. You really don't think he's going to start tearing the town apart to find me?"

Actually, this was a complete lie. With the events that took place earlier, he would probably just leave when I didn't answer the door. But part of me hoped Linc would look for me. Despite what he said, there was no flipping way I could feel this strongly about him and him not reciprocate at least a fraction of it. No way.

"That's exactly what I'm counting on. Which is why we need to get to work. Can't have you looking this good when he busts through that door." She sat back across from me on the bed, her look turning cynical as the snake of water turned to ice. *Shit on a stick.* She flicked her fingers toward me, and the sharp, knife point of the icicle stabbed my forearm. I winced, and a cry escaped. Looking at the sharp piece of ice sticking out of my arm, I was surprised not much blood trickled out.

"So, Maisy, what exactly is it that Linc sees in you? Huh? It's not your looks. So it must be that dazzling personality which I have yet to see." She cocked her head to the side, the ice turned in my arm like a screw, slowly. Warm crimson wetness started to drip to the floor.

My whole body tensed at the slow steady pain rippling through my arm and down through my body. My teeth were clenched so hard I had to be breaking molars. "I'm pretty sure the fact that I'm not a homicidal bitch is what he finds refreshing," I bit out through the pain.

Her arm flicked so fast I didn't even see the next icicle form before it slammed into my abdomen. This time, I held in the cry, but my eyes closed involuntary as the pain rocked through me. I was lucky these pieces of ice weren't penetrating much into my body, or I would probably bleed out. She seemed to know how much pressure to exert before they did any real damage. Ten bucks said I wasn't the first person she tortured.

She stood up, her black pants and boots splattered with blood, probably mine from when she cuffed me. Her white and black striped tank top was a little too tight and rode up, revealing more of her ghost like skin. She walked over to me, hulk stomping the whole way. Holding her hand above the bucket, the water gravitated up and wrapped around her hand. She sliced the air in front of her and all I felt was a slash of coldness hit my cheek. It took me a minute to even realize she sliced my cheek. I blinked. Linc needed to hurry the hell up, the bitch was going to bleed me dry at this rate.

"I'm surprised he hasn't figured out that you're here yet, or that I'm the one that's been fucking with you for the last couple months," she mused, holding her hand up and making a small tornado of water spin over her palm.

"He probably doesn't realize he dated a sadist," I whispered, my head falling forward as I tried to control my breathing.

The ice in my abdomen burned. Water hit the floor, and my head was ripped up by my hair. She was in my face, so close I could feel her breath.

"I'm really getting tired of that mouth of yours." She stared me down and I made sure I didn't break eye contact. I spit in her face, which she obviously wasn't prepared for, since it hit her square on the right cheek. Her fist connected with my face and the world dimmed again, dammit.

When I resurfaced to the hellhole, I woke to some old lady in my face, shining a small light into my eyes. Immediately, I threw my head back trying to get away from her and her tiny light that was making a big impact on my already growing migraine.

"Don't do that. You're going to give yourself another concussion, girl."

I blinked as she brought a bucket of water to my lips. I turned my head away in disgust. How the hell did I know if there wasn't something in the water?

"Drink, or you're going lose consciousness again."

Screw it. I drank.

The water flowed through me and reached my toes—heaven, pure heaven. I pulled the water bucket forward with my lips, trying to get more water, and winced in pain.

"Don't be hasty," the older woman said.

She wore a doctor's coat with her gray hair in a neat bun at the back or her head. She left the room as I stared after her. Who the heck was that and where did Caroline go? I squinted around the room. All I could manage was a slit of light through my right eye. Just a wild guess but I was betting my eye was swollen from the hit I took.

I knelt there for what felt like hours, when voices came from the other room. "She's awake now. I would advise no one hit her again. She has a mild concussion and has lost some blood."

Guess that was the doctor.

"Linc's going to fucking kill every single one of us. Every. Single. One," said a male voice I didn't recognize.

Good, I'm glad someone is scared of him.

"There's six of us. What is one Flodpoika really going to do?" asked a deep voice.

"Don't you remember what his dad did? What if he passed that along to him? Like Dixon said, he's going to kill us."

"I doubt Linc can do that without me or anyone else knowing. I was the guy's fiancée and before that his girl-friend for seven years. He can't. If someone stays by her, threatens her, he will comply with anything. I've seen the way he stares at her when she's not watching. The girl is his weakness," Caroline said, and then the door opened.

Looking at her, my body started trembling uncontrollably. I tried to remain calm, but nothing worked. The chains resting on my wrist jangled from the scared shitless shakes pulsing through my body. I pulled down hard to stop them from making noise, causing more blood to from wrists. Breathing deep, I focused on surviving this. I had to.

Raising my head, I stared at her. "Getting bored yet?"

She twisted her left wrist down at her side and pain shot through my abdomen again as she screwed an icicle into my side. Uncontrollable tears poured down my face. "I have to go take Marge home, so I'll be back to finish this little thing we've got going on. In the meantime, meet Henry."

A massive man came through the door, his dark hair pooling under his shoulders, and he had a dark mustache and a goatee. From the moment he walked in, I could smell the cigarette smoke clinging to his skin.

"Henry here will look after you while I'm gone." She patted him on the shoulder as she passed. "Have fun."

Henry lumbered over and knelt in front of me. He grabbed my face between his dirty hands. "Pretty." He moved his thumb across the scrape on my right cheek, smearing the warm blood over my chilled skin. I didn't meet his gaze. I had a really, really bad feeling about him.

"You have pretty legs, too."

And that was what my gut was telling me. I thrashed against him, trying to get away, throwing myself back into the wall. He grabbed my hips hard, and I screamed bloody fucking murder. Until then, I hadn't realized how deep the sharp ice was. I kicked my feet into his stomach as hard as I could, but he didn't even budge.

He smiled, revealing yellowing teeth; grabbed my hair; and ripped my head back. "Where do you think you're going?"

"No, god no. Get the fuck off of me," I screamed, picking both feet off the ground and throwing my heels into his chest. The strain from the cuffs should have hurt like a bitch, but I didn't notice. They weren't my biggest problem at the moment. Tears fell hard and fast down my face.

One hand stayed on my hip, as he ripped my shirt up toward my chest with the other.

That was when Linc came through the wall.

Chapter 22

Linc's body was engulfed in water. He shook his head, maybe from the impact, and looked over to where Henry and I were. Henry's hands hadn't moved, and his grip was so cruel I knew I was going to have bruises.

Water shot out, and ice pierced Henry's shoulders. Linc threw his arms toward us and ripped them back. Henry let out a grunt as he was yanked away from me and thrown against the wall, where he slumped down.

Linc was in front of me in an instant and broke the cuffs with his hands. "Maisy, I'm so sorry."

I thought I would hit the floor without the chains for support, but he caught me. Pulling me against his body, he scanned my face, and then removed the two icicles stuck in me. I gasped as each slid out easily. I couldn't stop shaking. My body was frozen, and I couldn't get warm, couldn't wrap my mind around what happened. Closing my eyes for a second, I let Linc check me out.

"Maisy, you have to stay awake, baby. Maisy, look at me, please. I'm so sorry. This wasn't supposed to happen. I—"

As I slowly peeled my eyes open, I saw Henry start to stand up from the wall. "Linc—"

I stared over his shoulder. Thank goodness he got the

picture, because I couldn't make my mouth form the words. He looked over his shoulder and picked me up as he stood and turned around. He shot his left arm out, and the drops of water turned into blades of ice, slicing Henry in the neck, head, stomach, and the groin area. Henry fell forward, blood pooling around his body.

Footsteps came from the hallway outside the room, and Linc ran to the hole in the wall. In the distance, his truck sat. It was still dark outside, the stars were shining bright, the moon looked like a tiger's claw, and we were by water, a creek.

"Leaving already, Linc?" a voice came from behind us.

Linc stopped, and I heard him curse. He put me gently on the ground in front of him and kissed my forehead. "Stay here, I'm going to get us out of here, I promise."

"That's cute, but I wouldn't make promises you can't keep."

I lifted my head to see five other men standing, each of them as strong and lethal looking as Linc.

Linc growled, full on growled, in the direction of the men. "I haven't. So which one of you fuckers wants to die next?" None of the men moved an inch, not even the one who ran his mouth. "No takers? I guess I'm just going to have to pick."

Linc's arms shot out, water from the creek shooting into one of the men, shoving him against the house.

Another man charged, grabbing water from the stream Linc used. The man threw his arms forward and shot ice daggers, that glistened at the tip, toward Linc. Linc stopped them all, centimeters from his face without lifting a hand. The ice daggers turned away and shot into the guy. He suffered the same fate as Henry.

"You guys have to bring more of a threat than this, if you're going to stand a chance," Linc called out. "I almost feel bad for you." Then he looked in my direction. "I take that back, I'm going to fucking kill every one of you."

One of the men smiled, a sickening sinister smile framed by his blond hair. "I don't think so. You're both going to die tonight. She's already half way there. It wouldn't take much to finish her off."

"I guess you're going to be the next." Linc lifted his hand and clutched the air. The ground shook, literally shook. Two trees were completely uprooted and floated behind him. He sent the trees at two of the three other Vedens. While they were distracted, Linc threw himself in the direction of the blond.

I tried my hardest to sit up on my knees, but each movement, each turn, sent violent pulses of agony through my body, making it hard to breathe—let alone stay conscious. Linc shadowed each of the blond man's fists as water and ice mixed into the swings and punches. They were too fast for me to track accurately. All I saw was flesh, water, and ice. Linc threw the attacker back into the house.

Linc stood in front of four remaining men, breathing heavily. He swiped his hand over the grass around him. The grass shriveled at the loss of water. Bullet-sized pieces of water flew through the air, each narrowly missing the targets as the men bolted out of the way at lightning speed.

Arms went under my armpits, and my breath caught in my throat. "Get the fuck off me!" My voice was hoarse as I struggled weakly.

"Maisy, calm down. Hey, it's me." Craig gave my body a small shake before trying to pull me toward the woods.

I relaxed for a fraction of a second. "No, let me go, Craig! Put me down, go help Linc!"

Craig looked at me and then toward where his brother stood, surrounded by four other Vedens.

"Go, Craig." I pushed him until he set me down as gently as he could and took off toward his brother. I blinked as Tommy appeared on the other side of Linc. I tried to breathe a small sigh of relief now that the odds were more evenly matched. Instead, I gagged, and blood rushed out of my mouth.

The fear I'd managed to purge from my body came back quickly as blood pooled in the grass in front of me. I looked back at Linc.

Another blond bulldozer of a man joined the fray. "So, I see all you boys came out to play today."

"Couldn't let Linc here have all the fun," Tommy smirked. "I haven't been in a good fight in years. No way was I missing a chance to kick someone's ass."

"They're not going to be as good competition as the Fiskares, Tommy. I've already taken out two," Linc said, and I could hear the venom in his voice.

"Well, that's fucking disappointing," Tommy said.

He and Craig called the water from the creek until it gravitated toward them to cover their arms.

"We'll see if you're as arrogant, when I'm slitting your throat," said one of the four blond men standing in front of them before they rushed Linc, Tommy, and Craig.

The ground started shaking once more, as trees, sticks, and roots flew over my head from the forest, adding a drenched earthy scent to the night. I thought Linc was the one uprooting everything and throwing the attackers back. It gave Tommy and Craig time to recuperate before attacking again.

Two of the attackers dodged the trees and water and sent back sharp daggers of their own. One hit Craig in the shoulder. He grunted, and the bullet of ice seeped out of his wound and fell to the floor. Linc and Tommy were on the blond in an instant. Tommy sent water toward the man's feet, forcing him stop for a second, long enough for Linc to take advantage of the situation. I watched him throw his hands around the guy's head.

I heard the crack before I saw it. The guy in Linc's hands fell to the ground, his head cocked in a way that was anything but normal. Linc had just broken the guy's neck. I coughed again, and more blood came out. My vision got a bit hazy, but there was no way I was going to go down before I knew that Linc was all right.

He flicked out of view for a second and reappeared behind another attacker in an instant. He brought his fist up, water following and covering it. When it turned to ice, he brought his fist down on the other guy's head. It looked like only two guys were left.

I crumpled from my kneeling position. My trembling extremities were unable to hold my body's weight, and I collapsed. There was a loud scream. I lifted my head to see Tommy on the ground. But the scream didn't come from him. It was coming from my mouth. At that moment, Linc and Craig's heads snapped to me, and one of the final two attackers flickered out of sight. I felt cold arms surround me as one yanked my body in front of him.

With Craig and Linc both distracted, the other attacker pounced on Craig, taking him down to the ground. I met Linc's gaze as a sharp blade pressed against my throat.

"Enough!" Linc yelled, throwing both of his hands up in the air.

The man holding me froze and so did the one holding Craig. Craig stood up and moved the frozen man off him. Strangely, the man didn't even blink as Craig kicked the fucker in the stomach and stabbed an icicle through his head. Holy crap, did Linc just freeze them? Why didn't he start with that?

Linc dropped his arm closest to Tommy and brought his other hand out in front of him palm up. He thrust his elbow toward his side, clenching his hand with the movement. The arm and knife pressing against my throat started to tremble. Finally, the man's hand swung away, sending the knife toward Linc, which he caught easily as if he was expecting it.

Linc appeared in front of us and gently untangled me from the man's hold. I slumped into him. Linc lowered his hand. I slightly turned to see the guy who was holding me kneel. Oh my god, Linc was controlling him. With one quick swipe of his hand, water connected with man. It happened so fast. The man's head rolled from his body and hit the ground with a thud. He was still kneeling as blood seeped from his severed neck. Linc put his other arm around me, shielding my eyes a little too late, and I heard the thud of the body hitting the ground.

Pushing away from Linc slightly, I saw Craig throwing Tommy's arm over his shoulder, helping him walk. Linc stumbled, and then he set me on the ground in front of him. "Maisy?" His voice was a barely there whisper.

I realized I was on my back, staring up at his face. It was blurry, even though I tried to focus. The sky behind his head was growing lighter, the moon and the stars fading.

I let out a shallow, ragged breath, my body starting to go numb. It should terrify me, but this blanket of contentment washed over me. Linc was okay. I could let go now. I could let go of all the bad and pain that was my body. I didn't have to fight anymore. He was okay. Tommy and Craig were okay.

"Maisy, don't you fucking leave me. Say something." Linc leaned toward me, so close he had to be pressing his forehead against mine, but I couldn't feel it. "Craig, get the fuck over here," he growled.

"Tommy's hurt, Linc. We're moving as fast as we can."

I could hear him, but couldn't see them. I couldn't see anything. More hands on my neck, my stomach, everywhere, touching me.

"Linc, I need you to get back while I try this," Craig said, sounding far away and out of breath. "I said back off," he growled.

I figured he was talking to Linc, because all I could feel was the damp grass on the back of my neck.

The next moment, I was floating, as water completely surrounded me. The coolness of it was welcome. I wasn't numb anymore. Instead, my insides tightened and warmth spread through me. Water washed into my mouth, down my throat, and coursed through my body, going into every nook and cranny. I dragged in a breath, but coughed from the water in my lungs. Water spewed up and out as I turned to my side. Opening my eyes, I could see, like really see clearly. My eyes widened as I pushed off the ground and sat up.

I let out a soft whimper once I got situated. My body was so sore, and the mark on my arm burned as if it was on fire. I stared at it as it darkened, turning so black it was as if someone ran a paintbrush of black metallic paint over my forearm. It didn't look real. I looked up to meet three pairs of wide eyes.

When mine landed on the pair the color of whiskey, they stayed there. "Linc?"

It came out more normal that I expected. My voice was hoarse and burned something fierce, but I could form words.

"Maisy?" He fell to his knees, running his large hand over his face and through his hair. The octopus tattoo moved with the flex of his bicep. He reached out and, as carefully as he could, dragged me toward him. Throwing my arms around his shoulders, I held on tight as tears started flowing.

I never wanted to let go, but I pulled back just a fraction. "Are you okay?" Panic rose as memories began to come back. "You're not hurt, right?" I looked down at his ripped shirt, running my hands down his chest and meeting the curves and dips of his abs.

"No, god, I'm fine. Maisy, I'm so fucking sorry." He pulled me closer and then hooked his hands under my knees and lifted, cradling me to his chest.

We made it back to his truck. He dug the keys out of his pocket and tossed them at Tommy. Craig hopped in front with Tommy, and Linc and I got into the back. Linc set me down in the middle seat and got in. Once he was settled, he tugged me to his side, and I fell into a deep sleep.

෴

I woke up in a sea of soft, cool cotton. I peeled my eyes open, and it was dark, really dark. I sat up, not realizing where I was, and instantly regretted that decision. My back cracked, and all my muscles ached—muscles I hadn't even known I had. As my eyes adjusted to the darkness, I realized I was in Linc's bedroom, alone.

Gently, I scooted out of bed, draping the sheets around me, since I only had my black panties on. I really hoped Linc or Eva had undressed me here, and not out in the field. Memories flooded back. I almost died, like really died. I yanked the sheet away and looked at my body. The stab wound in my abdomen was healing up nicely, as if it had been weeks instead of hours, barely bruised and a little scabbed.

Once in the bathroom, I took a deep breath and turned to the mirror. There was a small scar on my cheek, barely visible, and the swelling around my eye was gone. What the heck? Checking the rest of my body, I discovered I was spotted like a leopard with old yellow bruises. I couldn't have been sleeping for more than a day, right? Swallowing, I went to the bathtub and turned the water as hot as it could go.

A knock on the door came a second later, and Linc stood in the doorframe. He looked like shit, dark circles under his beautiful eyes, his facial hair longer than his usual scruff, and his skin pale.

"Hey," I squeaked and took off the little piece of clothing I on so I could slip into the too-hot water. I took a shaky breath while my body got used to the temperature.

"How are you feeling?" he asked softly, placing both hands on the top of the doorframe. The move made his biceps bulge and the tentacle on the back of his left arm move.

"Better than I should be." I looked away from him and into the water, breaking eye contact for a second before my eyes returned up to him. "What about you? You look like shit."

Linc ran his hand through his curls, walked over to the sink, leaned against it, and crossed his arms. The nylon shorts he wore were low, like too low, and his abs were at eye level. With his arms crossed like that, it accentuated his strength, his power. I squeezed my legs tighter together. *Glad to see almost dying didn't diminish my sexual appetite.*

"I haven't been better in the last three days than I am right now." He stared straight at me. Every nerve in my body was aware of his gaze roaming over me.

I looked up at him once more, taking him in, just staring.

He tipped one eyebrow up. "See something you like?"

I rolled my eyes and glanced away from his body.

He walked over to the tub, leaned down, and my heart rate soared. He kissed the top of my head. "We'll talk after you're done in here, and I'll put a shirt on."

I couldn't even think of a witty comeback as he walked out of the bathroom.

I closed my eyes. Damn right, he'd better put a shirt on.

After I cleaned up, I changed into some yoga pants and a clean tank before walking out of his room. I came down the steps and heard nothing. Going through the hall and into the kitchen, I spotted Linc carrying two plates of eggs, potatoes, and veggies.

He set them down on the table. "Come eat." He walked past me again and grabbed two water bottles out of the refrigerator.

I wanted to say no, but my stomach grumbled at the smell and demanded I put the food in my mouth. I sat down, and he sat across from me. Picking up my fork, I dove into the eggs. As I put them to my lips, I closed my eyes. Gosh, they tasted so flipping good. Seriously, it was the best food I had ever eaten in my life. Of course, at this point, raw kale would probably have made my mouth water. Once he was satisfied with the amount of food I consumed, he took the plates and tossed them into the sink.

I propped my elbows on the table. "So are we going to talk now?"

"We can do whatever you want," he said, turning toward me, and walked into the family room attached to the kitchen.

"How long was I sleeping for?" I blurted out.

"Three days. When Craig healed you, he accidentally knocked you out. We think."

I left my chair and joined him on the comfortable couch. "But I remember walking to the car. I wasn't knocked out yet," I whispered.

"We didn't know if it would work. He's never healed someone in your condition. Hell, I don't think he's ever healed a Veden before, let alone a human. We didn't know what to expect. I was happy when you seemed fine in the car, though."

"Wait, what? He's never healed anyone before?"

"Yeah, he's only healed animals. My parents don't know he can do it, though, only Tommy, Eva, and I."

"What—what else happened? Where's Caroline?" I winced at the sound of her name. She was the last person I wanted to see.

"You left my parents' and, once I figured that out, I left to try and stop you, to try to explain." He didn't meet my eyes. "You weren't here, so I started driving to Cindy's. Then I talked to you and realized you went to your actual home. I was so fucking mad, Maisy. I drove over there as fast as I could, and you were gone. I owe you a new door, by the way."

I stared at him, waiting for him to finish.

"I saw there was a glass of water knocked over in the kitchen. I ran through your house looking for you, and you weren't there. God, you weren't there, so I walked back out to my truck and noticed a pair of sunglasses in the middle of your driveway. I picked them up. They were the fucking same brand and style I gave Caro for her birthday last year. I fucking lost it. I drove over to her house, where she wasn't, but I remembered she had a guesthouse on her property. Once I got close, I heard you scream, and I—I went through the wall."

I pulled my knees to my chest and wrapped my arms around my legs, involuntary tears falling as everything came rushing back.

He reached out to move my hair out of my face, and I recoiled. His hand stopped immediately, and he dropped it.

"I'm sorry, Mais, I'm so fucking sorry. I killed people in front of you."

Yeah, he literally decapitated one of them.

"I completely understand if you're afraid of me," he continued, "but I won't hurt you. I could never hurt you." He put his forearms on his knees and his head in his hands.

We sat there in those positions for what felt like an eternity. I wasn't afraid of him, and I knew he wouldn't hurt me...well, not physically. And, honestly, I was relieved when he took their lives. I felt safe with him. I recoiled for a whole different reason. He hurt me, tore my heart into a million little pieces, and then set them on fire. I thought it was because I didn't see it coming, but that wasn't it. I was falling in love with him, was probably already in love, but no way in hell would I say that yet.

"I know you'd never hurt me," I whispered.

I was in his arms faster than a blink of an eye. "I thought I'd lost you. I don't know what I'd have done if that had been true. Don't ever run from me again," he said against my hair, his scent encircling me almost to the point of suffocation.

My body relaxed, not wanting to fight him, but the message didn't make it to my brain. "This is going to sound really selfish and make me seem like a total bitch, because I know you and your friends saved my life, and I am thankful. I am, but what you said to your parents...I...I don't know how to process that. When you're close like this, I have feelings I don't want to feel, and I'm confused, Linc."

He pulled back, and I saw his shirt was wet, and by wet, I mean soaked. I didn't realize I was crying that hard.

"Babe—" His voice faltered, and when I opened my eyes he was on his knees in front of me, his massive hands on both sides of my face. "The shit I said to my parents, it was a lie. You mean so fucking much to me, it hurts sometimes. The reason I didn't want to bring you over there in the first place was because of their reaction. I can't be with a normal human. It's not natural for the royals to mix with non-Vedens. I'm going to rule some-day, and I'm being pressured into finding a wife. Dating you, in their eyes, was a setback."

"It's fine." I tried not to let my crying turn into sob-bing. If I was a waste of time, then fine. "I get it." I tried to move out of his embrace.

"Obviously, you don't." He took a deep breath be-fore putting our foreheads together. "Maisy, I love you. You're the only one I want to be with, plan to be with. All the royal bullshit can suck my dick. I will be king someday, and I will change that stupid law."

"Linc. Stop," I cried, "please just stop." This had to be just the aftermath of everything. This couldn't be true. He told his parents I was nothing, for heaven's sake.

He pulled my face to his and pressed his lips softly against mine. My mind went blank. He lifted his head and looked at me, before lightly pushing me back on the couch, his tongue demanding entry to mine as one of his hands cupped my face. The other one was on the couch beside my head, supporting his weight.

We kissed for a while, and then he settled behind me on the couch and pulled a blanket over me. We just lay there. When his breathing finally evened out, and he was sleeping, he pulled me against him and squeezed me as if he was afraid I would disappear or leave. It freaked me out that I never wanted to leave his arms, but I was going to have to.

Chapter 23

Two weeks had passed since the attack, and we hadn't seen or heard from Caroline. Linc, Tommy, and Craig went out looking for her more than a handful of times, but nothing ever came of it. Linc thought she had probably run off, after finding her six bodyguards dead.

He vowed if she so much as set foot in this town, he would make sure she met the same fate.

It was the week before winter break, and I was re-registered for the classes I dropped, planning to retake them in the spring. Linc had one class left and was taking that during winter session.

He hadn't spoken to his parents since the night I ran off. I told him he would have to talk to them sooner or later if he wanted anything to work out—that, and they should probably know his ex was a psycho. I refused to be his dirty little secret, though. Craig told me Linc and his parents rarely fought. Mainly because they had to look and *be* united, or it would be perceived as a sign of weakness.

Craig still hadn't told Cindy anything about what happened or what he really was, but he promised me he'd do it soon. He really liked her and wanted her to accept who he was so he wouldn't have to hide it anymore. I was sure she could handle it. That girl was hell on wheels. She'd be fine.

Sara had finally quit housesitting for Todd and told him to find someone else. She and I were moving from our home into an apartment complex closer to campus. Linc's idea, not mine. I could see how this made sense, though, with all the events that had happened and Caroline still out there. He offered for us to move in with him but, with our relationship in shambles at the moment, I couldn't take him up on it.

Linc told me he loved me. I hadn't said it back, though. I didn't want to set myself up for a major heartbreak if something went wrong. I loved him. But saying it out loud made it too real, made me too vulnerable. I was now treating this relationship more like friends with benefits. Which there hadn't been many benefits lately. He was acting strange. He kissed me here and there, but he hadn't tried anything. Even his annoying, but admittedly attractive, cockiness had mellowed dramatically. I thought it might have to do with me not being able to trust him completely after what was said to his parents. I didn't think that would dim him this much, though. Maybe all the death that had happened? I honestly didn't know if he'd ever killed anyone before, but that had to take a toll on a person. Hell, I was still having nightmares.

And now, I was sitting in a pile of clothes and knick-knacks in my bedroom, with Sarah, going through all of our shit. We had way too much.

"You ready for this?" I asked. "It's going to be a lot noisier at the apartments."

She giggled and pulled her thick brown hair up into a ponytail. "It'll be better, though. Less gas wasting and we won't have to walk far to get bagels."

"Hey, I'm going out with Linc and his friends tonight. You should come. Tommy will be there." I wiggled my eyebrows at her as she tossed a shirt at my face.

"You know Todd isn't all that bad."

I huffed at her.

"He asked me to move in with him last semester, and I told him no because I didn't want to leave you alone. He didn't throw a fit or anything. Contrary to what you think, he isn't a bad guy."

I stared at her. The guy sucked. I didn't know if he was magical in the sack or what, because it had to be something to get Sarah to see past his douche-bagginess.

"You know, two weeks ago, Jake called me, asking about you again." She looked over at me while putting DVD's in a box.

I stopped, and I'm sure I paled a little bit. "What'd he say?"

"He said he had a bad dream about you, or something. He tried calling you multiple times, but you never answered. He was at the point of asking me to go over to Linc's to see you, but I told him you were fine. I had to promise him that you were okay. Then I called you the next day, and Linc said you were out shopping, but you were fine. I called Jake back and told him that I talked to you."

"So weird." I shook my head, trying not to look at her. How'd he know something was wrong? I looked down at the black mark on my forearm. There was no way this thing was giving him a direct link to me. That would be crazy, but since I was dating a guy who could manipulate water and rip trees from the ground, crazy wasn't a long stretch.

All the mark did was look ugly, and it had started itching badly yesterday. Today it started tingling. It was hard to explain. It almost felt like a mosquito's bite but didn't hurt. Still, it drove me absolutely nuts.

Linc said he didn't know what to think, because he'd never talked to anyone who was marked.

"Maisy!" Sarah yelled at me.

My head snapped in her direction so fast I felt my eyes widen and, before I knew it, I was standing. "What?" I finally got out.

"I've been talking to you, silly. I wanted to know if you wanted me to order pizza. Crazy person, are you okay? You've been acting jumpy all day."

"I'm good, and I have not been jumpy," I said to her as I gave her a trash bag filled with my clothes.

She snickered. "Umm, earlier I broke a light bulb and you all but dove behind the bed."

"Duh, I didn't want to get electrocuted." I turned red and focused on my bras.

"It wasn't even in the socket!" she snorted.

"Whatever, just order your pizza, fatty," I said.

She laughed, picked up a box, and walked out of the room, to add it to the pile of boxes by the front door. Linc and Tommy were coming over and loading up their trucks with all of our stuff.

There was no way she was a fatty. She was barely a hundred and ten pounds, lucky butt. I ran to stay halfway decent looking.

After Sarah ordered the pizza, we tackled the kitchen and dishes, which turned out to be easy, since everything in there was hers. It was our last room to box up. I was glad Linc let me do this without him. He had been so up in my business lately, I had to restrain myself from physically harming him.

It was exhausting not having a minute alone, and this was nice. I spent the whole day with Sarah, boxing up our home. I was totally going to miss this house. We'd been here the last three years. The land was beautiful, and it was quiet. I almost said *Screw it, I want to stay here*. But

I knew that would be a fight and not only with Sarah, who seemed giddy about being closer to civilization. Linc would probably have an aneurism over it.

Speaking of the devil, my phone started blaring his ring tone.

"Hey," I answered.

"Hey, I'm going to be a little longer than planned. Something went wrong with the job we're at," he huffed, annoyed.

I giggled. "Linc, it's fine. You know we could always just crash here another night."

"No." He nipped that in the butt right away.

"Whatever. What time do you think you'll be done?"

"Around seven? Maybe. I don't know. If I'm later, I'll have Eva swing by and get you guys. You guys could stay with us tonight if we don't get the bed's set up at the apartment."

"Sounds good," I said.

"I love you," he said, right before the line went dead.

I felt my eyes widen. He hadn't said it since the night I woke up. That probably had to do with how I reacted the day after everything happened. I'd insisted we slow things down because everything had really taken a toll on me emotionally.

For the next hour, we finished up boxing everything, and the mark on my arm had started itching even more horribly, all of a sudden. I scratched the ever-living crap out of it until I was sure I wouldn't drop a box. I grabbed a heavy box with pots and pans to put by the door when the doorbell rang.

"Mais, can you get that?" Sarah called from the pantry, too busy separating and boxing up canned food.

"Yup." I staggered out and all but dropped the box by the others.

I walked up to the door and opened it. My breath

caught, and my heart rate tripled. Stupid heart. Stupid feelings.

Linc strode through the door, kissing my forehead. "Hey, babe."

And damn if my heart didn't flutter over a forehead kiss. I raised my eyebrow at him. "Hey, I thought you were staying late on a job."

"Tommy called some of our team to take care of it. I just signed off on the paperwork."

Linc plopped down on the couch and threw his arm along the back of it. His head tilting to the seat next to him. His tan skin looked a shade paler than normal and there was slight purple underneath his dark translucent brown eyes.

I sighed, scurrying over and plopping down next to him. "W—What's wrong?"

His hand that was resting on the back of the couch dropped to my shoulder, and I was pulled against his masculine chest. A sigh escaped my lips as his scent washed over me. No matter how pissed at him I was, or how much trust had been lost between us, his presence still wound me up and calmed me down all at the same time. Stress released and lust surged. I got high off this feeling.

"I just need this right now." He nuzzled his head between his shoulder and my cheek, his scruff scratching a path down to my neck.

I sat there, holding this massive man, for what felt like an eternity. I glanced back to where the kitchen was and saw Sarah walk out and look at me. I shook my head at her, and she tiptoed back toward the bedrooms. I knew something was bothering him. I mean, everything that happened the last two weeks had to take a toll on someone. Hell, I didn't know how I was managing to keep it together. Which I guess technically I wasn't. Like Sarah had said, I was jumpy, I had nightmares, and I still watched over my shoulder while running errands.

"Question," Linc breathed into my neck.

I smiled lightly and felt the scruff of his cheek move upward. "Answer."

He sat back on the couch and grabbed my hand, interlacing our fingers. "Be with me again. I promise I'll be more upfront with you about things,"

"That wasn't a question."

"That wasn't an answer," he challenged.

"Linc, I can't. I can't go there with you right now." I sighed, pulling my hand from his grasp. I really wasn't up for this conversation right now, with Sarah in the house.

"Why not? I know I fucked up. I've apologized numerous times. I've told you how I feel." Linc ran his hand through his messy brown hair making the tentacles dance. I seriously loved that tattoo.

"Yes, and I told you 'apology accepted,' but it doesn't change what you said and how hurt I was. And I'm pretty sure the 'I love you' was due to the adrenaline from the night before."

"It was not." Annoyance colored his tone. He leaned forward and rested his strong forearms on his knees. "You know what? Fine, believe what you want. But I know you want this just as bad as I do. Ten bucks say's we'll be back on by Valentine's Day."

I laughed out loud and met his deep brown eyes. "You're seriously betting me right now? We were having a serious conversation, dumbass. And Valentine's Day is, like, a month and a half away. I'm not jumping into a relationship with you again. I told you we're going slow, like friends with benefits slow."

His smile reached his eyes. "We'll see."

"There's nothing to see, Linc. No."

He leaned in and pressed his full lips to mine, effectively shutting me up. It was like my brain short circuited, and I forgot that we were bickering. My hands raised up and looped around the back of his neck as he deepened the kiss. His right hand, that was now resting on the outside of my left thigh, started pulling me closer so that my legs were now on his lap.

He abruptly pulled his lips away, and I full-on whimpered. A half laugh escaped him as he rested his forehead against mine.

"This is going to be too easy," he whispered, his breath coming out in short and fast.

I pushed him away with a groan. This guy was going to be the death of me.

About the Author

Brittany Tollison is a wife and mother of two beautiful babies, and two fur babies. She grew up in California and holds a B.A. in Anthropology, with a minor in Humanities. Growing up she has always had a passion for the literary arts and decided after college to pursue writing. Tollison's understanding of human behavior, coupled with her interest in the unexplained happenings of the universe, drive her creative spark to provide readers with something more than your typical romance.

She enjoys spending time with her family, reading, writing, and soccer.